TERRY C. SIMPSON

The Shadowbearer

An Aegis
of The Gods
Book

Published by the author as a member of

The Alexandria Publishing Group

Golden Arm Press

Terry C. Simpson

Other Novels by Terry C. Simpson

AEGIS OF THE GODS
Prequel: The Shadowbearer
Book 1: Etchings of Power
Book 2: Ashes and Blood (Coming Soon)

TERRY **C.** SIMPSON

Copyright

THE SHADOWBEARER

this book and did not purchase it, or it was not purchased for your use only, then please return to author and purchase your own copy. Thank you for respecting the hard work of this author.

Find out more about the author and upcoming books online at terrycsimpson.wordpress.com or @TeeSimps on twitter or NovelistTCSimpson on facebook.

Second Print Edition
ISBN: 978-1-939172-04-4

Dedication

This book is dedicated to my daughter Kai. You keep me going and smiling through it all. Your enthusiasm even at 3 years old to pick up fantasy books inspire me.

TERRY C. SIMPSON

Map of Ostania

Part 1

Portents And Plots

CHAPTER 1

Knight Commander Stefan Dorn surveyed the battlefield below him from his vantage point astride his horse. The oncoming Astocan army stretched in a long line that disappeared into the shadows of the mountains behind them. The Setian Knight Commander grimaced. "Fools. They're dead." With a shake of his head, he let out a resigned sigh. "Prideful and stupid to the end." It pained him to see such a waste of good men even from his enemies. Their general should have listened to reason. Together they could have averted the upcoming bloodshed.

"The way the Astocans would tell it, it's bravery of the highest degree." Knight General Garrick Nagel shrugged, broad shoulders made even wider by the pauldrons of his plate armor. He twirled his mustache around his thick forefinger. "They give their lives for pride. To claim they bent knee to no one. They would say their gods and people deserve nothing less."

Atop his brown gelding, Knight General Kasimir Edsel snorted. "Too bad their gods aren't fighting the battle." With the recent sunny days, the Knight General's skin had tanned to a deep brown.

"Indeed." Stefan nodded. As a believer and leader of the Setian, he understood how a man might wish to have the deities on their side in a battle like this, especially if that man was an

Astocan. He pursed his lips as he scratched at the annoying black stubble under his chin and studied the enemy.

Spread like fangs, the peaks of the Sang Reaches cast long shadows as the sun blazed in the cloudless skies. From their depths, the Astocan army boiled in numbers to dwarf his Setian forces. The smell of horse, sweaty men, and metal choked the air as his cavalry spread to his left and right. Up ahead his infantry advanced.

"I still don't understand your concern for them," Garrick said.

"You wouldn't," Kasimir replied. "Not after what they did—"

Stefan cut Kasimir off with a glare. It served no purpose to remind Garrick of the past. "They're men with families and livelihoods like us."

"Never like us," Garrick snapped. "Lose this battle today and they would enslave us all, rape our women, and pillage our cities." Nostrils flaring as they often did when he was angry, Garrick pulled so hard on his mustache Stefan wondered if his friend felt any pain at all. "So you're right, Kas, I wouldn't understand, not after how they made me suffer. But I know what it means to you, Stefan." He nodded to the Knight Commander. "You have way more honor than I ever will."

"Thank you." Stefan dipped his head and let out a slow breath that Garrick held his temper in check. "You don't give yourself enough credit, old friend. You're as honorable a man as I have met, regardless of how you try to hide it." Out of the corner of his eye, he saw the thin form of Knight General Cerny as the man made to say something. The Knight Commander spurred his horse forward a few steps. The King's errand boy could wait a bit longer.

Drumbeats rolled from across the battlefield. Blaring horns and the stomp of marching feet joined in. The jangle of weapons and the trundle of carts from Stefan's army of Setian played accompaniment. In tight formations, armor dull and dusty, his infantry lines awaited their commands.

A buzz—like flies alighting on a bloody corpse—filled

the sweltering air. Arrows darkened the sky, shot from the blackness beneath the drab grey and green mountains.

"Incoming!" boomed the voices of the silver–armored Setian Knight Captains. Their warning rose unnaturally over the trumpets and drums echoing from the enemy's ranks.

Stefan's infantry legions brought forearms up to shield the eye ports of their helmets.

The buzz grew in intensity. Arrows began to land, pinging harmlessly off imbued steel plate.

"Be ready!" the Knight Captains yelled as the barrage ended.

Several horns blared down the cavalry lines to Stefan's sides.

He brushed a stray lock from his face then raised the looking glass to his eye. Despite their location at the base of the mountains some six hundred feet away, the encroaching Astocan soldiers sprang into his vision as if he stood among them. Their archers were preparing another volley.

"Infantry … Formations," Stefan called out.

The trumpets relayed his order.

Two ranks of shield–bearing swordsmen marched forward. Spread from left to right, they made up the vanguard. A similar formation of pikemen wielding twenty–foot spears followed them ahead of an additional double rank of swordsmen. Behind the column of foot soldiers were Stefan's ranged legion consisting of bowmen, operators, and Cardian slaves. In unison, over twenty thousand sabatons stomped. The impact with the parched earth resounded—a mocking challenge to the Astocan archers' efforts.

"Return fire," Stefan said.

Amid horns announcing the command, the trot of a horse's hooves accompanied Knight General Cerny's appearance next to him. Cerny made to speak, but Stefan spared the small man a look, eyebrows raised. Cerny's mouth snapped shut. With a gloved hand, Cerny dabbed at his sweaty forehead.

At the rear of the infantry, the small complement of bowmen stepped forward. They drew fletchings to ears. Bows twanged and arrows loosed.

Stefan's gaze followed the flight of the Setian arrows. As expected, they fell woefully short. No man could fire as far as the Astocans with the monster bows they wielded. A derisive cheer rose from the Astocan legions. Stefan smirked.

"Slow forward," Stefan said to Kasimir and Garrick arrayed on either side of him.

With nods, they called out the order. The Setian heavy foot surged ahead, a step at a time. Their boots drowned out all else.

Across the plain, in numbers like swarming brown ants, the leather–clad Astocans dispatched their infantry. Their cavalry spread to their flanks, lances upright, tassels blowing in the wind. Mounted bowmen moved among them. Stefan gave a wry smile. Renowned for their horseback archery, the large Astocan warriors could deftly handle their mounts while firing their oversized bows with deadly precision. The sight was a thing of beauty … or terror.

"Have the drays follow."

This time, there was no trumpeting the command. Bannermen brandished the Setian flags in a complicated pattern. The images of a forest with a quake splitting it down the middle swirled with the movements.

Each pulled by a pair of huge, tan–skinned Cardian slaves, the drays trundled forward. The two–wheeled, flat bed carts followed in the paths created by the infantry. The thin, gill–like slits on each side of the Cardians' necks flared open and closed with their exertion. Two Setian soldiers—the operators—followed behind every dray.

Scorpios sat atop each dray, positioned between the wheels. The weapons measured five–feet from their front to the end of their loading chambers. They were in essence massive crossbows with arms twice as long across. With two thousand scorpios at his disposal, the Astocans stood little chance. Stefan had hoped he wouldn't need to resort to their use today, but their general had rebuffed any further attempts to parley.

"You wish to speak, Cerny?" Stefan said to the red–faced

Knight General. *Why had King Nerian chosen to send this buffoon with his message?* The man couldn't lead a horse to a trough. Kissing the King's ass does have its benefits, he supposed.

"Why would you risk getting your men wounded by moving closer to the Astocans?" Cerny said in a huff. "You will not be able to reach them with your bowmen. Why use them anyway? You have the scorpios."

Stefan preferred not to waste his time or breath, but he still spoke. His answer might shut Cerny up. Gods knew he couldn't stand the man's mouth. "The Astocans are overconfident. They believe if they make us work, that by the time we engage, our men will be tired from marching in heavy plate armor. Add that to the wounded, and they think—"

"The armor is imbued," Cerny blurted, hairless brows rising. "It weighs no more than leather. And their arrows will not penetrate unless they get lucky."

"The Astocans know this how?" Stefan tilted his head toward Cerny. Explaining himself was a chore he'd rather not take up with the man, but he did so nonetheless. "They will continue to fire, maybe even take out a few slaves, thinking they have the advantage as we advance. In close combat, their general believes he can win because of the strength kinai gives them. Against lesser forces? Yes … but my men have had their fill of kinai juice as well. Their stamina is beyond what General Dedrick expects. I'll allow him to feel he can milk their superior range while we draw closer. By the time the scorpios begin, it will be too late for them to retreat."

"You're going to force them to charge," Cerny said, eyes widening.

Stefan gave a slight nod then resumed his attention of his army's advance.

The Knight Captains bellowed orders. Accordingly, the rearmost shieldbearers paused for the drays to catch up. They aligned themselves next to the wagonbeds in order to protect the slaves against a possible Astocan volley.

Again the buzz rose, the sky darkened, and a hail of arrows fell. Shafts landed among the drays in greater concentration. The Setian soldiers raised shields to protect not only themselves but also the Cardian slaves closest to them. The scorpio operators had their own shields on each dray, and they raised them as well. In some spots, a slave fell, an arrow protruding from his body. When the sky once again lightened, slaves in reserve dashed forward to replace their fallen comrades.

"Cavalry to the wide flanks," Stefan ordered.

"Hmmm," Kasimir mused, "you think we'll need them?"

"I doubt it, but one can never be too certain."

In response to the horns blaring the new order, several Knight Captains flapped their reins and detached themselves from the long line of horsemen stretching to Stefan's left and right. Their men followed hard on their heels as they rode toward the battlefield's eastern and westernmost edges.

The Astocans deployed more men to the wide flanks to outmatch any numbers Stefan produced. *Good, maybe I can save some of you.*

He judged the distance between his infantry and theirs. "Five hundred feet. Sound the last command for the men to prepare."

The call went out. Now, it was a simple matter of waiting for the battle to unfold. Despite the certainty that he already knew the outcome, a slight tingle of fear and anticipation ran through Stefan's body as the space between the armies closed.

"Four hundred and fifty feet or there about," Knight General Garrick said, a smile splitting his square face, his dark eyes twinkling.

Kasimir grunted his agreement. "No turning back for them now."

"Nope." Garrick's amusement grew to a toothy grin.

The roar and rumble of sixty thousand Astocans became thunderous. Their cavalry wheeled as if to begin their charge.

A feint.

"S–Sir," Cerny said, his voice shaky, sweat beading his brow. "Shouldn't you respond with our cav—?"

"And waste good horses to their mounted archers?" Stefan wrinkled his face in distaste at Cerny's suggestion. After a deliberate shake of his head, he refocused on his men.

"Watch and learn a thing or three," Garrick added as flippant as ever.

The Cardian slaves ran to the sides of each dray and began to work. There was the clack, clack, clack of winches being turned, closely followed by the grind of metal gears. The drays, with one operator on top, elevated another few feet. Within moments, two thousand scorpios were primed and ready.

The scorpio operators cranked the winches that drew the bowstring back into firing position. Once secure, they fed the large, steel–tipped bolts into the sliding chambers and declared their readiness.

Standard–bearers waved their flags all along the ranks.

A simultaneous twang followed as the scorpios fired. Indiscernible blurs in their flight, the bolts ripped into the Astocans.

The precision was uncanny. The majority struck true, punching through armor, flesh, and bone like paper. Blood sprayed. Men and horses screamed.

Within the first minute, a second and a third salvo ensued. If a bolt struck a man on horseback, it threw him from his mount. Those on foot simply crumbled before their brethren trampled them.

Two–handed great swords brandished, the Astocans' pace began to increase in tiny increments. Behind their ranks, the drumbeats also sped up.

Stefan's army advanced at an almost leisurely rate, one pronounced step at a time.

The air hummed with another flight of death from the scorpios.

Soon the Astocans were trotting. A horn blew from among them. The drums rose to an incessant roll, unfaltering. A roar went up from the enemy ranks, and their speed increased to a sprint. The cacophony of the Astocan charge—hooves, boots, rolling drums, screams, and shouts rolled across the plain in a living wave.

Stefan's men stood fast, staring down the incoming

enemy that outnumbered them at least two to one. Not a single man among the Setian shifted or flinched. They simply waited.

Another flight of bolts tore into the Astocans. Empowered by battle rage and kinai, those pierced in the chest managed a few more steps before they fell. Where the steel–tipped projectiles sliced or severed a limb, that Astocan still attempted to drag himself to the melee.

Ignoring the onrushing forces, Stefan focused on his men and studied the smoothness of their reaction. His soldiers shifted positions instinctively. Their ranks curved at the far ends and collapsed inward with the shieldbearers taking up the foremost positions. Behind them, the pikemen formed a column four lines deep with more swordsmen at their back. To the rear stood the ordered scorpio file, still shooting.

More steel bolts thrummed death into the Astocans.

Yet, their charge did not falter.

Neither did the scorpios.

The Astocan cavalry drove forward, well ahead of their infantry now. When the enemy reached within forty feet, the Setian shieldbearers shifted. The pikemen adjusted their stances and dropped down to brace the pikes into the ground behind them, using the small bucklers at their elbows for support. Into the small spaces opened by the shieldbearers, the twenty–foot spears jutted out.

Too late and moving too fast to pull up, the Astocan cavalry slammed into steel instead of men. Horses died and sent soldiers crashing to the ground. The force of some of the sudden impacts propelled Astocans into the Setian ranks.

The Setian front line took a step back. Simultaneously, the pikemen yanked out their spears from the dead or dying. They shifted, allowing a space between each man, and the next file assumed their places. The movement was seamless. Unable to breach the formation, the next wave of horsemen died, impaled on steel.

Stefan saw he was wrong about one thing.

The Astocan cavalry were not simply archers but trained infantry also. Roaring as their battle rage took them, the ones who flew into the Setian lines that hadn't sustained grievous wounds lay about them with short swords. Their blows sheared through steel and lopped off limbs. More often than not, it took three or more of his men to down one crazed Astocan. When the last one fell, the Knight Commander let out a relieved breath. The second rank of his swordsmen replaced the first. Stefan shifted his attention to the remainder of the Astocans.

Depleted by more than half, the charge waned while their men still died to the firing scorpios. The drum rolls and triumphant horns faltered, cutting off mid note. By the fifteenth flight of steel bolts, before their main infantry ever reached the Setian front lines, the Astocans broke.

The barrage of projectiles did not end. The Astocans were well within the scorpios' thirteen hundred foot range. Winches cranked to increase their trajectory. The machines fired again and again. Bolts split skulls, punched through backs, and some cut limbs in half. Fleeing men fell.

Out of habit, Stefan took the pendant that hung from the chain around his neck and kissed the likeness of his wife. Soon, they would be together, but for now, there was a little work left. If they were lucky, maybe a quarter of the Astocans survived. Face a mask, Stefan said, "Call off the scorpios. Kasimir, Garrick, leave as many alive as you can, but bring me their General's head."

"King Nerian's orders were to kill everyone," Cerny protested.

Garrick clapped the smaller man on the back. "Do that and who would tell of our glorious victory then?"

"But the King—"

"Doesn't command this field." Stefan spared a glare for Cerny. He nodded to Kasimir and Garrick. "Send eagles to the other forces and let them know we no longer need them here. Have them head to Castere and take control of what's left of the Astocan government. I'll see you back at my pavilion when it's done."

"What of the King's tithe as well as the number to be enslaved?" Garrick raised a questioning eyebrow.

The thought of slavery curdled Stefan's insides. He

didn't object openly, but his refusal to partake in the negotiations after the victories spoke for itself. Once in a great while someone mistook his concern for softness until his sword proved differently. "Send word to the King that as usual he can have one of the High Council relay his demands." Nerian wouldn't be pleased, but then again, he was accustomed to Stefan's way of doing things. Sweeping victories in return for some leeway was a good tradeoff.

The two Knight Generals put fists to hearts and rode toward their legions.

"Cerny," Stefan said, the corner of his lips curling. "I don't care if you're slotted to be the next Knight Commander. Object to my commands in front my men again, and I will have you flogged and sent home to the King with your back and ass bloody."

At first, Cerny's mouth dropped open, and his complexion paled. Then he gathered himself and stiffened. "I'll have—"

"Are we clear?" Stefan made his eyes blank pits, his features expressionless.

"Yes, sir, Knight Commander Dorn."

Without another word, Stefan signaled to his escorts. Not caring if Cerny followed, he wheeled his mount to face the neat Setian tent lines spread before him less than a mile away. He set off at a trot.

Inside his tent, Stefan's gaze drifted to the map of Ostania and all its kingdoms. Three of them now belonged to Seti—the three that mattered the most. Next to the map was an artist's impression of the Great Divide far to the north in Everland—a jagged tear in the earth that went on for miles. Depicted crawling from the edges, creatures of pure night slunk up from the chasm. Shadelings, every one of them. People fled before certain death. He kept the artwork there as a constant memorial of the darkness that once plagued Ostania. A reminder of why he fought these campaigns.

As he stroked the prickly stubble under his chin, Stefan

mulled over the message Cerny had delivered from the King. "Is that all? I need to let my men know they have earned their peace."

"Look," Cerny whispered, eyes shifting nervously to the tent's entrance. "I advise against this."

Stefan scowled at the man. "And I advise you to keep this news to yourself. If I even hear a word of it from any of my men … an inkling … a whisper …." He let his voice trail off but deliberately slid a hand to his sword.

Cerny's head bobbed up and down as he averted his eyes. "As you say, sir. How soon will you speak to your men so Selentis and I can be on our way?"

"Cerny." Stefan took a deep breath. "You're trying my patience. Stop, please. Also, I don't care if she's outside or how you feel about them … when speaking of Alzari in my presence use the proper title and show respect."

After sparing the Knight General an additional glare, Stefan stepped outside, his armor clinking as he ducked through his tent's flaps. Overhead, Denestia's twin moons shone in a cloudless sky, casting the surrounding countryside in silvery blue. He breathed deep, rolled his neck, and worked the tightness from his back and shoulders. The smell of food, the cackle of laughter, raucous song of drunken soldiers, the tinkle of music, and the giggle of women greeted him. Campfires and torches lit the encampment as his men reveled in their victory. They drank, gambled, gorged themselves on a myriad of dishes, or rutted with whores.

He signaled to the green and gold robed Alzari Matus who stood guard outside his tent—one of King Nerian's own. The woman, who along with Cerny, had brought the news from the King. News he never expected. "Zar Selentis, if you will be so kind, I need everyone to hear me."

The Alzari Matus' face wrinkled in concentration. As with any other of her kind who could delve into the elements of Mater said to reside within everything in the world, Stefan was certain she was doing just that. The ability allowed her to touch the essences within those elements and shape them by the force of her will.

He wanted so much to open up his own senses to see the wonder of what she Forged. But he cringed with the thought of what might await him there. Yet, he couldn't help but frown. Did she Forge air alone to carry his voice? Or more?

In his youth, he'd often dreamed of wielding the same power as an Alzari Matus or any other Forger. They were lauded as being blessed among the gods, and as a boy of faith, he could not think of a greater honor. Gifted with the ability to harness the elements of Mater like the gods themselves, able to create, to destroy, or to save lives. How he'd dreamed. Until he witnessed what awaited those who succumbed to the very power they wielded. Those horrors had etched themselves into his mind. He shuddered.

"It is done, Knight Commander. You may speak," the Zar said, her voice showing no strain.

"Thank you, Zar Selentis," Stefan said. He closed his eyes to quell the emotions warring inside him. Words from *The Disciplines* echoed in his head. *'As a leader, be careful what you promise your men. Failure to deliver can be as costly as defeat. Glory, the spoils of war, and the worship of the commoners are good forms of motivation, but use such rewards sparingly. The trust of your men hinges on their belief in you. In turn, victory hinges on that same belief. Break that trust but once, and the damage may be irreparable.'*

"Men," he called as he opened his eyes.

Enhanced by the Alzari Matus' power, his voice boomed across the encampment to every corner, certain to reach all thirty thousand soldiers. The celebratory noises dwindled away, leaving only the crackle of fire and the scuff of a boot here or there. Heads shifted and eyes focused in his direction.

"For thirty years, you have followed me. You have feasted with me before every battle and after every victory. You have obeyed my commands without question. In turn, I have walked in the footsteps and listened to the words of a great man, a man more like a father to me than the father I knew. To King Nerian the Lightbearer!" Stefan raised his cup of kinai wine and downed it in one gulp.

"To King Nerian the Lightbearer!" his men echoed, cheering each other on as they drank.

The liquor wasn't as refined as his wife's was, but it did the job. The kinai wine's heat flared down his gullet, bringing with it a sense of renewed vigor. Tasting the drink brought on a longing to be with Thania, conjuring memories of her dark hair, coppery skin and golden eyes. Stefan smiled despite the heaviness in his heart. "Men." The noise died once more. "Tonight, we feast together again, but for another reason. I was a mere youth, my nineteenth naming day when I earned my first command."

"Are you saying you're an old man now?" called a gruff voice.

All around, soldiers barely stifled their laughter.

"Not quite, Carim," Stefan said to the smooth–faced Knight. "But I could whip you and any other youngster who think they can best me with a sword. Wait …" He grinned. "Isn't that exactly what I did to you two days ago? It was four of you, wasn't it?"

Guffaws and good–natured ribbing came from the men around Carim. Red faced but smiling, the Knight bowed.

"Anyway," Stefan said. The men quieted. "When the King began his campaigns, I assured him we would be victorious—I promised YOU victory."

"Stefan the Undefeated, Stefan the Steadfast," someone shouted. Picked up by other voices, the names rolled through the camp.

The Knight Commander raised his cup, and the shouts lessened until the men drifted into silence once more. "The victories are not mine alone or the Knight General's." He gestured to Garrick, Kasimir and the others. "But yours." He pointed to the soldiers. "You men made this possible. Your willingness to believe in us, to stand before superior numbers undaunted, and battle to the last breath. Your fortitude to train until your body burns and you can no longer take a step much less lift a weapon has carried us to this point." Chest heaving, he paused. "YOU … have made the name Setian a name to be feared, a name to be held in awe, a name to be revered for all time!"

A cheer went up then, building into a deafening roar. Stefan allowed it to continue for a few moments. They deserved their elation.

"Today," Stefan said, his words rising above the din to wash it away. "You won the last victory in our campaign to make Ostania whole once more. We can stand against the shade and any other enemies as one people, one nation, unified. Today, we routed the Astocans like their cousins the Cardians before them. Coupled with the Banai surrender, we have prevailed. Today, we can truly consider ourselves an empire." Amid the wild whoops that followed, Stefan rolled the word around on his tongue, loving the taste.

"I promised you something else back then. For those of you who remember that day and have witnessed me repeat the same time and again … I promised you peace … a chance to raise your families, to love your wives, to find a wife, start a family, to ensure our future as a people.

"I said you would have a chance to go home to Seti one day to live a different life. Not as soldiers, but as merchants, miners, farmers and teachers, or simply to relax, enjoy life and your children until the end of your days."

The camp reached a palpable silence.

"You." He pointed out to his men, drawing his hand from left to right to encompass them all. "You. Every single one of you. The ones before you who have shed blood, who have given an arm, a leg, a life, for the King, for Seti, for victory, deserve this day.

"Men of the Unvanquished …" it was the name many had begun calling them, and although he resisted it, and often said he never wanted to hear the name in his presence, right now, the title fit. "I give you peace."

When the triumphant cries bellowed, Stefan could no longer hear himself think. He allowed the feeling to wash over him, reveling in the tingle it brought. Not only the cheers and belief of his men but the word peace itself.

It meant he should have been able to finally go home to Seti, be with Thania, and maybe, just maybe, start a family. A smile that did not touch his eyes bloomed on his face. However, as he turned and entered his pavilion with Garrick and Kasimir close on his heels, his expression crumpled.

CHAPTER 2

Several hours later, after Cerny and Zar Selentis left to return to the capital, Stefan sat at the table in his pavilion. Two candles in glass holders occupied the table's center, their perfumed scent overriding that of the untouched food before him. Illuminated by flickering light, a map next to his plate displayed his forces. He removed the pins representing the Alzari Matii. By now, they were well on their way back to Benez under Cerny's command.

Men were going to die because of the King's order for their withdrawal. A great many.

In the days to come, the first to perish would mainly be Astocans. Some might say their deaths weren't much of a loss, but eventually, his own men would number among the dead. A sense of helplessness crowded over him, and he sighed. Yet, he harbored no regrets for his announcement. Somehow, some way, he needed to stay true to his word.

"So what now?" Kasimir asked.

In his brooding, Stefan had almost forgotten about him and Garrick. "We do as we have always done ... save as many of the enemy as we can."

Garrick grumbled a protest under his breath.

"I know how you feel about them, Garrick." Stefan recalled the sight of Garrick's mangled body and face after his torture by the Astocans. "However, this was the one thing King Nerian, myself, and the High Council agreed upon. We would be different from other conquerors. We decided to save as many of those we defeated and give their people some choice in how we rule. This way, the common folk won't think of us as tyrants—a lesson history taught us."

"Use force as necessary for victory and compassion when the battle is won," Kasimir said. A quote from Henden's *The Disciplines of Soldiering*.

"Exactly."

"I understand." Garrick let out a resigned breath. "I still don't like it."

"If that's the case, what I don't get," Kasimir shifted in his seat and peered at the map, "is why the King ordered us to kill them all and now has withdrawn our Alzari menders."

Stefan nodded. "Yes, that's been troubling me also. I can't remember Nerian changing plans without conferring with me in person. So why now? I swear ... I feel as if something is amiss back home. I don't trust Cerny. Any man who is so quick to do anything without questioning motives often has his own plans."

"You think he had a hand in this?" Garrick scowled.

"Not likely," Stefan said. "The man barely knows the ass end of a horse. Someone else may be using him."

"Or he's smarter than any of us suspects," Kasimir added.

"Still," Stefan said, "until I speak to Nerian himself, I'm not changing how we do things. We'll mend as many Astocans as we can."

"How are you going to accomplish that without our Alzari?" Kasimir leaned back in his chair, armor creaking as he did so.

"We do possess other Matii besides them," Stefan reminded him. His thoughts drifted to the crimson-garbed

Ashishin Matii sent by the Granadian Tribunal. Considering the old hostilities between Ostania and Granadia, the Tribunal's willingness to help and their accepting King Nerian among their ranks had come as a shock. It had taken a while for his men to adjust to the Ashishin. The fact that the Pathfinders—whose job it was to kill any Ashishin who succumbed to their power— accompanied them, had not helped.

Initially, his own Alzari had protested the Pathfinders' presence. When orders arrived from Nerian himself, stating that the Pathfinders would also decide the fate of the Alzari, the outrage grew. It hadn't lessened, but they did tread with fear around the silver-armored Pathfinders. Stefan was certain Nerian's new orders relieved the majority of them. However, he harbored his own doubts as to the results of the King's command. He shook off the thought to hear Garrick speaking.

"Mending as many folk as we gathered might be a bit much for them. Ashishin Matii may be stronger than Alzari, but I doubt they'd be able to do the job without going mad, even if they got it done at all."

As much as Stefan hated to admit it, the big Knight General was right. Forging Mater varied by Matus, requiring a certain proportion of essences to be available in relation to the Forger's strength. One could not simply create something from nothing. The Matus, in this case Forgers like the Ashishin or Alzari, either used what existed around them or enhanced that which was inside them for what they wanted to Forge. Centuries before, this was one of the reasons the Alzari had defeated the Namazzi, whose strength lay in water. On land, and without a rainstorm, the Alzari outlasted them until the Namazzi used up whatever liquids they'd stored. The Battle of Blood, it had been aptly named.

From the little Stefan understood, mending worked in the same fashion. The Matus had to use a liquid essence, preferably water or blood, some type of solid, preferably tissue, be it plant, human, or animal, as well as a touch of the essences required for life from either their patient or themselves, in order to mend a wound. Unlike a sickness, which they could simply drive from a body. He was certain the process was much more complicated, but that was the best explanation he ever received.

"You also seem to forget the Shins aren't exactly ours," Garrick added.

Considering Garrick's disposition towards Ashishin, Stefan was surprised to hear the man use their honorary title. "Maybe, but they are all we have. The risk is worth it. At least to save the soldiers who are worse off. For the ones with minor wounds, we gather apothecaries from the surrounding villages. It's paramount we do something to gain the people's trust."

"What if one of the Ashishin does go mad?" Kasimir arched an eyebrow.

"We let their Pathfinders deal with them," Stefan answered.

"I don't know." Garrick shook his head skpetically. "The Pathfinders themselves worry me. What makes them so different from a Shin, Zar, or any other Forger? Why are they immune to the elements' effects? Another thing, if they do know a way to keep their madness at bay, why keep it secret?"

"Does it matter?" Stefan shrugged. "The Pathfinders never fail to do their jobs."

"Not that we're aware of," Garrick countered.

"Regardless," Stefan spared a glare for his big friend, "they're the ones we rely on. Now, if you two don't mind, I need you to visit the villages, collect the apothecaries, and head to the encampment. When you leave, send in Pathfinder Kaden."

The two Knight Generals stood, bowed, and left the tent.

Stefan rubbed at his throbbing temple. Other than the difference in elements each could Forge, Alzari, Ashishin and Pathfinders were the same or should be. So why were they so far apart in control? Did their strength in particular essences within each element create the disparity, decided who went mad? No, he doubted that. Someone would have resolved such an issue long ago. He'd inquired after the Pathfinders and the Ashishin in general once, but his questions resulted in silence. On more than one occasion, he was told to direct his questions to their ruling Tribunal. Stefan shook his head. As a free Ostanian, setting foot in Granadia was not an option. Not if he wished to live.

Still, the plan to mend the Astocans was a risky business. Chances were they might overwork the Ashishin. Doing so could result in more bloodshed. But the lives saved by their work and the modicum of trust such a compassionate act brought was what mattered. Ostania needed to be whole again. For that to occur, the Astocans must see the Setian meant well.

Stefan closed his eyes and worked his neck from side to side to relieve some tightness. He wondered what his wife was doing at home in Benez right now. The sweet scent of bellflowers from the candles tickled at his nose. Thania's and his favorite. He sighed. Gods knew he wanted to be in his villa again. He pictured his triumphant return and the cheering masses. More than them, he anticipated the sight of Thania on the wall awaiting his arrival.

A rustle announced the tent's flap opening. Stefan eased his eyes open. A smooth–faced cadet stepped inside.

The young man placed a fist to his heart and gave a stiff bow. "Sir, Pathfinder Kaden is here."

"Send him in."

The cadet ducked outside and moments later, Kaden entered. As with all other Pathfinders, he wore filigreed silversteel armor. The torchlight played off its surface, highlighting the fine craftsmanship. At Kaden's hip rested a sword in a leather scabbard chased with the same metal. The Pathfinder's eyes were dark things obscured within the port of his full plate helm. The small golden shield worked into Kaden's breastplate was the only thing differentiating his armor from his fellow Pathfinders.

King Nerian's words rose fresh in Stefan's mind: *'The Pathfinders protect us from the Ashishin and the Ashishin from themselves.'* The words lent Stefan some comfort. Things existed that were beyond men like himself or his Knight Generals. For those, he needed Matii like the Ashishin or the Alzari and inevitably men like Kaden and those he led.

Kaden knuckled his forehead to Stefan. "Sir, I assume

this means we leave for the encampment at dawn?" Despite the helmet enclosing his face, Kaden's voice was deep, clear, and vibrant.

To the point. Stefan nodded. "Yes. There are more wounded Astocans than expected. Quite a few from our earlier skirmishes, in fact. Your Shins will be mending near fifteen thousand men." Stefan wished the Pathfinder's entire face was visible, but the narrowing of Kaden's eyes told him enough. "Can they can manage?"

"If we had a few weeks or if I had more than a thousand Ashishin *plus* your Alzari, yes, but you want this done in days. Why? It's not only the lives of these Astocans at stake. There is a possibility I will lose some of my own men as well."

"I understand, Pathfinder Kaden." Stefan stared through the slit of an entrance to his tent and into the night. "A King once said to me, 'a good commander is one who shows an interest in the plight of his enemy, especially after their defeat. Such an act goes a long way in turning the mind of one's enemy to seeing more than a simple conqueror.' "

"A wise man. But what of my Ashishin? Essentially, you might be working them to death, and putting your men as well as what's left of the enemy you're trying to save at risk at the same time."

"Doesn't your Tribunal proclaim the Shins as servants to all?"

Kaden regarded him in silence for a moment. "Fair enough." The Pathfinder tipped his head. "Whatever is the Tribunal's wish, I am but an extension of their orders."

"Good. Now, do you think your Pathfinders will be able to prevent any Shins from losing control?"

"We can try, but there are no guarantees in this. However, *if* one of them does succumb, we should be able to stop them before they do any damage."

"That will have to do," Stefan said.

"Knight Commander?"

"Yes?"

"Why did King Nerian summon the Alzari back to Seti?"

"I'm wondering the same thing myself," Stefan answered.

"If something should go wrong tomorrow, Nerian's decision will be partly to blame."

"Then let's make sure nothing does."

Chapter 3

In the shadow of the Sang Reaches, Stefan surveyed what remained of the Astocan encampment. Located in a vale with a tiny pass for an entrance, the expanse of fields had been quite defensible with an easy retreat into the mountains. Too bad the positioning was all for nothing.

Burned and ripped canvas, broken poles, and ramshackle wagons spread in a haphazard fashion about the ground. Hanging from a tree branch was the corpse of one of the Astocan captains. Below him, another soldier leaned on the trunk, a spear driven through his chest. The acrid pall of smoke hung so thick Stefan covered his mouth to choke down a cough. Brown, tattered brush crowded once verdant fields. Pieces of weapons glinted amongst the trampled grass. Stefan's men had gathered the majority of the Astocan soldiers and led them off. A few of the remaining officers had managed to flee into the mountains. The ones left behind were incapacitated by their wounds. Some lay on makeshift litters, while others rested on grassy mounds. Moans and groans echoed among them. Many were unmoving and silent—eyes staring sightlessly.

One Astocan—skin so dark it shone—coughed and attempted to rise to his feet as Stefan approached. Several punctures from what must have been scorpio bolts and a missing arm prevented the soldier from doing much more than getting to his knees. The man clasped a hand to the two thin slits at the side of his neck that always reminded Stefan of a fish's gills. The matching ones on the other side fluttered open and closed. Red trickled between the Astocan's fingers, and he crumpled.

An Ashishin wearing the colors of a Devout priest hurried to his side. She placed a hand on the soldier's chest. Blood oozed from the wounds and bubbled from the man's mouth. Head down, the Devout prayed. An answering rattle issued from his lips. He gave a final kick and lay still.

Robes a brighter red than the dried blood on the ground, Ashishin Matii moved from one man to the next, mending those not too far gone. Soldiers beyond the point of saving were passed on to the Devout. Dressed in white and gold, these higher ranked Ashishin bent to offer prayers for the dead and dying. More often than not, the mortally wounded chose to convert to the Streamean religion the Devout preached and accepted the blessing of a god whose warriors bested theirs.

In close proximity to the menders were the Pathfinders. Displayed on their cloaks as well on each Ashishin's breast was the Lightstorm insignia of the Granadian Tribunal—an illustration of three lightning bolts striking in front of the sun. Each Pathfinder's hand rested on his sword. They had eyes only for the Ashishin.

Seeing the Matii at work with their guardians keeping watch, Stefan wondered again about the King's message and his actions. Why did Nerian withdraw all his Alzari? This was the last battle. He knew they needed them to save as many Astocans as possible. Why did Nerian require the few Forgers they possessed? And for what campaign? Why was the King willing to risk the men's ire by having them go off to war once more? The questions roiled on. Only one threat came to mind that would need the attacking power and prowess of the Matii.

Shadelings.

A chill passed through Stefan, and he shivered, covering the tingle by running his hand up the back of his neck and stroking the hair standing on end. He breathed easier knowing that the combined might of the Ostanian kingdoms had driven back the black monstrosities years ago. Thanks to the Tribunal's

help. On rare occasion, a report came in from the far north
or northeast of a sighting. A massive hunt followed until they
destroyed the creature in question. Stefan found it hard to believe
a sizable incursion had occurred without his knowledge. At least
not one dangerous enough to warrant the King's actions and the
message of a new call to arms that Cerny had delivered.

Controlling his mount with his legs, Stefan shifted to
get a better look at Kasimir and Garrick. "I still can't decide if
I should break the news to the men or how." He'd spent the
previous night mired in sleeplessness and nightmares. In his
dreams, his soldiers mutinied and caused a war that brought Seti
to its knees. Hopefully, events would not be so bad. The thought
did little to lessen his sense of dread or his dislike for the King's
orders. Such had been the dreams that he'd awoke red–eyed and
weary.

"Do as you always have," Garrick said. His mount sniffed
at the ground then snorted. "Tell it like it is."

Kasimir nodded his agreement.

"Maybe that would be best," Stefan said. Impaled on
a pike not far from him was General Dedrick's head. A slight
breeze ruffled the Setian Quaking Forest banner tied to the shaft
below the ragged stump of a neck. "I still can't help the sense
that many of our men won't be pleased. I feel as if I failed them."

"Nonsense," Garrick said. "The men followed your
command because of who you are and what you have done.
They'll know you wouldn't force them back into duty if it could
be avoided."

"I still don't understand why the King feels the need to
continue the campaigns," Kasimir added. "Except for the Harnan
and Svenzar lands, we have claimed all of Ostania for ourselves.
Does he intend to attack those two again?"

"Don't forget the Felani," Garrick said.

"Meh, the Felani are the Felani. They will continue to
hide behind the Vallum of Light."

"Unless he's found a way to root the Harnan and Svenzar
out of their mountain strongholds, I don't see why he would

bother," Stefan said. "Such a feat would take more Matii than we have." He nodded toward the Ashishin.

"Involving that many Forgers in an active battle wouldn't be worth the risk," Garrick said with a shake of his head. "At least I don't think so. Why—"

A scream cut off Garrick's words. Stefan whipped his head around to peer in the direction of the sound, twisting slightly in his saddle.

In the middle of the encampment a young Ashishin Forger stood with her hands and face raised to the gray skies. Her keening intensified until his ears hurt. The slight breeze rapidly became a gale.

Ragged, tearing sounds followed as canvas, dirt, debris, and fragmented weapons swirled into the air around the woman as if a miniature tornado formed. The wind snatched the pike bearing Dedrick's head and flung it into the sky. Corpses flew from the ground. Wounded soldiers clung to the closest things at hand, even if it was only brush. When their hold failed or the gale ripped the foliage from the earth, the soldiers screamed as the storm swept them away. Their voices lasted only moments before the wind's howls drowned them out.

Stefan's horse whinnied and pranced. Cloak whipping about him, he yanked on his reins as he realized his mount was being drawn inexorably toward the tempest's center and the lone Ashishin. Pebbles pinged off his armor, and dust stung his eyes. The clouds above rotated to match the wind, forming a gray maelstrom. From its center, the sun shone through to illuminate the Ashishin's form shrouded within the mass of glinting metal, swirling debris, and bodies.

A man–shaped glint of silver crashed through the vortex to land a step behind the Ashishin. One of the Pathfinders. The soldier's sword flashed up.

One hand formed into a fist, the Ashishin spun. The silver–armored Pathfinder's blade took her head in a spurt of blood. In the same motion, he dropped to one knee and stabbed the earth.

As the Ashishin toppled, the storm died. The debris swirling around her fell. Bodies, stone, dirt, wood, and weapons rained to the ground in a deadly deluge. Stefan sucked in a breath as they dropped toward the Pathfinder.

But the man simply kneeled, both hands on his sword hilt. Anything falling toward him spilled to the side without touching him. It appeared as if a small dome had formed two feet above the Pathfinder. Not once did anything strike him. The debris piled until it hid him from view.

The rain of rubble ended, and Pathfinder Kaden stepped forward. "Shin!" he yelled and pointed at the mound of rubble burying his brethren. "Shield."

Four Ashishin gave nervous bows as they hurried over. Each one took up a position to form a rough box at the four corners of the mound.

"Free yourself, Pathfinder Clarus," Kaden called from where he stood a few steps beyond the Ashishin.

The mound exploded outwards. Rubble struck invisible walls between each Matii. Clarus staggered to his feet.

"Help him," Kaden ordered, "and have your fellow Shin take a break until tonight."

The Ashishin bowed and hurried to Clarus' side. Kaden wheeled his mount and headed toward Stefan.

The Knight Commander glanced around to check on Garrick and Kasimir. Dust coated their armor and their faces were grimy, but beyond that and their unkempt hair, they seemed no worse for wear. Both Knight Generals peered toward the other Ashishin as if expecting another outburst.

Garrick was the first to turn to Stefan. "This is why they're not worth the risk in a battle."

"There would be no risk if your King hadn't pulled the Alzari." Pathfinder Kaden reined in next to them. His eyes glittered deep within his helm. "With the amount of wounded here what did you expect?"

"Bah. A few more Astocans dying here or there would have been fine," Garrick countered. "The blame is partly yours too. If you hadn't allowed your Matii to Forge for so many hours without rest—"

"Stop it, Garrick," Stefan commanded. "I asked Kaden to do this. It's my fault this happened as much as it is the King's for withdrawing the Alzari."

Garrick gave a grudging nod and mumbled an apology to Kaden.

Stefan focused on the damage the Matus had inflicted. Not as many bodies as he expected stood out in the rubble. He'd once before seen what happened to a battlefield when a Forger lost control and went insane with no Pathfinder to hold them in check. The results were blood, mangled flesh, and death on an unimaginable scale. He shuddered. If Clarus had been a moment longer, everyone in the vale would have perished. *Maybe, I should count us lucky the man reacted when he did.* However, he simply couldn't. The prone forms of the dead Astocans gnawed at him. "Although I blame myself, Kaden, we spoke on this." Stefan eyed the Pathfinder coolly. "What took so long?"

Kaden shifted in his saddle and gazed at the Ashishin who were heading toward tents clustered near the entrance to the vale. Their Pathfinders escorted them. "That one was stronger than she should have been. Not to mention the elements here have been acting strange. See for yourself."

Stefan paused for a moment as he considered what Kaden asked. As with any Dagodin like himself or Garrick and Kasimir, he had the ability to see or rather, sense the elements of Mater and their essences. However, he was unable to manipulate them—to Forge. A deficiency he was thankful for, but what he witnessed moments before still made him uncertain. Suppose the voices that haunted Mater, those he'd heard at one time during his training all those years ago, surfaced? What if he failed to resist their temptation?

"I can assure you, Knight Commander, that in all my years as a Pathfinder, traveling with various Matii, I have yet to see a Dagodin fall to the madness." Kaden's voice was filled with certainty, and not once did he blink.

Stefan sucked in several breaths, and then opened his Matersense. Power swirled in bands representing the three elements of Mater. Inside those bands, the individual essences within each element stood out in a myriad of colors. They existed in everything, from the ones he recognized to those he could not discern. They twisted, stretched, and congealed in a chaotic mass.

Many hues of blue and transparencies represented water and air essences contained within the liquid element of Flows. They threaded upon the breeze, the coolness of which promised rain. Within the murky blanket above, they coiled.

Among the fields, the sheer rock faces, and the forested slopes of the Sang Reaches the tiny differences in browns, greens, and metallic glints stood out. Those displayed earth, wood, and metal essences within the solids that were the element of Forms.

The sun's glow peeked through a crack in the clouds. Gold and white brightened the sky for the briefest moment. Darkness wavered in and out of view among the shadows. The humidity from the day still hung in reddish orange. Those hues and bands represented light, shade, and heat essences—all belonging to the energy from within the element of Streams.

As he took in the wonder of his Matersense, Stefan became aware of what Kaden meant. There was an overflow of power among the essences. It was almost too much to bear—as if they reached for him, swirled within his head, his sight and sucked at him. With a gasp, he released his sense.

"What you saw there, we can feel a hundredfold," Kaden said.

Stefan took a moment to ease his heavy breathing. When his heart calmed, he asked, "If it's that bad, why did you still allow your Ashishin to go on for so long?"

"We have seen the like before and were able to work around the influence of Mater by rotating menders and extending the time between each Forge." Kaden stared toward the body of the dead Shin. A Devout priest gathered the head to the corpse and bowed in prayer.

"So what happened?"

A slow, deep breath resonated within Kaden's faceplate. "She attempted the impossible."

Stefan frowned then opened his eyes wide. "She attempted to Forge all three elements at once?"

"I'm afraid so." Kaden shook his head. "Shin Rotesa was as young and strong as she was imprudent. She let the task of saving these men overcome her sense of limitation. When the essences took her, she was too weak to resist."

Stefan recognized the pain in the man's voice. "I'm sorry for your loss." He paused. "I don't want to seem crude, but in ways this helps us. I can send an eagle to the King informing him of the issue. With Mater this unstable, he should understand. It will give you some time, at least a week. Please do your best to make sure the Shin recover."

"As you wish, sir." Kaden wheeled his mount and rode toward the tents.

Stefan studied the man in silence. He turned at the snort of a horse to see Kasimir and Garrick eying him. "What?"

"Do you think the King knew of the change in the essences, and that's why he recalled our Alzari?" Kasimir asked.

"Maybe, but why didn't he have me informed? Why didn't he warn the Ashishin?"

"Why should he?" Garrick shrugged. "They're Matii. They can sense what is happening as much as any other."

"Not to mention that he did command us to kill the Astocans," Kasimir added. "So the use of menders should have been limited to our own wounded."

"An order I disobeyed," Stefan said, voice low. He flapped his reins and sent his horse trotting toward the Setian camp. *Nerian knows how I feel about saving men. If there was a problem with the elements, why didn't he send a warning? In fact, why hadn't Cerny or any of the other Alzari?* The question swirled through Stefan's mind all the way back to their encampment.

CHAPTER 4

Days later, Stefan sat in his pavilion tapping time on his helmet. Raindrops drummed on the canvas, while the winds howled and buffeted the gray–white walls. The rain was a welcome respite to the sweltering heat the past few weeks. So far, there had been no more incidents with the Ashishin, but the breaks needed by them brought the entire process of mending the Astocans to a crawl.

To make issues worse, if the elements didn't stabilize sometime soon, the Travelshafts would be of no use. His army would have to march from the Sang Reaches across some two thousand miles or more to Benez. Although the trip was mainly through farmland and grassy plains, it could take at least three weeks and that was if he took only his cavalry. Waiting for the entire army meant adding another three months.

"The bloody gods of Flows laugh at the plans of men," he grumbled under his breath as he stared at the map.

Stefan glanced up at the rustle from the pavilion's entrance. The rain became a roar and the wind a wail as Kasimir's slim form ducked inside, water streaming down his armor.

The Knight General cleared the hair plastered to his forehead and cheek before he spoke. "Sir, a report arrived from Kaden. The elements calmed overnight. The Shin have been able to mend all the Astocans."

Stefan's lips twitched into a smile. "And here I was cursing the gods."

"I knew you'd like that." Kasimir grinned. "Garrick and the Knight Captains are gathering the men. We assumed you weren't planning on waiting out the storm."

"You know me too well." Stefan stood and pulled on his gloves. Lips pursed, he traced a finger south from the Sang Reaches through the swamps and into Castere. "With the storm, the Sinking Swamps will be too treacherous to pass if we wanted to use the Travelshafts at Castere. The next closest city is Konele, here." He moved his hand west. "Have a contingent stay behind to take apart the tents and follow when they're done. Send the scorpios and wagons through first with enough men to protect them should the Svenzar decide this is a good place for a raid."

"Do you really think they will strike this far south?"

"We have seen how quickly the Svenzar can traverse any mountain range. Considering they built the shafts, who is to say they don't have a way to reach them easier than we do?"

"If that's the case, why not wait?"

"And risk Mater becoming unstable again? No. We leave now."

Kasimir nodded. "I'll make sure all is ready." The Knight General turned on his heels and left.

After Stefan pulled on his helmet, he took one last look around his pavilion. In ways, he would miss his tent, but he was also glad to be heading home. Thania's silky hair and golden eyes called to him. With a sigh, he pulled back the tent flap and stepped outside.

Immediately, the rain pattered on his helm and the wind snatched at his cloak. He ignored both and slogged through mud to where his horse was tethered. Despite the weather, the camp had a purposeful bustle about it as soldiers and Cardian slaves hurried along with their preparations. They were taking apart tents while others had the wagons and drays with their scorpios already in a line. To the west of the camp, a long snake of infantry waited. Ahead of them, horses stomping their impatience, the cavalry formed.

The storm had done a good job of washing away the stench of thirty thousand soldiers. No longer did the pungent smells of piss, shit, or sweat hang. Instead, Stefan drew in a breath of freshness. Muddy freshness but satisfying all the same. He was mounting when the sound of racing hooves reached him.

Silversteel armor unmistakable even with the deluge and dark clouds that made the afternoon more akin to dusk, a Pathfinder raced through the camp. When the man drew closer, Stefan made out the golden shield chased into the breastplate.

Kaden yanked on his reins and brought his horse to a jarring halt several feet from Stefan.

"What's the matter?" Stefan was unable to see Kaden's face, but from the way the Pathfinder kept his back straight and head high as he approached closer something wasn't right. The Knight Commander tensed.

"Apparently your King has forbidden the Ashishin from entering Benez. He went so far as to banish any who serve the Tribunal," Kaden shouted over the wind's howls.

"What?"

"Word came by eagle sent from the Tribunal themselves. They ordered us home to Granadia immediately."

Stunned, Stefan stared through the rain at his army. *Nerian, What in Ilumni's name are you doing? First, you recalled the Alzari without saying why and now you banish the Ashishin from Seti?*

"I took the liberty of sending the Astocan survivors to Castere," Kaden said. "Without Pathfinders, I wish you the best of luck, Knight Commander. May Ilumni shine his light on you." Without another word, he flapped his reins and thundered back the way he came.

Stefan watched the man ride off. Without Pathfinders, they would need more than luck or Ilumni's blessings. Managing the Alzari to make sure none went insane, or to limit the damage when one did, once again fell to whatever method King Nerian chose. In the past, none worked half as well as having the Pathfinders.

Kasimir rode over, his horse's hooves splashing through puddles formed within the ruts from wagon wheels. "What was that about?" he yelled.

A hand stroking the stubble on his chin, Stefan gave a slow shake of his head. "Nerian has banished all Ashishin from Seti."

Kasimir's eyes widened. "Hydae's Flames, what's he thinking?"

Coming from Kasimir, the curse caught Stefan off-guard, but he sympathized. "I was standing here saying the same thing. The Tribunal won't take kindly to this."

"That's an understatement. I wouldn't be surprised if this sparked a war."

At the words, Stefan frowned. "You don't think that is—"

"N–No, it couldn't be." Kasimir's face drained of color.

"Let's hope not," the Knight Commander said. "There's no way we can win a war against the Tribunal with all of Granadia's might behind them. Even Nerian knows that."

"What if he believes differently?"

"I guess we'll find out when we get to Benez. Is the cavalry ready?"

Kasimir nodded.

"Good, we head out now. Leave a quarter of them behind with the infantry and the scorpios. We can't afford to wait. Whenever they make it back is fine." With a jerk of his reins, Stefan set off through the downpour.

By the time they reached Konele's outskirts, the rain was dwindling to a drizzle. The drum of hooves drew Stefan's attention to a fenced field near an abandoned farm—one of the many in the area. Head down, a horse galloped across the muddy pasture.

A loud mewl made Stefan whip his head around in the opposite direction. Body a blur, a six–legged creature crashed through the fence. Splintered wood flew into the air. The beast slowed as it gained the field. Stefan recognized the mottled carapace, the humped shell on its back, the long swinging, snake—like neck, and a head with a mouth lined with sharp teeth. It was a dartan.

The beast stopped, peered at Stefan and his men, and then toward the lone horse. It mewled once more before bounding forward, muddy water splashing as its feet churned. As tall and wide as dartan's were, one would expect them to be slow and lumbering, but they were as much that as they were docile. This one ran three times faster than the horse, and it was several times larger. Kept by farmers for their speed and strength, dartans needed to be beat into submission to maintain a semblance of control. Even then, such control was often fleeting. Yet their workload was worth the risk. Not to mention their use in prizefights.

Before the horse gained the fence to the pasture's far side, the dartan caught up. The creature crashed into the horse's side. The horse went toppling, its body carving a path through the sodden earth. With a whinny, the horse attempted to scramble to its feet.

The dartan rushed forward, head snaked out. Its jaws snapped onto its prey's neck. A sudden twist and the horse stilled and sank back onto its knees. The dartan tore a chunk of flesh and mewled in content.

Whenever Stefan saw the beasts, he marveled at them. He had sworn to find a way to harness their aggression and speed into something his army could use. Alas, such a process eluded him. The arrival of one of his scouts drew him away from the dartan at its meal.

Garbed in dark leather, the scout drew rein. "Sir, they have withdrawn everyone into Konele."

"Good." Stefan gave one last glance to where the dartan stood tearing another chunk of meat. "Head down to the Travelshaft. It's past time we were home."

Similar to their other locations the Travelshaft's entrance

sat outside the town with three, smooth–paved roads sloping down into it. The stone of the roads weren't cobble or large flagstones. It was as if one layer of rock had been laid down in a stretch a thousand feet long. The surface showed no signs of erosion nor did precipitation collect. Instead, rain flowed off as the streets declined slightly from the middle to the sides. Despite their smooth surfaces, the roads never became slippery. They were an ancient marvel none appeared able to reproduce. And there was no discussing the construction with the Sevnzar even when they did happen to speak to a human.

As the scout reported, the central road itself was empty. Unmanned, heavy stone fortifications stood sentinel along the way. Next to those were several ballistae aimed at the portal tunnel that was the Travelshaft's entrance.

Ahead, the yawning maw of the shaft towered. Rock covered the exterior forming what looked like a short hallway hewn into stone and angling down into the earth. Nearly forty feet tall and twice as wide, the surface of the portal gave off an ethereal glow, power resonating from it in rhythmic pulses. Any Matii could feel the pull of energy as soon as they set foot onto the ramp's beginning. Beyond the glow was a black so pure it stood out at night.

Stefan waited for Garrick and Kasimir to draw abreast of him. Once they began the downhill dash, there would be no stopping. The speed altering effect of the road leading to the portal was immediate, triggered by some unknown link between Matii and the essences around them. According to researchers, most creatures seemed to have the link innately. Any normal man would feel nothing. After a deep breath, Stefan hunkered deeper into the saddle, raised his hand, and dropped it. He slapped his reins at the same time.

His horse leaped forward, head down and stretched like an arrow shot from a bow. Legs churning, its speed increased until it ran at twice a normal gallop. Then three times as fast.

Behind him, his cavalry thundered. Unbidden tears came to Stefan's eyes, but he could not manage to lift a finger to wipe them away. His face contorted and his hair and cloak streamed out behind him. He hunched into the saddle.

In moments, the Travelshaft reared up in front of him. He plunged into the pits of its blackness.

As Stefan crossed the portal's obsidian surface, his movement slowed from a breakneck lunge to a crawl. Tendrils of cold prickled across his skin as if tiny creatures attempted to leech all warmth from him. Then he was through to the other side and his men with him.

Inside, a dim glow lit the three channels—the wide thoroughfare they ran on and a lesser one to each side. The channels consisted of link upon link of interconnected metal each in the shape of an H. Rocky slabs filled the open spaces at the top and bottom of each H like smooth, rectangular flagstones. Only the difference in the silver of the metal and the brown of the stone told where one began and the other ended. Tracks, the Svenzar called them. The channels stretched for miles into impenetrable darkness.

To the outskirts were walls that made Stefan feel as if he rode in cavernous mine deep within a mountain. Bleached bones showed in a few locations against the rock faces. Sometimes he wondered if this was how it looked within a tomb. The thought made him shudder. One thing he was happy for was the Travelshafts' scent. Their interiors did not carry the stench of death or of a space enclosed for too long. They were practically odorless. So much so, that he could smell his own sweat and his horse.

Along one of the other paths, a contingent of guards on foot surrounded several supply wagons. The tracks didn't appear to move, but the soldiers slid along all the same, apparently at an incremental pace. Stefan knew the sensation was deceiving. Their actual speed would be more in comparison to ten times a horse's gallop. Everything always seemed to slow when within range of the exit.

Stefan braced himself for the lurching rush that would send his stomach into his mouth when he passed beyond the entrance's threshold. Fifty feet in, he crossed. His horse leapt forward under him in a speed that made what it did on the roadway outside seem slow by comparison.

Blood rushed to his ears in a roar, a tingle shot through his body, his stomach threatened to spew its contents, and he thought his heart would jump from his chest. He squeezed his eyes shut against the sensation of blinding speed, knowing within a few moments it would settle as if it were a part of him. Those moments seemed to last an eternity, but once his heart and his stomach calmed, he eased his eyes open.

In this section of the Travelshaft, the glow was much brighter, like early afternoon suffused by a light mist. Even after all these years, he still marveled that no lamps or lightstones produced the effect. The luminescence simply existed. The air rushed by in a steady swish, a gentle breeze against his face, the one thing louder than his or his horse's breaths.

The channels stretched on, but for all the light within the Travelshaft's confines, Stefan couldn't see more than thirty feet ahead. The walls lining either side were an unchanging gray and black mass. Occasionally, another channel intersected the main ones, leading off to a city or town. The journey continued this way, almost devoid of time's passage, one steady flow where he stood still while the rest of the world moved around him.

As they made their way in silence, they encountered several convoys passing on the other channels. Most consisted of soldiers escorting wagons and supplies, while others were merchants and their guard contingents. No one used the Travelshafts without protection. Not with the Svenzar raiding them at will.

"Stay on guard," Stefan shouted to Kasimir and Garrick. "The way things have been going the past few days, it would only be fitting if we encounter the Svenzar here."

Before they were able to pass the word, the ground lurched. Ahead, a wave of earth flowed in an undulating mass from the rocky walls. The movement came to an abrupt stop in the open space between their channel and the outer one. Then dirt and rock spewed upward.

"Svenzar!" Stefan yelled. "Take positions." Eyes fixed on the creature he leapt from his mount and snatched his bow from below the saddle.

A head the size of a wagonbed formed. The ground continued to flow up, pushing the head higher and higher until it stood upon a mass of stone well over twenty–feet in height.

Arrow nocked, Stefan aimed for where he expected the eyes to appear.

The Svenzar's stoneform body continued to grow. The ground rumbled and the chamber shook as the being created itself from the earth. Different colors of sediment layered its body, accompanied by metallic glints. Rigid, square shoulders formed, quickly followed by muscled arms a dozen or more feet across. Fingers clenched and unclenched. The wide chest matched the head in proportion. A hollow boom echoed as the rest of the Svenzar from the abdomen down hewed itself from the dirt, stone, and metal in one motion that ended with its feet appearing. Debris showered the channel.

The ground rumbled again, and smaller waves, hundreds in all, appeared within the cavernous Travelshaft. They grew along the walls. Pebbles, small rocks, and dirt rained down. Stefan cast his gaze up to the roof high above them. There, the humps in the stone existed also.

Mouth agape, he stared as the humps formed into smaller versions of the Svenzar—their young counterparts, the Sven. They inhabited the walls, standing sideways or hanging upside down from the roof like bats made of stone.

Stefan raised a hand to signal to his men. They knew to fire as soon as the creatures opened their eyes. He focused on the Svenzar.

The Svenzar's eyes did not open. A voice like musical notes put to speech but at the same time, a basso rumble, said, "Put away your weapons, Knight Commander Dorn. We seek an audience."

CHAPTER 5

*H*ow, in all that's righteous, does the creature know my name? Stefan wondered

"Don't trust them," Garrick cautioned as he stepped up next to Stefan, his bow drawn, fletching to ear.

"Look around us, Garrick." Stefan lowered his bow. "Even if we wanted to try hold out until the infantry and the scorpios arrived, we couldn't. Not without Alzari or Ashishin."

"What if they decided to take you?" Kasimir's weapon still pointed at the stoneform creatures.

"We wouldn't be able to stop them if that was their wish."

"I hate being helpless," Garrick said.

Stefan nodded. "Me too. Me too." He raised his voice. "Men, lower your weapons." Exhalations and the creak of strained wood easing on either side of him confirmed Kasimir and Garrick followed the order. Stefan glanced behind to make sure the rest of the cavalry complied, and then he faced the Svenzar once more. Fissures and cracks were appearing on the creature's body in patterns he couldn't quite place. "Svenzar, how do we do this?"

Stony chips fell away from the Svenzar's eyes as they

opened to reveal emerald pools. The eyes reminded Stefan of his own. "I wish to speak to you alone, Knight Commander Dorn. Come to me. Leave your men behind."

"How do I know you don't mean me harm?"

"You do not."

"I'm supposed to trust such an answer?"

Voice tinkling in those musical notes, the Svenzar gave what sounded like a chuckle, "What choice do you have?" The Svenzar gestured a massive rocky hand to the Sven surrounding Stefan's men. "Our young are more than enough to handle your men. Within the stone, we hold power. All you see here is ours to do with as we will."

As if in emphasis, the creature waved its hand, and the ground shook. Walls grew from the earth, spouting up until they blocked off any possible retreat. For the first time Stefan also noted the sense of motion that persisted inside the Travelshafts had come to a complete stop. The sensation was as if the entire world paused and waited for a command.

"Point taken," Stefan said aloud. Under his breath he said, "Should they do anything to me, fight to the death."

"Yes, sir," both men replied solemnly.

Stefan exhaled, let his bow drop to the ground, and strode forward. He refused to unsheathe his sword. A measure of command was necessary. Feet crunching on smaller portions of rubble, he picked his way through the rock chips and debris littering the floor until he found a clear path along the metal tracks. As he strode to the Svenzar, he kept his back straight, his chest out and paced himself with an easy grace. In this situation, he would show no fear.

When he drew within a dozen feet of the creature, Stefan realized the fissures and cracks on its body *did* form lines and patterns. In fact, they appeared to be more like tattoos. He strained his eyes and was able to pick out images of men, creatures he'd never seen before, landscapes, scenes of great battles, and sparkling celestial bodies. The intricacy of the artwork made him gasp. Even the murals along the walls in the Royal Palace paled by comparison. This was the first time he ever witnessed such a vibrant tapestry.

"I have watched you and your people for years." The Svenzar's voice was softer now, more musical than before, and conversational.

Stefan stopped. The Svenzar's stoneform body stretched so high Stefan needed to crane his neck to peer into its face. Up close, the tattoos wormed and shifted. They gave off the impression the men and creatures watched his every move. "Why?"

The Svenzar chuckled. "So impatient your race is. You often want answers to questions you already know and to those well beyond you. It must be a trait of having a shorter life span."

"If I knew the answer I wouldn't ask."

With a sigh that drifted upon the windless air, the creature said, "I have monitored you because you shape the future. Your decisions and choices affect all around you."

"Isn't that the same for everyone?" Stefan frowned. The conversation somehow felt off, a little odd.

"Yes, but for your kind more so than any other. Look at what your conquering of Ostanian lands has done. In Granadia you have changed the life patterns of countless millions."

"I almost get the sense you aren't pleased," Stefan said.

"Upheaval, instability, fates in constant change …." The Svenzar cocked its head. Boulders fell from its face in a rumble, but when they struck the shoulders and chest, they clung as if snagged in mud and were absorbed into its body. "I would not say I am not pleased … more … concerned. Such events take thousands of years to occur among the Svenzar. For you, it takes hundreds."

Stefan shrugged. "So is this the reason you hindered my passage? To inquire about my race and how we live?"

"No. I am here to give you a choice to change the course your people are set upon."

"My people? The Setian?"

"Who else could I mean?"

"I'm not sure. For a moment there I got the strange sense you meant all of Denestia."

The Svenzar smiled, mouth a maw of jagged stone teeth.

"So what's this choice," Stefan asked. "My people's future has never been brighter." He focused on the creatures eyes, trying his best not to cringe as the mouth eased shut.

"I would disagree about the future, but arguing is pointless. We need you to serve the Svenzar. In so doing you serve your people."

Stefan gave a cynical chuckle. He shook his head at the absurdity of the Svenzar's statement. "Even if I considered such a thing ... not that I am ... why would I want to serve you?" He brought his hand up with the thumb and forefinger almost touching. "We were this close to defeating you and the Harnan."

"If that is what you believe." Again, the creature gave a jagged smile. "Your choices here may doom your people."

"Really? How so?"

"Power seeping into the world from the Nether. Unstable Mater ... well, at least for your kind it is unstable. I am sure you have encountered such already."

"The same Nether where the gods are supposed to be imprisoned?" Stefan tilted his head as he regarded the creature.

"Yes. The very same one." The Svenzar frowned. "You do not believe in the gods?"

Stefan raised his brows. "Of course I do. I have seen enough to believe they exist. I simply doubt their ability to affect anything in this world."

"A shame," the Svenzar said. "You have seen their power at work. A young Matii and several others are now dead because of it. Choosing to serve us can help prevent some of what is to come."

Stefan kept his face smooth to hide his shock at the Svenzar's knowledge. "Tell me, Svenzar—"

"Call me Kalvor."

"Tell me, Kalvor, why did you choose me for this news or this offer?"

"Because that is the way of things. The fate of your people rests with you. It is a chance before a step is made from which there is no return."

"What if I refuse?"

"Your people are doomed."

"As simple as that?"

"Like death, most things are simple."

The statement sent a chill through Stefan's spine. The words were eerily similar to those Nerian often uttered. "Who or what will bring this doom?"

"Your own and the shade," Kalvor said.

Lips curling, Stefan resisted the urge to reach for his sword. He took a moment to calm himself before he replied. "My people are more unified now than they have been in ages. As for the shade … we defeated them before … we can do so again. This," he pointed at the Svenzar and the hundreds of Sven, "show of strength feels like a general laying out an army before an enemy in an attempt to instill fear." He tilted his head slowly until his gaze met the Svenzar's eyes. "There is little for the Setian to fear from you or any others. I won't betray my people to serve you. In fact, we will conquer you and the Harnan."

"So be it," the Svenzar said, his voice once again a basso rumble. "Let it be known the choice was given and refused."

With those words, the walls shook. The stones and dirt covering the floor rushed toward Kalvor. As they touched the Svenzar, they became one. Kalvor's body began to melt, taking on the appearance of thick mud as it slid to the ground. Around the walls and the roof, the Sven once more became humps of earth. When the process completed, no traces of their presence remained.

Jaw unhinged Stefan stared all around, fully expecting the creatures to reappear again, but nothing happened. Finally, he turned and headed toward his men, his mind swirling with all the Svenzar had said. What did Kalvor mean by the fate of his people rested with him? That by choosing not to serve he had doomed the Setian? It was as if the creature was revealing some distant future. Stefan dismissed the thought. More likely, the Svenzar and the Harnan had an abundance of forces at their disposal no one expected. This was too close to the odd happenings with King Nerian. If the King did intend to resume the old campaign in the Nevermore Heights against the two peoples, he might be walking into a slaughter. Nerain needed to be warned. *With news of this encounter, I can save my men after all.*

"What did the beast want?" Kasimir asked.

Stefan relayed much of what the Svenzar requested.

"Serve them?" Garrick snorted. "We had them beat if the Tribunal's Ashishin hadn't refused to help our Matii."

Even as he nodded his agreement, Stefan gazed at the area where moments before hundreds of Sven and a Svenzar had been. Not a stone appeared out of place. *Were we really close to winning?*

"So what now?" Kasimir held out the reins to Stefan's horse.

"We go home," answered the Knight Commander as he took them. He swung up into his saddle and set off at a trot. He was so preoccupied with all the occurrences of the last few days he almost spewed the contents of his stomach when the Travelshaft's speed altering effect restarted.

The remainder of the trip was uneventful, the monotony of the channels broken only by the occasional merchants or soldiers on another path. The first gong to warn them they had entered the arrival area broke him from his pondering. Ahead, the exit's white light beckoned. Taking a deep breath, he plunged into the glow.

Instead of feeling as if it slowed upon entering, the horse exited already at maximum speed along the roadway. The sensation from a steady, almost leisurely pace to the sudden blur of movement brought a rush of bile to Stefan's throat. He bit back on the sensation, squeezing his eyes tight. The effect lasted little more than a few moments but seemed to stretch on forever. The easing of the pressure on his stomach was a welcome relief.

Slowly, elongated shapes outside resolved into people,

fortifications, wagons, coaches, and animals. Colors that once bled became solid. Here, the green of cohorts marching down lanes between the three roadways, there, the many shades and differing styles of clothing worn by the Setian and other peoples who were congregating for arrivals or departures. Large and small buildings lined the roads. The cacophony of several thousand conversations in a myriad of tongues as well as the trundle of wheels and clang of smithies resounded. The activity reminded him of a hive—roiling yet organized.

The arrival in Benez chased away his other thoughts. His only wish was to see his wife again. All else could wait.

CHAPTER 6

Helmet under one arm, back straight in his burnished armor, Stefan and his army marched to Benez's gates and its walls hewn from black feldspar. The clop of their horses' hooves on the cobbles matched the outpouring of celebration from the people. He smiled as he took in the cheering masses, but his wife's absence overshadowed his triumphant moment. Absently, he raised a gloved hand to rub tenderly at the charm. Long ago, when they had identical pendants crafted, he and Thania made an agreement: Whenever he returned from battle, she would wait on the ramparts directly above the gates next to the King. Stefan checked the parapet again. There was no sign of Thania.

King Nerian, black hair done in long braids, golden armor gleaming, was on the battlements in his usual place though. A smile plastered on his face, the King stared down at Stefan and the Setian army. Stefan acknowledged the King with a nod and placed a fist to his heart. The sight of his mentor—a man he thought of as a father—brought a jumble of emotions flooding through him. He hoped all was well.

Stefan peered farther along the walls trying to make out if any of the noblewomen in their frilly, colorful dresses was his wife. Unable to pick her out, he searched among the crowds on the King's Road before the yawning black gates and the portcullis.

Peasants and the less fortunate, many in their feast day best, lined the street, breaths rising in feathery mists with autumn's chill. Their jubilation brought a fleeting smile to his face. Admittedly, the sweaty stink from the press of so many friendly bodies was something Stefan did indeed miss.

But none were his wife. Not the folk held in check on the street by lines of guards, not the ones at the windows of the shabby buildings, or crowded on the rooftops. Children ran beside the path, waving, and dogs darted back and forth, barking and nipping at the horses as if they too reveled in greeting the Unvanquished.

"Feels good to be home," Garrick shouted. He clapped Stefan on the shoulder.

"Yes, it does." Stefan offered a strained smile to his friend.

The procession continued up Benez's winding streets with the Cogal Drin Mountains looming above and behind, the city ascending on the lower slopes. The crowds grew thicker as they drew closer to the massive amphitheater built squarely between the ending of the slums and the beginning of the middle class' brick and mortar edifices. People hung out the amphitheater's windows, cheers rising in a roar to drown out all else. They showered the soldiers with flowers. A few women flashed their privates to the amusement and appreciation of several warriors.

Their surroundings changed to more affluent neighborhoods, cleaner streets and a network of drains to carry the stink of sewage away from the city, and so did the people's garb. Rich wool and moleskin blends became the main fare among the folk. Choice of clothing again altered as they trekked even farther into the Upper City. The people here wore the most expensive silks and satins but made certain to cover their shoulders in ermine scarves or cloaks. The avenues widened, became pristine, and lined by gardens, fountains, colonnades, and villas, many with spires rising into the sky against the backdrop of the Cogal Drin's expansive fangs.

The Royal Palace sprouted before them, Seti's Quaking Forest flying from the highest points. Stefan frowned at the omission of the Tribunal's Lightstorm banner. The castle reminded Stefan of a delicate off–white flower tinged with blue on its towers, spires, and parapets. The rugged battlements, the guards with watchful eyes, hands on weapons, and the many murder holes lining the castle's surface proved the appearance to be a lie. The Royal Palace was a fortress.

Still, no sign of his wife. Hopeful that one woman he picked out with velvet hair almost to her waist and a lithe frame could be Thania, he paced a little ways from his men. His heart sank when she turned, and an unknown face greeted him.

"People of Benez." Nerian's voice boomed above the din. The King stood on the palace's walls with his arms outstretched, golden armor glinting. His lone bodyguard, dressed all in black with a long cloak to match, was only a few feet away. The noise from the crowd died. "I give you … the Unvanquished."

Wild cheers followed. People danced and capered in the streets and threw hats high. Many showered the army with flowers.

"In honor of their return," the King's deep voice rose higher still over the cacophony, "games will be held in two months."

The jubilation pitched to new heights. A tap on Stefan' arm made him glance down.

"The King requires your presence immediately." The man who spoke wore black. He was of average height with a face plain enough to fit in anywhere, but Stefan never forgot those eyes. The way the silver flecks within them shifted to hide the green of his irises was disconcerting and made them appear to witness everything at once. The man was Nerian's bodyguard, Kahar.

How had he gotten down from the walls so quickly? Taken aback, Stefan paused for a few moments before he nodded, tossed his helm to Garrick, then dismounted to follow Kahar.

Without the bodyguard speaking or even making a

gesture, the crowds parted before the sinuous man. Each person appeared oblivious to his presence, yet still made room for him to pass. Together, they strode up the steps, into the western tower, around winding stairs, and onto the battlements.

"Stefan," King Nerian proclaimed. A wide smile on a face still wearing the past summer's tan made him appear a darker shade than his usual olive. The King did not look as if he aged a day.

"Sire," Stefan replied, going to one knee.

"Oh, my son, stop, no need for formality. Not here." Nerian strode over, and they embraced, the King having to bend a ways to get his arms around Stefan.

Stefan was not a small man. At a little over six feet, he was taller than many a Setian, but next to the King he always felt small and not only from the man's stature. Nerian was at least a foot, maybe two, taller than him. The King often reminded Stefan of the pictures of giants from books in his youth. In the three years since Stefan was last home, Nerian's chest was wider, face more angular, his eyes harder. When Stefan met the King's gaze, emerald beads came to mind.

"Let me look at you." Nerian held him at arm's length. "Not bad." He pursed his lips. "A little worse for wear, but you look … healthy."

"Same to you, sire. You're more fit than I remember."

"Ah, if only I felt that way."

Mind drifting to Thania, Stefan gave a pensive frown.

"What troubles you?" Nerian asked.

"Where's Thania? She's never missed a day when I return."

"Ah. Yes." Nerian was grinning now. "She is well." His voice lowered. "I am not supposed to be telling you this, but she prepared a surprise for you."

Stefan arched an eyebrow.

"Not to worry. Trust me. You will love it."

"Yes, sire." Stefan still couldn't help the trepidation gnawing at him.

"So," the King's demeanor became serious, "Cerny said you did not receive his message well."

"The man's overbearing and incompetent. Why did you promote him anyway? Because he's an Alzari?"

"Yes, he can be." The King paused for a moment. "Still, I had my reasons beyond him being a powerful Matii. Walk with me. Let us escape the crowds." He nodded out toward the revelers in the streets.

A wind nipping at them, they walked in silence for some time until the palace's battlements met with the city walls. Guards greeted them, bowing deeply to the King and putting fists to hearts at the sight of their Knight Commander.

They were traveling along the southern wall when finally Nerian spoke. "What do you think of what Cerny had to say?"

"Nothing good," Stefan admitted, breath rising in feathery mists from the evening's chill. "Why another war so soon? And against whom?"

The sun played off the King's resplendent golden armor of interlocking plates as he stopped. His oversized hands gestured out to the vast city from the slums before the gates here in the south to the villas and spires rising up the slopes of the Cogal Drin Mountains to the north. Citizens crowded the streets. "For them of course, the people, the Setian. We deserve to rule all of Ostania as we did in the days of old."

I thought you'd given up on that. Stefan suppressed a sigh.

A time existed when he and Nerian plotted on how to bring Seti and Ostania to their former glory, holding dominion over most of Denestia. But the Tribunal shattered those dreams when they united the Granadian kingdoms in its present empire under the ideals of Streamean worship. During the Luminance War, when the shade swept out of the Great Divide in Everland, Felan and then Seti itself ceded to the Tribunal for protection and assistance. The Felani, however, had recently broken away from the Tribunal. Still, with its influence stretching far into Ostania, the Tribunal was a near immovable force now.

As the thoughts flitted through his mind, a sense of

satisfaction overcame Stefan. He and Nerian had managed to carve an empire for the Setian within Ostania. He could live with such success. A whisper of sound made him look over his shoulder.

A few steps behind, Kahar trailed. The King's bodyguard was like a ghost, always seeming to fit in wherever he went, and most did not notice he was there until it was too late. The man's too plain appearance, placid demeanor, and shifty eyes glinting with the dying sun gave Stefan the chills.

Bracing himself against the King's possible anger, the Knight Commander said, "The men deserve a break, a time to rest. Haven't enough died a hard death already?"

"Death's always simple. We spend our entire lives dying." Nerian shrugged.

Those words again. "Do you intend to resume our attempt to conquer the Nevermore Heights?"

Nerian's brow wrinkled. "One day, not now. Our campaign starts in Everland with Erastonia's fall."

The words brought a slight relief to Stefan. He considered warning Nerian about the Svenzar, but first, he needed to voice a protest for his men. "I promised my men—"

"I know what you promised, and I commend you. Your words gave them something to fight for besides simple glory. 'Give a man a purpose he believes in with all his heart, and he shall accomplish great things.' You have taken *the Disciplines* and implemented them in ways well beyond my imagining when I taught them to you."

Despite the concern for his men, Stefan's chest swelled with pride. "So you'll let them have some time before you start this new campaign? Or, at least seek volunteers first? Plenty among them would gladly remain soldiers."

Nerian paused and rested a hand on Stefan's shoulder. In his mentor's shadow, Stefan felt inconsequential as if caught up by some irresistible force. A glimpse of regret flashed across Nerian's emerald eyes.

"You are like a son to me, but I cannot promise you

anything," Nerian said. "I will try to limit how this reflects on you, but I must do what is best for our budding empire."

"I understand." Stefan resisted the urge to pull away from the King's grip. "But it's not right."

"Come now." Nerian chuckled and gave Stefan's shoulder a squeeze before releasing. "You sound almost like the little boy I met all those years ago. Sometimes we need to be hard."

"I know." Stefan gave a half–hearted shrug as he stared off at nothing. "If there's anything commanding men has taught me, it's that one constant. Still, I don't have to like this or what it means for men who have already spent most of their lives in service."

"Duty," Nerian said, his expression thoughtful, "can weigh on a man until it buries him like an avalanche of snow. Yet, if you strive hard enough, if you keep working, you will find a way to dig out from under its weight."

"Unless it kills you first."

"There is that."

"Are you sure there's no other way around this?" Stefan glanced out to the setting sun, its glow lighting the sky in purple shades that made the Cogal Drin's rocky shoulders even more beautiful. "Maybe leave it to the Granadian Tribunal? They owe much to you. After all, you backed them for years. Without you, they would not have a presence in Ostania."

"I would not take it that far. I believe they would have found a way at some point." Nerian stroked his oiled beard. "Their refusal is partially why I am undertaking this action."

"They refused to help? Why? This concerns the shade, and it's not as if they know of your plans for Seti's full revival."

Nerian clasped his hands behind his back. "According to their High Ashishin, we effectively drove the shade back into Everland and the Rotted Forest. They feel invading Everland itself and breaching the Great Divide to eradicate the shade's minions once and for all is not worth the risk."

"Despite the ruin the beasts brought the world since their creation?"

Nerian pointed out to the southwest where a distant white glow suffused the horizon. "The Granadians think they are safe behind their precious Vallum of Light. Why should they feel any different when the Sanctums of Shelter has protected them from the Great Divide for countless centuries?" A sneer played across the King's face. "They are not overly concerned with what happens to this part of the world, unless it interferes with their plans."

Stefan almost said he agreed. They themselves might be better served leaving well enough alone. Ostania had survived for a millennia defending against the shadelings. Either the giant, black–haired wraithwolves that at times stood like men, or the darkwraiths—creatures of smoky mist in the shape of men. More often than not, the shade's taint transformed some hapless adventurer seeking fame or fortune in the crevasse that was the Great Divide into one of the beasts. Stefan cringed at the pictures his mind conjured from the years he'd done battle against the monsters.

However, the tomes of the Chronicles spoke of a time when the creatures would rise again to scour Denestia. Supposedly, if the prophecies were to be believed, the Setian would pave the path to free the world from doom. Thinking of the books conjured memories of Stefan's old wet nurse, Shin Galiana who often told him the stories. To many, they were little more than myths. Stefan wasn't so sure.

Part of Nerian's words rang true for the Knight Commander. Granadia's Tribunal had done what none else accomplished: Their Dagodin, Ashishin, and High Ashishin had driven the creatures from their land and helped Ostania accomplish the same. Why should they risk more for kingdoms unwilling to convert to the Streamean religion despite all they'd done to help in the past?

"Would you care if you were them?" Stefan asked.

"If I were them, the world would already be mine to do with as I wish," Nerian replied absently, his gaze seemingly locked on something in the distance.

Stefan frowned. This was not the Nerian he remembered before going off to war. Sure, they were both ambitious and both lived for glory, but the sound in the King's voice spoke of a longing, a need to make the entire world bow to him. When they shared their dreams in the past, they wanted the Setian to stand above all but without oppression, without tyranny. Nerian sounded almost … jealous. "You intend to take on the Tribunal, don't you?"

Nerian's gaze shifted to the Knight Commander.

Stefan almost flinched at the cold pits there. "Why? They helped to give us much of what we hold now."

"Give?" Nerian scowled, showing his teeth. "They gave me nothing. All I have I took." He paused. "You helped me take. You, my son, are the only one I need to thank for what we Setian accomplished. The rest are fodder."

Stefan opened his mouth to tell the King he was wrong. Without the men who worshipped them, the men Stefan convinced to follow him and the King's wishes to their death, they would have nothing. The same men Nerian now denied the peace Stefan had promised them. Had it not been for them, the Setian would be a shell of their current glory. How had the King changed so much in three years? The man spoke as if life was little more than a tool to be sharpened, used until it broke, cast away, and then replaced. Stefan bit his tongue. Instead, he said, "Thank you, sire. You honor me."

Eyes again drawing to something distant, King Nerian nodded as if he expected nothing less than gratitude. "The Tribunal wishes to make it seem as if they have no real interest in Ostania or even Everland, but indeed they do. They may not be able to rule us by force yet, but they conquered many Ostanians mentally. If only I saw it sooner."

"What do you mean?"

"Streamean worship, of course." Nerian pointed toward the towering statues of Ilumni and the other gods at the temples in Benez. "With their Devout priests and priestesses, the Tribunal has accomplished what no army could. They have subverted the rule of the Ostanian kingdoms with their promises of unity of the gods, harmony between the three religions, and equality between men and women." Nerian spat. "They tout compulsory education and universal language as if we are semi–intelligent beasts. Through the knowledge they garnered from the Chronicles, they lead people to think the gods reveal their will through the Devout. The fact every one of the priests is also a mender only helps to make that more believable. Look around you some time. Their influence is rampant. Despite their promise of unity, which god do most of us pray to? Ilumni. When something ill happens, to whom do we direct our curses, our blasphemy?" Nerian turned to meet Stefan's gaze, letting the answer hang.

Amuni, Stefan thought, but kept silent.

"I see you begin to understand," Nerian said.

"You might be right, but they also brought stability with them. Denestia has thrived from a world wreathed in war to one more prosperous. Take Granadia for example. When was the last time you heard of a major war there? They have small conflicts, sure, but nothing on a scale like we do."

"Because the Tribunal rule their own as we should. Absolutely."

Stefan shook his head. "Let's say this is true, that the Tribunal does intend to rule all of Denestia. How would you begin to stop them?"

The faraway expression clouded the King's face once more. "A concentration of Mater exists in the Great Divide. It must be why the Erastonians guard it so rabidly. I will have that power even if it means defeating the Erastonians themselves. Not that I would need much excuse to fight them. Their inability to prevent shadelings emerging from the Divide has led to enough damage to other lands. The time has come for someone else to take on the responsibility." Nerian's gaze shifted to Stefan. "You saw how powerful a few shadelings can be. Imagine if we managed to harness their power without the taint attached. We would not only complete a conquest of all Ostania but Granadia as well."

Creeping, cold fingers eased down Stefan's spine. The King had lost his senses. To dream of controlling Mater? The power legend said the gods created? One that had turned mountains into flatlands, forests into plains, seas into deserts, created the Vallum of Light and the Great Divide itself? The power existing within everything, but as the madness that eventually took all Matii who wielded it proved, was unstable at best and needed to be handled with extreme caution? Either the King's ascent was corrupting him or he was going mad. Stefan had heard the voices inhabiting the essences as they whispered their malevolence in his days of training to become a Dagodin. He cringed. Could such an ailment be afflicting the King?

"I see that look in your eyes, son." A smile on his lips, Nerian shook his head. "I am not insane. And yes, I believe a way exists to completely control Mater. The Pathfinders are a perfect example. They may not have full control yet, but they are more powerful than almost any other Matii. The answers lie in the Great Divide. I am certain of it. Why else would the Tribunal seek to bring Ostania under their rule?"

"How are you so sure conquering Mater is their intention?"

"Come now. You witnessed what happened when their Ashishin handled unstable elements. Imagine the possibilities if a way existed to prevent such a thing from happening."

A world in chaos, Stefan thought, as he pictured Forgers abusing their power without its limitations. Then his eyes widened. "So you did know," he exclaimed, staring at Nerian in disbelief. "And you withdrew our Alzari without warning me."

"You would have tried to mend those Astocans anyway."

Stefan frowned. "Who told you I did?"

"I have my ways. Remember when you were young and you and Kasimir stole kinai fruit from that merchant?"

Brow wrinkling, Stefan recalled the time vividly. He and Kasimir had waited until Master Sena placed the sweet, fist-sized, red fruit in his warehouse before using the hole they'd dug the night before to crawl in and gorge themselves. Before they could leave, Nerian called to them, stepping out from the dark. The King had kept it quiet, but he'd put a whipping on the two of them they'd never forget. For weeks after, they both found it difficult to sit. Involuntarily, Stefan's hand reached toward his butt. "Yes," he said. "Garrick told on us then. Did he … is he—"

"No, he did not and is not. I asked and he refused me." Nerian gave him a wry smile. "Do not worry yourself, but what happened at the Sang Reaches was confirmation of things I expected. I was already aware of much of the Tribunal's plans."

Stefan's mouth fell open. "A spy within their ranks? Not just anyone, at least a High Shin." Stefan's brows climbed his forehead. "Galiana," he whispered. Another knowing smirk from Nerian was all the confirmation he needed.

"Don't look at me that way," Nerian admonished. "She volunteered for the task. Besides, the Tribunal has been spying on us this entire time. I cannot trust any of their Matii."

"Despite all the years they helped in our battle against the shadelings?"

"Do not be naïve," Nerian chided. "We use who we must as they do us. Alone, we could never muster enough Matii or weapons to fight the shade's last invasion, but together, a united Ostania did. In taking credit for bringing us together, the Tribunal gained their hold in Ostania."

"And we're united now, aren't we," Stefan said, finally understanding some of the purpose of his last few years of service. "On our own." He couldn't bear to look at Nerian with the knowledge of how the King used him.

"Not quite," Nerian said. "But we are close, oh so close." His voice gained a sudden fervor. "Don't you see? We are stronger now. We no longer need to rely on the Tribunal to defend us. We can protect ourselves. Eventually, we can chase them back across the sea where they belong. Ostania can once again be whole."

Stefan regarded the man he once held in such high esteem. "What then?"

King Nerian chuckled. "After that my son, the world is ours."

"A dream, sire. You're living a dream. I guess the Granadians will simply bend knee and let you claim their lands. Their Matii will no longer fight for their cause but for ours instead." Stefan made no attempt to hide his sarcasm.

"That my son is the beauty of it all. Come."

His body tense, Stefan followed at the King's heels.

Nerian strode with purpose, head held high. He stopped at the edge of the battlements. "There, this is why I needed you to come home." The King pointed out to the fields beyond the eastern walls.

An army numbering in the tens of thousands, no, hundreds of thousands covered the plains. The Quaking Forest of Setian flew from every battle standard. The absence of flags displaying lightning bolts striking in front of the sun was more than a little disconcerting. That absence, the lack of the Tribunal's Lightstorm, was a stark revelation of the King's intention.

"What—"

"Matii," the King declared. "Our own."

Stefan stared dumbly at the mass of bodies below. The green with crimson sleeves represented Dagodin, and from the unnatural gleam of their swords and spears, they wielded *divya*. How had the King found enough Matii to imbue so many weapons? Next to them he counted several legions in green and gold tunics and pants—Alzari. "How did you find so many Forgers?"

"Because of you, son." A wild grin split Nerian's face. "Once you defeated the Astocans, it gave us the last supply of Matii we needed. We may have warred with each other, but long ago, the kingdoms came to an agreement. Whoever conquered all of us would lead a united Ostania to overthrow the Tribunal. The other kingdoms decreed that all Matii must enter military service. Here in Seti, we sent out High Alzari to recruit Matii or forcefully take any who would dare shun my commands. I chose not to make the requirement public until I thought we were ready to face the Tribunal."

Or to avoid any Matii fleeing beforehand.

"Now, that day is here," Nerian continued. "All that remains is for you to say yes, you will lead them."

"I thought Cerny was next in line."

"He has proven to be a tad unworthy."

"What if I refuse?"

Nerian gave him a mirthless smile. "Come now. You will not refuse. I have done away with titles endowed by the Tribunal. We shall revert to our own. From now on, you are no longer Knight Commander, but General Stefan Dorn."

Stefan shook his head in denial. *How could Nerian have changed this much?*

"Go home to your wife and think things over."

"I don't need to—"

"Trust me, General. Think about the decree for service from all Matii."

Stefan's eyes narrowed. Thania was a Matus, once a Shin within the Tribunal. A sinking feeling rippled through the pit of his stomach. "You can't mean to force—"

"Go home to your wife. She needs you."

Stefan stiffened at the empty tone of the King's voice. The pendant of his wife became as heavy as the sudden weight threatening to crush his heart.

CHAPTER 7

Cold autumn air whipping at his face, his mount's hooves beating thunder onto the flagstones, Stefan rode hard for home. Yet, the chill wasn't what sent shivers through his body, and his speed wasn't what spurred on his racing heart as he dashed past mostly empty side streets in Benez's Upper City. Concern for his wife was the cause. Another time and place he would not have believed King Nerian could have meant Thania harm, but the look in the man's eyes, his voice and his apparent insanity sent doubts whirling through the Knight Commander's mind. Nerian's mention of his distrust for the Tribunal and their Matii, his revelation of mandatory service, coupled with the fact Thania once served as a High Ashishin only added to Stefan's trepidation.

This was supposed to be a time of enjoyment for him and his men. Music feathered through the air. All across the city, the people celebrated. Even here, along the avenue with its expansive villas, nobles dressed in layered silks and satins hurried on their way to join those cavorting on the King's Road or to the ball at the Royal Palace. Some paused to cheer him on. At any other time, Stefan would have stopped to enjoy the festivities, the foods, the dancing. His expression soured with the thought of revelry.

He whipped his reins and dug his heels harder into his

horse's sides. Head down, neck outstretched the animal bounded forward. The world became a blur as he raced up the avenue, his anxiety growing the closer he came to home. When the square columns, the manicured gardens, and the roof of his villa appeared over a rise, he willed himself to go faster. Heart aflutter, the last vestiges of the daylight dipping below the horizon and Denestia's twin moons casting long shadows around him, Stefan reached the premises.

Down the small incline he went and through the gates, ignoring the servants who waited there to take his mount. He did not stop whipping his reins until he reached the stairs before the wide, mahogany doors. Not waiting for the attendants to take his mount, he leaped off its back and ran up the stairs.

"Thania," Stefan yelled. "Thania!" He threw the doors open and entered.

A long lamp–lit hallway stretched before him. Dressed in the blue of the Dorn house and bowing profusely, his serving men and women greeted him.

"Thania!"

"Good to see you, Lord Dorn. It is—"

"Perta," Stefan grabbed the steward by his shoulders. "Where's my wife? Is she well?"

"Why yes, my lord." The balding man's forehead wrinkled. "Why wouldn't she be?"

Stefan expelled a long breath and smiled, a gloved hand gripping his chest as a tightness he had not noticed before eased. "King Nerian, he," Stefan began. "Never mind. Where is she?"

"I'm not sure, my lord."

"What? What do you mean?"

"M–My lord, M–Master D–Dorn, sir." Perta grimaced. He pointed to where Stefan's other hand still held his shoulder, squeezing.

"I'm sorry," Stefan said, releasing his hold. He shed his gloves and tossed them to one of the attendants.

Perta rubbed at the spot, taking slow breaths. "It's fine, my lord. What I meant was I'm not sure where she is in the house.

It's been a lot of commotion since your arrival was announced."

Stefan nodded. He rounded on the other servants lining the hall. "Do any of you know where she is?"

A chorus of murmured 'No, my lord' spread throughout the foyer. One servant stepped forward. Stefan didn't recognize the diminutive woman.

Head down, she said, "Lady Dorn went to her rooms to prepare for your arrival, sir."

Relief swept through him for the second time in a few moments. "Thank you. What's your name?"

"Clesi, my lord."

"Thank you, Clesi."

"Lord Dorn," Perta said, "is there anything we can get you right now? Food? A drink? Maybe you would like a bath before you see Lady Dorn."

Stefan cocked his head and raised a quizzical eyebrow at the steward's suggestion. The man knew Stefan always spent time with Thania first before doing anything of the sort. "Perta."

"Yes, my lord?"

"Walk with me. The rest of you continue with whatever my wife had you doing."

After they bowed, the servants hurried away.

Stefan noted the sweat beading on Perta's forehead. He made sure all the other servants were out of earshot before he deliberately rested his hand on his sword's hilt. "Now, would you mind telling me why you're stalling me from seeing my wife?"

Perta's mouth opened then closed. He dabbed at the perspiration with a powdered cloth.

"You have another moment to answer me ..." Stefan allowed the implied threat to linger.

"The Mistress, sir. She ordered me to delay you."

"Why?"

"It's supposed to be a surprise, my lord. I cannot tell you."

Stefan quirked an eyebrow at Perta and tapped a finger on his sword hilt.

"Mistress's orders ... she forbid it," the steward said quickly.

For a moment, Stefan considered commanding Perta to reveal what he knew, but by the stubborn set of the man's jaw, he saw he would be wasting his time. The steward's loyalty was unquestioned. And it belonged to Thania. With a resigned sigh, his earlier urgency washing away completely, Stefan said, "Fine. Take me to her."

After a deep bow, Perta led the way. They walked along the hall, their footsteps muted by the thick carpet. The paintings on the walls were still in the same places Stefan remembered leaving them. In the main greeting area, he couldn't help but smile. It had been three years, but again Thania had made sure the same soft, cushioned chairs and benches were against the walls. The vast area rug they now walked on was also as he left it. The artwork woven into the material showed an ancient war between the Eztezians and other Matii as they battled against each other and the shade's armies. Materforgings scoured the land in lightning bolts, waves of earth, fountains of flame, maelstroms, and tornadoes. Around the entire scene, a massive forest burned. Shadelings were being herded into an enormous rent in the earth that supposedly represented the Great Divide.

The house smelled of bellflowers and spices, and sure enough, around the room on short pillars were vases filled with the blue and yellow blooms. Candles, smoke rising from them in lazy wisps that carried the nose tickling scent of the spices, burned in small holders on the three long tables set to either side of the room's center. Servants hurried to the tables upon which sat various appetizers, from fruits to breads to meats.

As Stefan and Perta made their way across the room to the wide marble steps, several attendants came to offer Stefan fruit or small pastries of rolled meat. The mouthwatering aromas brought a grumble to his stomach. Hunger denied his temptation to shoo them away. Soon he was gulping down food while washing it down with his wife's kinai wine. Whatever Thania had planned, she intended to have his attention held until she was ready. *My dear wife, what are you up to now?*

The last time Thania had gone to this extent, she'd thought she was with child. When she found out she wasn't, she'd been devastated. Stefan's shoulders slumped with the thought. With the threat of another campaign in the way, he wondered if they would ever get to experience the joys of parenthood. At eighty, his chances were rapidly dwindling. Although she kept her age a closely guarded secret, Thania was much older by far, but she had the advantage of being a powerful Ashishin on her side, while he was only a Dagodin.

They reached the landing, followed the balustrade to the right, and entered an alcove with a staircase to the uppermost floors. Two flights up, they exited and strode down a short lamp lined hall to the main bedroom. Perta knocked on the door.

"Come in."

Stefan's heart sped up at the sound of Thania's melodious voice.

Perta entered, and Stefan frowned at a noise much like a child's laughter.

A moment later, the steward announced, "The lord is here, my lady."

The urge to push open the doors almost overwhelmed him, but Stefan decided to let his wife have her fun. She'd gone to extreme lengths to prepare for his homecoming. The last thing he wished to do was ruin her surprise. One boot tapping on the rug, he waited.

The giggling reached him again, but this time a child did appear, peeking out from the door. Hair midnight black, green eyes twinkling, something about the child seemed disturbingly familiar. Stefan growled under his breath. Now he knew why the whole delay. Thania had once again taken in one of the servant's children. Had one of them died like last time? He shook his head. When last this occurred, his wife had become irrationally attached to the baby. When the child's family arrived to claim him from Southern Felan almost a year later, it had taken months for her to recover from her sorrow.

"My lady says you may enter, sir," Perta said from where

he stood holding the door open.

Stefan stepped inside, his heart suddenly racing at the prospect of seeing his wife after so many years away. The door closed behind him, and it was only himself, Perta, the tiny boy who couldn't be more than three and …. Was that another child sitting at a small table playing with a doll eyeing him curiously? Stefan's eyebrows climbed up his forehead. *What, in Ilumni's name, is going on?*

Rather than question Perta again, Stefan studied the room. Similar to the rest of his home, his wife had kept the room as he remembered: the wide bed, the paintings on the walls and the lamps in their sconces. The familiar rug under his feet showed some battle between the gods. A bundle wrapped in an oiled cloth sat on a table near the door to the sitting room. A pinging noise made him look down. A smile on his face, the boy was knocking on his armor.

Smiling in return, Stefan peered around the room and called out, "Thania? Love?"

The door to the adjoining sitting room opened, light pooling in to match that from the glass lamps adorning the room's walls. In glided Thania, radiant as ever, her hair falling in velvet waves down past the mounds of her tanned bosom and the deep V−neck of her layered silk dress with its many ruffles. Between her ample cleavage rested the twin to his pendant. To add to her appearance, she'd made up her face with powders and paints the way he liked. Upon her entry, Stefan's pendant bloomed with warmth. Thania did not appear an hour past twenty−five naming days. She was perfect. Blue always looked best on her.

"My love," she said, all sweet innocence, a smile that would brighten the dreariest day lighting up her face.

The thoughts of the King, the children, and all else fled Stefan's mind. In several brisk steps, he strode to her and swept her from her feet. She smelled of saffron and bellflowers. He gazed into the golden pools of her eyes and kissed her deeply. Soft lips, so soft, like spun silk, greeted his chapped monstrosities. He couldn't tell how long the kiss lasted but it felt like forever as her tongue played against his own and on his lips, moistening them. When he let her go for a moment to stare into her eyes, they were both breathless.

The pinging noise came again, and Stefan glanced down. The boy stood there knocking on his armor. Next to him was the girl.

Innocent eyes peered back up at him then over to Thania. "Mommy, who is this?"

The familiarity struck Stefan then, and he gasped, releasing his wife. Except for the green eyes, the child, no, both children were splitting images of her.

"Yes," Thania said. "They are my ... no, correction, they are our children. Stefan, this is your son, Anton and your daughter Celina."

Stefan promptly sat on the floor, armor and all.

CHAPTER 8

"How?" Stefan stared dumbly. "How can I have children when I wasn't here for three years?"

A cough came from Perta's direction. "My lord, my lady … if it is not too much, I beg your leave."

"Yes, you may go," Thania said.

The two infants were clutching her dress. As doubtful as he felt, Stefan could see some of him in them, and they certainly had his eyes.

"As to how," Thania said, "The last night before you left …"

Stefan remembered well. Passionate did not quite begin to describe their lovemaking. Raunchy, salacious, maybe lecherous would be a better word. He flushed. Not once that night did he attempt to hold back.

"Twins," he whispered. He rolled the word around on his tongue. "Praise Ilumni." A sudden outpouring of love almost overwhelmed him. Tears welled up in his eyes, and he allowed the sobs to come. "Thank you, Ilumni. In your light I walk." Then he began to laugh, low in his throat at first until he bellowed with joy and thumped the floor where he sat.

"Go to your father, children," Thania said.

Stefan held out his hands, but neither Anton nor Celina moved. They both still held fast to their mother's dress, eyes wide and bewildered. A stab of pain built in his chest. If only he'd been there for them since their birth. If only he'd been there to *see* them born.

A rustle of movement from Thania made him look up at her. She was clutching the charm, and her eyes narrowed for a moment. Stefan knew she was Materforging.

A moment later, an image sprang to life next to her. Standing a foot taller than her, lean and broad–shouldered, dressed in the crisp uniform of a newly promoted Knight, it was Stefan's exact likeness of the pendant down to his dark green eyes. His hair was a little longer and his face had the vigor of youth, but it was him all the same.

The children giggled and as one said, "Da." Their gazes went from the image to Stefan, their eyes twinkled, and the next moment they were leaping into his arms. The image winked out.

Tears streamed down Stefan's cheeks. Before he could stop, he was openly sobbing with joy. He hugged his children tighter, reveling in their smell and warmth.

The boy, Anton, pushed back from him a little and peered into his face. Brow knitting, he said, "Da, you sads? Why you crying?"

Stefan pulled him close. "No, son. I'm not sad. I'm very happy. I have never been happier in my entire life because I have you and your sister." He took in Thania's beaming face. Their gazes locked. He mouthed, "Thank you. I love you."

She whispered. "I love you too." Thania hiked up her dress and joined them on the floor, one hand around Stefan's back and the other hugging Celina.

While enjoying the feel of his new family, basking in how complete he felt inside after so many years he and Thania spent avoiding the prospect of children, a sense of dread crept within Stefan. *I finally have a full family to come home to, and Nerian wants to force me to leave again. NO. I can't afford to be away from my children. I missed their birth. I will not miss their lives.* But there was something worse than him having to go away on another campaign. Nerian's command. *All Matii must enter military service.*

"What's wrong, honey?" Voice filled with concern, Thania eased up from him. "Why are you so tense?"

Ever so slowly, Stefan gently held the children away from him. He peered into their fair faces and innocent eyes. Anton's dark hair sat on his head in small curls, while Celina's had already grown down to her neck. They gazed back up at him, their expressions joyful. "They have inherited our power haven't they?" His throat constricted.

"Yes," Thania whispered. "Like any other Matii, it may not manifest until after they turn thirteen, but their ability is there. I can sense it. They are going to be strong, love. Very strong."

A great fist squeezed at Stefan's heart with each word. Tears began to trickle down his face again, in happiness and sorrow. "Can you tell if they will succumb to the madness?"

"Honey, they're too young to tell." Thania gave his shoulder a squeeze. "But if their ability to already control their emotions this young is any sign, they should be fine. But that isn't all that's troubling you, is it?"

Stefan shook his head. "I spent the evening with Nerian. He told me about the decree. And he wants me to lead this new army of his. He went so far as to tell me I wouldn't refuse him then told me to go home to you, that you needed me." Stefan stood. Hands ruffling his children's hair, he stared into Thania's face.

Thania's eyes closed, and she took a deep breath. When she opened them again, they were moist. "Cerny said the King promised he wouldn't enforce the new law on me if you agreed to lead."

The pain Stefan witnessed in her eyes, the fear written across her crestfallen face meant only one thing. He asked anyway. "And the children?" He stopped playing in their hair, sliding his hands away.

The tears that had welled up in his wife's eyes began to flow freely, leaving streaks in her makeup. Thania's face contorted.

Her lower lip quivered. "Cerny said the King would take them as part of that law should you refuse," she said in a barely audible whisper.

Stefan folded her tenderly into his arms. Head lost in his shoulder, she wept even harder. A tug on his trousers revealed Anton on one side and Celina on the other, hugging onto both him and their mother. Although he fought against the urge to clench his fists, he could not help grinding his teeth or the smoldering he felt deep within the pit of his stomach. The heat of his emotions crawled across his body like a living beast, clawing its way to get out.

He wondered if those really were Nerian's orders. Cerny wouldn't dare threaten his family without the King's blessing, would he? Stefan found it hard to fathom. None of it sounded like the man who'd helped raise him and taught him what he knew, being there more than his own father. Yet, the meeting with Nerian gave him pause and clouded his mind with doubt. Somewhere deep inside, he knew one thing. He would not hesitate to kill either Cerny or Nerian if they touched his family.

"We could run away," Stefan said into the silky, perfumed tresses of his wife's hair. "We could go to Granadia."

It took a few sniffles before Thania answered. "The house is watched. Who knows what he'll do if we tried to escape and were captured. What I used to produce the image is the extent of power any Matii can Forge within the city. Somehow, the King has found a way to dampen our Forgings here. It's enough to train with but not near enough to Materialize us away from here."

"Besides," a female voice said from the sitting room's direction, "you are needed here. It is more important than ever that you make sure your children are safe."

Stefan slid his hand to his sword hilt. He eased a step from Thania and the children to face the voice.

High Ashishin Galiana Calestis stood in the open doorway. Stefan squinted. Or was she High Alzari? Or both. The same chiseled face, ember hair, and golden stare from when she left twelve years ago greeted him. Dressed in green and gold robes, hair in a tight bun, she kept her gaze focused on him. Twelve years and still the woman did not appear to have aged a day from when she mentored him. Her complexion was a little pale as if she'd spent too much time out of the sun, but that was to be expected when one visited Granadia, even more so when the visit meant an extended stay at the Tribunal's Iluminus.

Galiana's brow quirked as her gaze shifted from his face to his sword hand then back to meet his eyes once more. "What a way to greet your old teacher and wet nurse."

"Is that all you are?" Hand still on his hilt, Stefan shifted, placing himself between his family and Galiana.

A pained expression crossed Galiana's face. "I should paddle your bottom."

Stefan ignored the quip. "According to Nerian you were key in setting him on his current path." He kept his tone conversational despite the angry heat inside. "A path that may yet cost me my family, my happiness, and hundreds of thousands if not millions of Setian lives."

"He said that?"

"Not in so many words, but you provided him with information you gained in your infiltration of the Tribunal."

Galiana's lips twitched into a smile, but her eyes were frozen pinpoints. "Have you ever killed for your King, Stefan?"

"Of course I have."

"Have you ever disobeyed your King's orders?"

"How dare you? Never!"

The smile wilted from Galiana's face. Her lips became a tight slit. "Good. The same for me. Until now."

"What?"

A change came across her then. Galiana's shoulders slumped, and she appeared tired, older, lines of worry about her eyes. "I gave King Nerian copies of several tomes the Tribunal kept in the Iluminus' most guarded libraries. The tomes of the Chronicles. You remember those, correct? Written by philosophers and fortune–tellers countless years ago, they tell of things in the past and of events to come. Events that occurred since the Chronicles were written."

"Are the stories really true?"

Galiana shrugged. "Apparently, they are. According to the Iluminus' researchers, the people who wrote the tomes were the Eztezians and their direct descendants."

Stefan frowned. The Eztezians were great warriors, the most powerful Matii to grace Denestia. Said to be a part of the gods' lineage, they were tasked with protecting Denestia from the shade. And from itself. Driven mad by their overuse of Mater however, they almost destroyed the world. Eventually, they created the Great Divide, which brought about the shade's defeat. Then they turned on their masters, sealing the gods in the Nether to prevent future wars and the creation of more creatures like the shadelings. Stefan could not picture such men and women sitting down to write anything. If they did, what else had they included in such texts?

"I see you understand the importance," Galiana said.

"And you gave them to the King. Why?" Stefan asked.

"The Tribunal has been using The Chronicles for years to maintain their empire. It is how they can tell who would be their greatest threats and eliminate them beforehand. Seti is one of those threats. In fact, the Chronicles state Seti will overthrow the Tribunal's rule but not how. That part is written in ancient Seti, a language several millennia old. No one knew how to read it."

Stefan eased his hand from his sword and began to pace. Some things began to make sense to him now. What Galiana said would explain why of all the kingdoms, the Tribunal had chosen Seti to be its main ally in Ostania. He stopped and faced her. "Does King Nerian know how to read it?"

Galiana hung her head for a moment and then raised it to meet his gaze once more. "He found a way."

"And he's using it to bring the words to pass even if it means sacrificing his own," Stefan concluded.

"I swear to you, I did not know. When I found out about the tomes and how the Tribunal used them, I saw this as a threat to our survival. I did what you would do. I made sure to manipulate events to see we would outlast whatever they intended. My loyalty is to our people first. When Nerian brought forward his plan for Everland and the Great Divide, I realized the chance to secure power beyond the Tribunal's had corrupted him." She squeezed her eyes tight. "Stefan." Her voice was a hoarse whisper. "I saw Nerian's translations. If he stays on this course, the Setian as we know them will perish."

Mind whirling, Stefan glanced over to Anton, Celina and Thania. His wife did not appear at all surprised by Galiana's news. "She discussed this with you already."

Thania nodded. "It's why I wasn't at the celebrations."

"So what do we do?" He began pacing again. "What can we do?" Even as he asked the question, he wondered if he could trust Galiana. Everything she said so far was based on translations only she knew. But what if they were true? What if this was Kalvor's warning?

"Well, for the first question," Galiana said. "You will have to do as Nerian says and lead his armies. For now, it is the only way to keep your family safe."

Stefan stopped pacing, his hand sliding to his sword. "I could gather the men loyal to me—"

"I know what you are thinking," Galiana said. "You cannot flee and you cannot fight him right now. You need to give me time to devise a plan."

"What if none of this is his doing?" Stefan found it hard to believe Nerian could have changed this much even from the conversation he had with the King. There had to be another catalyst. "I have my suspicions concerning Cerny. The way the man has come into power and the fact he's an Alzari."

"I had my people inquire after him years ago," Galiana answered. "They came up with nothing out of the ordinary. Which leaves Nerian."

"You believe you can find a way to stop him?"

"To stop him? No. To limit the damage he does … Yes."

"How?"

"The Chronicles lay out many possible futures. They also hint at events not within the books. The possibility for change is endless if caught before a certain point."

Again, possibilities revealed by Galiana alone. Stefan mulled the information over. If he was to act, he needed confirmation. Finding a way to draw it out of the King may be the only way to be sure. Galiana may have been his mentor, but Nerian had been like a father. "If changes can occur, we can save our people."

"Not exactly. The tome foretells that once Nerian received his copy of the Chronicles, that the Setian are doomed. There was talk of a remnant being able to survive."

"Does Nerian know of this?"

"Yes."

"And it didn't change his mind?"

"He never wavered. I spent the last two years learning ancient Seti using the King's own translations. When I went back to the Iluminus, there were a few more texts dealing with the demise of Seti. Nerian's actions will bring about a cataclysm caused by a cult worshipping Amuni and using shadelings for their armies."

Stefan's eyebrows shot up his forehead. "Dear Ilumni save us." As he said the words though, more doubts concerning Galiana's intentions crowded his mind. Her knowledge seemed all too convenient. And it made Nerian appear as vile a man as any. Something Stefan could not believe. "What did Nerian say when you told him?" he asked, voice soft.

"He said that is but one path. He believes he can prevent whatever is coming. At that point, I knew he had to be stopped. Which brings me to the second part of what you can do." Galiana strode over to the table with the wrapped bundle.

Frowning, Stefan watched as she picked up the cloth and gingerly unwrapped it. When the material fell away, it revealed a plain leather scabbard and a simple hilt. Stefan's brows drew together tighter. *A sword?*

"This," Galiana said, reverently, "is the key, not only for

your children but the Setian as a people."

Eyes full of hope she unsheathed a sword, its metal carrying the high silver shine of imbuement. A *divya*. But the way she held it out like some offering before the altar of a god spoke of something special.

CHAPTER 9

Unimpressed, Stefan shrugged. "It's a *divya*. The King's armies carry thousands of them much like the one on my hip." He indicated his sword. "What's so different about this one?"

"According to the Chronicles this is an Access Key to another, greater *divya*," Galiana said. "One able to unleash a power to rival the gods themselves. The tomes also state this is the way to ensure a remnant of the Setian will survive the coming times."

"Can it be used to defeat Nerian?"

Galiana shrugged. "No one knows how powerful he is, not even me, and I trained against him on several occasions. I lost every session."

Stefan shook his head in resignation. "If a High Shin like yourself cannot defeat him, how do you expect me, a simple Dagodin, to succeed? The *divya* is useless to me. Nerian would kill me the moment he senses I'm a threat."

Galiana snorted. "I never understood why you Dagodin underestimate yourselves. You can do what we Ashishin or any other Forger cannot, yet, you complain."

"I think you overestimate us. Honestly, do you think wielding some weapon imbued with Mater is better than being able to Forge?"

"Pwah." Galiana's eyes glittered angrily. "Has a Dagodin gone mad or died from the influence of the essences? For too long now you have allowed your fear of being a Matii and of Matii in general cloud your judgment. On some days, Stefan, we would trade our places with yours for some semblance of a normal life. The knowledge that our deaths will inevitably come because of our gift is a thing we struggle with every day. Imagine doing so while living to my age."

"Sometimes I wish I could live to your age," Stefan retorted. "Many would give themselves for such a chance."

"Honey." Thania's supple fingers touched his shoulder. "She's right. I dread the day when I won't recognize any of the people I love. One moment I'll be well … the next … I'll be gone."

His wife's pain resonated in her eyes. Truth be told, he wouldn't trade his ability or his shorter life span for the longevity of any Shin. He couldn't imagine not recognizing Thania's beautiful face or her sweet voice. He was almost overwhelmed as he studied his children and thought of losing what he'd gained. "So how does the sword work?"

"I'm not certain. The Chronicles were not specific about its use. There was a picture of a Dagodin wielding the weapon and the three elements of Mater flying off into a spire. I …" Galiana shook her head, "I think he was using the sword to Forge."

"Impossible," Stefan whispered. The possibility of a Dagodin using a *divya* to Forge Mater in this fashion would change the scope of every war.

"Normally, I would agree," Galiana said with a slight nod, "but I'm inclined to believe the Chronicles." She held out the sword to him.

Gingerly, he took the weapon, turning the scabbard in his hands. The leather was of simple yet intricate craftsmanship. Nothing stood out at first, but upon closer inspection, he could not discern where one part of the material joined with the other. The pieces appeared seamless. He unsheathed the sword. Lamplight glittered off the blade's edge. He was willing to bet the sword would cut metal if he tried. Runes and glyphs ran up and down the flat of the blade. A tingling sensation crept up his arm and through the rest of his body. He held the weapon out before him and frowned. The sword felt as if he'd wielded the thing for years, one with his arm, like an old lover's tender caress.

"One other thing about this," Galiana said.

"Hmm?"

"It is said to be able to warn you if a shadeling is close."

Mouth dropping open, Stefan was at a loss for words. *A weapon able to identify shadelings?* A hand stroking his chin, he shook his head as he considered the sword. No wonder the Tribunal had kept such a thing hidden deep within the Iluminus. *How many of these did they possess?*

"I can see your mind work, Stefan," Galiana said. "I checked myself. The Tribunal's Imbuers attempted to duplicate this for nearly two hundred years. Every one of them failed. This is the only *divya* of its kind."

"Makes sense then. They would have conquered the rest of the world long ago if they had more." He sheathed the sword, unclipped his own weapon from his sword belt, and attached the new one. The scabbard felt as if it belonged. "How did you manage to escape with this anyway?"

Galiana smiled mischievously. "I Forged a construct that was an exact duplicate. By the time they realized, I was long gone."

A sudden thought struck Stefan. "Why do you think this was meant for me?"

"Part of the passage concerning the weapon … it said:

When the Setian once again become an empire,
A King shall be blinded by memory lost and desire
To wield the power the gods wrought
He shall sow chaos as his lot
Under the influence and with armies of shade,
Man and child sacrificed for the way laid
Mater feeds life, Darkness descends,
Ever encroaching until the light transcends,
Wielded by a warrior from the line of thorns

The first part of the Aegis will see their ancient line reborn.'

One eyebrow arched, Stefan asked, "That refers to me how?"

"One from the line of thorns," Galiana explained. "In ancient Seti, your name Dorn means thorn. Your lineage is what the passage speaks of. This sword belongs to the Dorns. Supposedly, only one of you can harness the power residing within it. Coupled with your triumph over the Astocans when the King officially declared Seti to now be an empire, and considering his plans, the conclusion seemed obvious."

"But you also suggested he will turn to the shade," Stefan said. "That, I cannot believe."

Shin Galiana shrugged. "I would not believe he would try to tap into the Forging used to create The Great Divide either, but that is his intention. No one can tell what will happen then. The power in the Divide is as unfathomable and unstable as anything I have ever witnessed."

"Maybe he knows something you don't? That none of us do?" Thania said, lips pursed.

"Possible," Galiana said, "which is why I wonder about the mention of the sword being the first part of the Aegis. If he found out what the Aegis is, that would explain some of his interest in The Chronicles."

"What is this Aegis?" Stefan asked.

"The Chronicles refer to it very vaguely. It is some type of weapon or power strong enough to defend against or to protect the gods."

"You seem to suggest they'll escape the Nether somehow or if they did, would need protection." Stefan smirked as he touched the sword. "They're gods. This is simple silversteel."

"Why the gods would need protection is beyond any of us, my dear," Thania said.

"Are you certain he isn't aware of this?" Stefan touched the new weapon's hilt.

"Unless he can get someone into the heart and soul of the Iluminus past several dozen High Ashishin, Raijin and worse, then, no."

Stefan whistled. "They moved the Chronicles into the Halls of the Exalted?"

"Indeed," Galiana replied.

"So, until we find out how to use the sword, what do I do?" Stefan regarded Anton and Celina even now doubting the decision he was being led to make.

"Nerian is willing to give you a year to spend with your family before he begins his campaign," Galiana said. "He will use the time to recruit. I will translate the other parts of the Chronicles I have copied by then."

Stefan paced across the room. "I don't know. If all this is true, if Nerian is threatening my family, if he is now a lunatic like you say …." He shook his head. "Pretending to side with him, hiding my feelings might be beyond me." Every fiber of his being told him to take his family and flee, but he also knew he could no such thing without guaranteed safety. Not to mention his men to whom he'd promised peace and a prosperous future. If this was all true, the lives of many rested on his shoulders. He stopped. *What if Galiana is lying and this is some Tribunal plot? What if it isn't?* Stefan squeezed his eyes shut.

"My dear heart, I don't think you will need to hide how you feel," Thania said. "For this to work, for you to keep us safe, you must let Nerian see your anger. Let him be aware of how this situation fuels you. Only then will he believe you're sincere in aiding him in this endeavor. Anything less and he will be suspicious. Not only will he not let you close to him then, but he may take us anyway."

Stefan stared tenderly at his children, gritting his teeth against hopelessness. "What if he decides to take you all regardless of what I do?"

"Until now Nerian has followed the teachings of *the Disciplines* more closely than anyone," Galiana said, "including you."

"'Demand honor but first show righteousness,'" Stefan quoted, temper flaring. "His recent actions violate the third

Discipline."

"Unless he thinks what he's doing is righteous," Thania countered.

Stefan bristled at his wife's words.

She shrugged. "There's no distinction to determine exactly what's righteous."

He looked to Galiana for support but the wry smile on her face told whose side she supported. "Fine," he said grudgingly. They were correct. Some of *the Disciplines* were left open to their moral interpretation. This allowed some freedom in the decision–making process for any leader who followed them. One thing became evident over the passage of years. A leader who followed them developed a strong belief from his men that led to victories skill alone could not achieve His own Unvanquished were living proof. Following this line of thought, Nerian would allow him to lead because the men fought with a fervor for Stefan they might not have for their King.

"One year." Stefan sighed, and then peered longingly toward Anton and Celina.

Self–sacrifice is often the greatest motivator for man and nation. Another of *the Disciplines*. He would treasure the time he had left with his children; it could be his last. When Perta entered moments later with a flagon of his wife's kinai wine, Stefan barely noticed the taste.

After Galiana left, and Perta reported she'd been escorted from the premises, Stefan turned to Thania in the privacy of their room. Both Anton and Celina were asleep on their own bed. "Do you believe her?"

The lamplight shone more golden in his wife's eyes. "As far as?"

"About all of it. Nerian's intentions, her translations of the Chronicles … this sword. This is so convenient it must be a trap. Better yet, one of the Tribunal's intricate conspiracies."

"Galiana and I have been friends for over a century. In that time, I have yet to see her so adamant about anything except when she led the Tribunal's Matii against the shade." Thania kept her gaze locked on his. "But I also know better than to completely trust anyone but you, my love. Whatever you decide, I'll be here to back you. At least consider what she asked of you." She glanced away from him toward the children's bed. "We have more than us to think about now. If you must, give Nerian the benefit of the doubt. I realize what he means to you. Maybe there is more to the Tribunal than Galiana is letting on. Even when I was among them, they kept many secrets. Whatever it is, for our children's sake, we must support the correct side. And we must be careful in doing so."

"What if this *is* some prophecy come true?"

Thania looked at him askance. "You? Believing in gods shaping fate?"

"Not necessarily, but ..." Stefan told her about his encounter with the Svenzar.

When he finished, Thania seemed lost in thought.

"Well?" he asked.

"I have seen enough in my life to believe in the gods and their touch on the world, both good and bad. A balance exists in all things, but as far as prophecies go, I'm uncertain." Thania focused on him. "If we follow the teachings of our philosophers, fate and prophecy are nothing more than the paths a man may weave for himself. It is similar to math: adding or taking away from something produces a certain result. Are the paths limited?" She shrugged. "Who knows? However, I do believe, even more so now since being with you, that whatever it is, a man shapes his own fortune. You made the decision you thought was best. Whatever comes of it we will face that storm together for the sake of our children's future. Nothing and no one can stand in the way. Not Galiana, not Nerian, not the Svenzar ... no one."

Stefan nodded. For the first time in a while, tightness eased from his shoulders. With Thania's support, difficulty became a trifle. Patience was his strong point. He strode over to her and took her hand. When he bent to kiss her, all thoughts of his troubles left him for a moment. All that existed was her smell, her silky hair, her body pressing against his as he pushed her down onto the bed.

But as they made love, the meeting with the Svenzar wormed its way into his head. He hoped for the sake of his people he'd made the correct choice.

CHAPTER 10

As the sun drifted high enough to illuminate the broad shoulders and soaring peaks of the Cogal Drin Mountains, Celina and Anton skipped along the garden path. Rose vines climbed up one side of the villa, the red and yellow blooms adding color to the otherwise drab sandstone and granite walls. Two months had passed since Stefan came home, and these daily walks with his children were now a routine he anticipated. His children brought a smile to his face, made him laugh outright at some new antic, or caused him to stare in wide–eyed amazement at how quickly they learned. More often than not, they grasped the wrong things the fastest especially swear words. He needed to remember to watch his mouth in front of them.

A squeal from Celina, followed by Anton's giggle, revealed the boy chasing her while brandishing some new insect he discovered. They ran around a circular hedge of blue bellflowers. When they returned from the other side, Anton was still after her, but this time she had somehow gotten his favorite toy soldier crafted by one of Benez's woodworkers from him. Her own doll in her other hand, Celina was the one laughing.

Stefan basked in the joy of watching them at play while inhaling the sweet scents. Blue and yellow bellflowers highlighted most of the hedges. Carved in circles and squares, the gardens extended several hundred feet, sloping down from the villa toward Tezian Avenue. Servants tended to the flowers and small trees, making sure each stayed uniform. Beyond the gardens grew Thania's small kinai orchard. The red fruit stood out in the bright sunlight as several workers under Perta's direction harvested them. The day was another good one, not chilly like the past week.

The synchronous thud of marching feet announced another five-guard patrol travelling down Tezian Avenue. *Right on time this evening,* Stefan noted. He still had difficulty adjusting to their regularity. At night, a watch joined them. His inquiries about the increased security revealed assassination attempts on the King and several of his court members. Since the first attack, when Nerian lost the Knight General that Cerny had replaced, there had been no further deaths. Cerny's promotion still bothered him. Despite the Knight General being a powerful Alzari who seemed to enjoy kissing royal ass, Stefan could not picture the benefits, not when other competent Alzari made up the King's High Council. The Nerian he knew was meticulous in making his choices; there had to be some special factor he simply was missing.

"Papa."

Stefan glanced down to Celina's voice and the pull of tiny hands on his trousers. The patter of small feet announced Anton's arrival next to his sister. With her doll, Celina pointed toward the colonnade at the villa's entrance.

Stefan allowed his gaze to follow her toy. What he thought had been the usual patrol was marching through the gate. They took up positions next to the columns. Ahead of them rode Knight General Cerny on a roan gelding. *Speak of a shadeling and one will appear.* Stefan shook his head.

Back straight, chest puffed out like the prideful fool he was, Cerny wore a formal green jacket with silver scrollwork on the sleeves. Sunlight glinted off the three golden knots of his station attached at the chest. One of Stefan's guards approached the Knight General. The guard bowed and a conversation ensued between the two. Cerny gave a dismissive wave of his hand then continued up the colonnade.

Stefan's lips curled—both at the Knight General's presence and for not hearing the horse's hooves ringing on the flagstones when the patrol approached. "Children go inside to your mother." He peered over to the kinai orchard. Perta was riding hard toward the villa's stables and its rear entrance. Knowing Cerny could not see him yet, Stefan hurried toward the front door.

This section of hedge was taller than the rest. Unable to catch a glimpse of the Knight General any longer, Stefan waited. Time passed as he listened to the unhurried clip–clop of hooves. As the sound drew closer, his hand drifted to his sword. He inhaled a deep breath and forced himself to relax.

"Greetings, Lord Cerny. Welcome to the Dorn home," said Perta's high–pitched voice.

"Thank you. I have come for your master ... at the King's request."

"Ah," Perta said. "Clesi, Dani, fetch some spiced wine and fruit for the Knight General. I'm sure he must be a tad warm on a day like this."

"Thank you."

A rustle of sound reached Stefan.

"No. I won't be staying long so taking my mount is unnecessary. Perta, is it?"

"Yes, my lord."

"Lord Dorn?"

"Ah, yes. Pardon me, I forgot that quickly. He's in the gardens I think. One moment, let me send someone to find him."

Head tilted as if he was inspecting the mix of bellflowers and the rose bush winding up the trellis, Stefan stepped around the hedge and onto the colonnade.

"No need," Cerny said.

As Stefan turned toward Cerny, he widened his eyes. "Knight General Cerny? What a surprise. No one informed me you were coming today."

"The King sent me for you ... sir."

"Oh? Why?"

Cerny's thin brows rose. "Did you forget? The games?"

"Actually, I did," Stefan said. "I have not been able to think about much besides my children." He gave a warm smile. "Perta, fetch my mount, please."

"Yes, my lord." Perta bowed and hurried away.

"I see you are taking special care of your gardens once again," Cerny said.

"They're Thania's pride and joy. When she's happy so am I."

"I'd find that kind of attachment burdensome." Cerny's gaze roved across the grounds. "I would much rather go hunting."

"You? Hunting?" Stefan stifled a laugh.

"What about it?"

"I'm sorry," Stefan said with a shake of his head. "I have a hard time picturing you as a hunter."

Cerny's eyes narrowed. "What is that supposed to mean?"

"Exactly as it sounds. You don't appear the type who goes out to the forests to hunt."

"Who said anything about the forest?" Cerny's lips spread in a slow smile. "My hunts are more subtle. I have a nose for sniffing out conspiracies and the like against the King."

Stefan kept his face straight and regarded Cerny with a cool expression. "Sounds useful but I much rather hunting in the wild myself."

"There's no more challenging game than man," Cerny said, his eyes searching Stefan's face.

"On that we agree." The Knight General appeared far too comfortable for Stefan's liking, like a cat batting around a mouse. "Speaking of games … what were you playing at by not informing me of the instability in the elements and the reason you took the Alzari? Was my warning about undermining my authority not clear enough?"

"My task wasn't to inform you. As for why I took the Alzari," Cerny shrugged, "I did tell you they were the King's orders, did I not? But you wanted to flaunt your authority in front of your men."

"Do you always follow those commands to the letter?"

"Don't you?" Cerny still smiled. "Wait, no you don't. Your orders were to kill all the Astocans. Whatever lives were lost because of you disobeying the King's orders are on your hands. My sole purpose is administering the King's wishes—for as he goes so does Seti."

Stefan wanted to reach out and choke the man when he thought about the crazed Ashishin and the dead, but in ways, what happened was his fault, at least partially. "You should have warned me instead of allowing my men and innocents to die."

Cerny leaned forward. "What innocents? There is Seti then the enemy. Remember that." Cerny straightened. "Look, we can both stop pretending. You don't like me, and my sentiments for you are the same. As for the Astocans, you did as expected." Cerny let out an amused grunt. "You think me a fool, Stefan. You may have made a good Knight Commander at one time, but you are losing touch, becoming soft. Do not allow it to be the end of you. You hold your post for now … but know this, one day it will be mine."

Stefan arched an eyebrow at Cerny's boldness. Forcing his hand to stroke his clean–shaven chin rather than reach for his sword took a great deal of effort. A time existed when none dared speak to him in such a fashion. While he often returned from war to many changes, this one in particular he did not anticipate. Added to how different Nerian had grown, Cerny's direct challenge let Stefan know he needed to tread with caution.

He'd miscalculated much about the Knight General. The man was more adept than he let on. Cerny had used that against him. *By mending the Astocans, not only did I appear rebellious, but I cost a few lives. Then I came home and refused the King's request to lead his army. What must Nerian be thinking of me now?* Stefan couldn't help the twitch of his lips. The Knight General might be a terrible strategist when it came to war, but he seemed to be a master at manipulation. How much of the events happening in Seti were the King's own doing and how much was Cerny's influence? Worse yet, were the rumored assassination attempts on the King and those achieved on some members of the court any of Cerny's plots?

"What's to stop me from striking your head from your shoulders right now?" Stefan asked, playing the part of his old self.

"Other than the fact I'm an Alzari?" Cerny scoffed. "I have the King's ear and men who will say you attacked me without provocation." His head gave a slight shift toward the guards near the pillars. "And well, then there's your family to think about. You—"

"You're the second person to make me feel as if they're threatening my family," Stefan said softly. He gave the Knight General a dead–eyed stare. "Be warned, Cerny. Neither the King nor the gods themselves can save you if you make such a mistake again."

Cerny licked his lips. "You misunderstand. I was pointing out your family would struggle without your presence."

"Where am I going? I don't plan to leave or retire any time soon. In all honesty, it's you who misunderstood. In my family, I'm the weakest. I wouldn't wish Thania's wrath on my worst enemy. You're far from that." Stefan allowed himself a slow smile.

Hooves on the cobbles announced Perta's return with the mount. Stefan purposefully turned his back to Cerny, took the reins to his favorite black stallion, and mounted. When he met the little man's gaze once more, Cerny's eyes were tight and his face dark with anger.

"It's been a nice chat, but as you say, the King awaits. Shall we?" With a flick of his hand, Stefan shooed the Knight General away, making it plain he no longer wanted the man's presence on his premises.

CHAPTER 11

The journey to the amphitheater dragged by without any further conversation. Although he didn't fear Cerny, Stefan still kept an eye on him. He would be a fool to overlook the man now. He'd considered bringing his own guard complement, but that would have played into Cerny's hands. He much preferred the man to be confident. Overconfident, if possible. For now, he intended to keep up appearances that Cerny's maneuvering did not bother him. He doubted the Knight General would have the nerve to make an attempt on his life in daylight anyway. Cerny was more the type to brandish a knife in the dark.

Marching ahead of them, the Dagodin guards kept the avenues and roads clear of people on their way to the games. From the way the men managed to stay in front of the trotting horses without appearing to tire, Stefan figured they must have drank some kinai concoction before the trip. Dressed in vibrant colors and designs, the townsfolk bowed as he and Cerny rode past. The stench of sweat and unwashed bodies made him glad to be riding. Children pointed from roofs and windows, and the occasional dog's bark echoed amongst the murmuring crowds.

"Make way! Make way!" yelled one of three soldiers at a

crossroad. The other two helped to funnel people to one side or another, keeping the intersection as clear as possible.

Thousands of conversations droned in an incessant buzz. Ahead of them, a coach carrying some noble trundled along the cobbles, its driver dressed in red and gold livery. Stefan had lost count of how many such carriages they'd passed. It appeared everyone but he had remembered the games. Not that it bothered him. Dartan fights and duels between slaves did not hold his attention as they once did as a youth. However, he did understand the need for sport, especially, the games. They brought the Setian together. The coin gained filled the city's coffers as people from all across Seti and the surrounding lands attended and spent lavishly on everything from clothes, to food, to wagers.

The huge sandstone and alabaster construction of the amphitheater dominated the landscape below as they turned onto the King's Road. Here, the throngs packed to the sides in a milling mass as they inched forward in the lines leading to the arena's main entrance. At certain sections, food vendors shouted out their wares beside their carts and stalls either by themselves or with criers. Their calls added to the cacophony. Smoke and steam rose from pots and cook fires. Meat roasted on spits, and stews and soups boiled in large pots. Spicy smells of peppered deer, quail, and roast chicken drifted through the air. Stefan's stomach growled in protest. He hadn't eaten yet. An image of the feast the King always provided brought on another grumble.

He hadn't seen Nerian since the day he returned from Astoca. Not that he minded. The time had given him a chance to think. Whereas the Chronicles mentioned a link to the Dorn line, who was to say the King they referred to might not be someone who overthrew Nerian? Maybe even Cerny. Or could it all be some grand Tribunal scheme Galiana was unwittingly tied up in? All the years spent under her tutelage and upbringing made him doubt she involved herself in a conspiracy to harm not only the man he thought of as a father but the Seti people as well.

Whether or not the Eztezians could see all these different threads of the future was something he couldn't simply dismiss.

The Svenzar, Kalvor, seemed to believe, and so did Galiana. Head throbbing from the way his thoughts spun, he was still undecided as they rode into the amphitheater's shadow.

"A moment, General, Lieutenant," a gold clad guard announced.

At first, Stefan didn't acknowledge the soldier. Then he realized the guard had used the new titles attributed by the King. Stefan gave a slight dip of his head to the man. The guard nodded toward a line of dartans crossing the street. They headed toward the ramp that led to the arena's bowels.

Stefan frowned at the sight of the beasts. Prize fighting dartans were nothing new, but the way the handlers dealt with these ones certainly was. Normally, it took several armored men prodding and poking at the animals with long lances to keep them in line. Even then, he'd witnessed once when a creature went wild and ignored the sharp points that too often did not penetrate their tough hides. The dartan snaked its head out, snatched the closest handler, and ripped him in two. Another time, a dartan plopped to the ground and withdrew its head and six limbs inside of its shell. No amount of stabbing or poking bothered the beast. It took an Alzari's Forging to make the animal move.

These handlers bore some kind of lengthy metal rod with a thick rubber handle. Anytime a dartan stepped the wrong direction, the handler gave the beast a jab. A jolt of blue light, much like the lightning Forgers called from the sky, arced across the rod's tip. The beast mewled in pain, put its head down, and followed almost as docilely as a newly broken horse.

Amazing.

"Shocksticks," Cerny said.

Stefan narrowed his eyes.

"Some Ashishin Imbuer came up with the idea." Cerny shrugged. "They took the essences of energy during a lightning storm and infused them into the metal like any other *divya*. Then they attuned it to the dartans. Rather than needing a Dagodin to wield this type of *divya*, anyone can. Simply place the shock end onto a dartan's skin and the reaction is instant. As you can see, quite effective at controlling those monsters."

The practicality of such a discovery wasn't lost on Stefan, but right away he considered other possible uses if such *divya* as the shockstick could be attuned to other things besides dartans. Before he drew any conclusions, what he saw next left his mouth agape.

A merchant dressed in silks was riding a dartan.

Seated in a hollow carved deep into the animal's shell, the man waved to children and other folk who pointed and stared as Stefan did. Occasionally, the dartan swung its head around to reach the rider, but the merchant's position prevented it from doing so. A shorter version of the shockstick dissuaded the dartan on such occasions. The man's head and shoulders stuck up beyond the shell to give him an ample view of his surroundings. He tugged on reins made from silvery chain, and the dartan leaped forward in an easy lope that took it past the others and down the ramp.

"Show off," the guard said.

"Who is he?" Stefan managed to ask.

"That's Merchant Vencel. He loves to make a spectacle since he figured out a way to ride them things." The guard shook his head. "I still wouldn't risk it. Got these fool youngsters all over the place trying. Many of 'em are dying too, behind that foolishness."

Thoughts still swirling Stefan said nothing. He promised himself to have a talk with this merchant at some point.

"Well," the guard said, "the way's clear. You may go now, sir. Enjoy the games."

With a nod, Stefan spurred his mount forward and crossed Humelen Avenue with its huge statues of giants carrying mountains on their shoulders—some builder's representation of the god of Forms after whom the street got its name. He entered through the wide entrance meant for nobles only, nodding to the guards as he did so. Whether Cerny followed or not, he didn't care. Now that he was within the amphitheater, his hunger pangs took on more urgency.

After leaving his mount with a young stable boy, Stefan entered the main hall. Dignitaries, merchants, and court members crowded the area, smoke from pipes floating lazily. The sweet scent from the giana pipes mingled with the perfumes of the women and created an almost sickly odor. As Stefan stepped into the room, the chatter paused as minor nobles acknowledged his entrance. Moments later the conversation buzzed on once more.

Several times Stefan swore there was a weird thrumming from the sword against his leg. However, when he attempted to focus, it disappeared. Soon, he dismissed the sensation as a residual effect from the stomping and yelling in the arena outside. A glance over his shoulder revealed Cerny had stopped to chat. Stefan took food from a platter a servant carried and continued to weave his way through the men and women to the door leading upstairs.

"Stefan," a raspy voice said.

A smile on his face at his recognition of the voice, Stefan turned. Although bald, Knight General Senden still looked half his ninety years. His shoulders were straight and broad in his immaculate white jacket with green scrollwork down the sleeves. Next to him was Knight General Renaida. The twenty years of youth he had on Senden did not show. The man's eyes were sunken sockets and pockmarks marred his face. His hair was as white as Senden's jacket.

"Walk with us," Senden said.

Renaida's eyes shifted from side to side. Sweat beaded his forehead, running a trail through the bronze powder he used to give color to his skin.

Stefan frowned at the man's apparent worry. "After the games." He rubbed his stomach. "Right now, I could eat an entire dartan."

"No," Senden said with a hint of urgency, "before you visit the King."

"Fine. Let me—"

"Ah, there are you are, Lord Dorn," called Cerny from a few steps behind.

Renaida gave a slight twitch at the sound of Cerny's voice but quickly covered the reaction.

"I have been told the King is in his chambers already, awaiting your presence." Cerny stepped up beside them, a serene smile on his face. "If you Lieutenants will excuse us?"

"Sure." Senden smiled, but from his eyes, the expression was forced. "We would not want to delay the General. After the games then, Stefan." Senden bowed, motioned to Renaida and the two eased their way into the crowd.

A thumb stroking his chin, Stefan eyed the two men until they disappeared from view. He'd spent years on many a campaign with them. Never did they appear as fearful as they did now, not even when they faced shadelings.

"I'd be careful associating with them," Cerny said. "They are the only ones on the High Council who openly criticize the King's new campaign."

"Now you're going to suggest who I keep as friends?"

"Not at all, sir. Not at all." Cerny wore the same smile on his face. "But as I said, the King awaits. Shall we?" He spun with a flourish and stepped through the door.

CHAPTER 12

Several flights up winding stairs that held one soldier at each landing brought Stefan and Cerny to the King's chamber. Two red and blue clad Royal Guards at the door gave slight nods before they allowed them in. Stomach growling in earnest, Stefan strode through the foyer.

Members of the High Council and special dignitaries from prominent neighboring cities occupied the Royal chambers. Dressed in their finest, they milled about chatting quietly, not even giving a nod as Stefan passed. He recognized they were Council members by the insignias on their lapels and sleeves. Not one among them were people who held their positions before he left for the last war. The thought was so troubling, he found himself stroking his chin again.

Distant jeers drew his attention away from the nobles and to the four doorways ahead. Guards stood before each. The largest door led to the Royal Box from which Nerian oversaw the games. No action had started yet, of that, Stefan was sure, but the noise meant the crowd was growing impatient.

Not waiting for Cerny to lead the way, he headed toward the door. The King's guards allowed him through and into the hall. More soldiers stood along the walls on either side making the spacious area feel uncomfortably small. Up ahead, sunlight shone through the entrance to the arena's stands.

Stefan stepped out onto the stairs. Bright sunlight and a cool breeze greeted him. Shading his eyes, he waited a few moments for his vision to adjust. When it did, he took in the walls of people packed into the stands. In too many colors to count, they spread down the eastern and western sides of the arena, waving and yelling.

Set in the middle of the lower section of the stands, the King's Box took up several seating levels. In silversteel armor, which glinted like a precious jewel, King Nerian sat on a cushioned throne. The giant man's presence made everything else trivial.

"Finally," shouted Nerian, a grin splitting his face. "I was beginning to wonder if Cerny and you ran off to some whorehouse."

"Not at all, sire. The crowds ... you know how they can be," Stefan answered.

"Ah. To be expected with such a glorious event." Nerian gestured out to the spectators. "Come, sit." The King indicated one of the empty chairs next to his throne.

At least ten flights of seats above the King were clear of anyone but guards and two green liveried servants. After the space came the High Council then the other nobles in their personal chairs. Oddly, Kahar was absent. Servants weaved their way among the nobles, serving fruit, drinks, meats, and bread. Stefan's gaze followed one particular platter heaped with what appeared to be venison. He licked his lips as his stomach protested mightily.

"Knowing your habits like I do, you have not eaten yet today." King Nerian snapped his fingers as Stefan took the seat. Without looking at the servants, the King said, "Our guest of honor is here, and he is famished. Cerny," the King's gaze flickered to the reed thin man who'd approached as Stefan sat, "leave us."

For a moment, Cerny's eyes glittered, and then he bowed and headed up to the next level and the members of the High Council. Renaida and Senden were conspicuously missing from their number.

The King stood, his massive form casting a shadow

that stretched up several seats. Almost immediately, the crowds silenced and rose to their feet.

"People of the Setian Empire." Nerian's voice boomed across the arena so clear and crisp Stefan knew he was Forging.

The crowd's answering ovation rippled through the stadium.

Nerian raised a hand and the din simmered.

"People. Of. The. Setian. Empire."

This time, the reply was defeaning.

Nerian's grin and twinkling emerald eyes told how much he savored the words. Hand still in the air he turned as if basking in the glow of his people's elation. He drew his hand across as if slicing the air and the cheers lessened. When all were silent once again, he continued, "It feels good to finally say that after all these years. Your loyalty and willingness to sacrifice has brought us the greatest reward possible. In appreciation for our General Dorn who has led the way in our campaign, I honor you, the people, with these games. Long live Seti."

The crowd roared the sentiment. Thousands upon thousands of stomping feet shook the stonework beneath Stefan's feet.

Still smiling, Nerian sat. The spectators' celebration continued as the metal gates on either side of the arena slid up and two dartans entered. Carried by a Forging, an announcer's voice rose over the racket to proclaim the upcoming fight. The look on the King's face conjured memories of a time when the man reveled in leading Seti for the good of its people. Stefan wondered if that man still existed beneath the armor.

"So," Nerian said. "Fatherhood appears to have been good to you. You enjoy your children and those gardens of yours so much you have yet to come visit me."

Stefan lounged back in his chair and allowed his limbs to relax. The King was letting him know he had someone within his house. Any sign of emotion now served no purpose. Stefan briefly considered which guard or servant might be the spy, but speculation was a pointless exercise. Even if he did discover the one responsible, Nerian would find another. "Yes. It's been wonderful. Better than I ever imagined." He studied the empty throne next to Nerian. The man had never taken a wife as far as Stefan knew. "Maybe it's time you find a queen and have an heir."

"Why?" Nerian shrugged. "I rather enjoy my rule. Considering that I have no intention of relinquishing the crown or dying anytime soon, I do not have a need for one. You are the closest thing I will ever have to a son."

Despite the King's nonchalance, Stefan caught the quick glimmer of sadness in his eyes. As with most of the Alzari on the High Council, Nerian lived an extended life. Stefan had traced the King's ancestors once and how long he'd ruled. The annals went back at least five hundred years before they became too disjointed to tell who held the throne before Nerian. One of the biggest issues with all Matii was that they often had only one chance to give birth. Most took advantage of the opportunity to pass down their power and extend their lineage. Others preferred to allow their line to die off rather than have their children experience the walk at the edge of sanity that burdened them all. Nerian's last words confirmed he'd made such a choice long ago.

"If you only knew what it is like …" the King's voice softened. "A gift but so much more a curse." He looked out to the crowds, but his expression was as if he saw nothing. "You have heard the voices once, I'm sure, when you first touched Mater—the way they whisper, goad you, make promises, seep into your core—all Matii have. But to live with them every day, every waking moment, invading your dreams, your nightmares … Such a burden becomes unbearable. Such a life might make a man want to kill himself, yet the same things that drive you mad also prevent you from taking such a course." A solitary tear dripped down Nerian's cheek. "Why would I want to bring a child into that?" With his thumb, he flicked the wetness away. "You are a braver man than me, by far. You have brought two."

Mouth open, Stefan broke eye contact with the King. This was the first time Nerian revealed such sentiments to him. The man he saw now was more the person he remembered if a bit more emotional. He thought back to when he first returned to Benez, and felt as if two completely different people inhabited the King's body. Absently, Stefan glanced down into the arena where the two dartans were tearing into each other to the crowd's delight. When he met the King's emerald eyes again, an icy coolness had replaced the melancholy.

"Does this mean you will let me live in peace to raise them?" Without blinking, Stefan held the King's gaze.

"You and I both know that is not possible." No hint of emotion resided in Nerian's tone. "For me to succeed, the men need you. They believe in you. The people believe in you. Stefan the Undefeated and his Unvanquished are names that strike fear into many an enemy's heart."

"If I refuse, will you force Thania and the children into service?" Stefan tensed.

A frown clouded Nerian's features. "Why would you ask such a thing?"

"The last time we spoke, you—"

"Not once did I make such a threat nor would I."

"So Galiana is lying?"

Nerian arched an eyebrow.

"She said you're willing to allow me a year with my family before I make a decision."

"I am."

"So it's true. Coupled with what you implied that day—"

"Do not try to read me," Nerian's face became a blank slate, "or read anything into my words. If I wanted to say I would force your family to serve in the coming wars because they are powerful Matii, I would have."

Stefan thought back to that day and what Galiana said. He'd judged everything from Nerian's mood and what he thought the King meant. *What if I was wrong?*

"This is not to say that they," Nerian tilted his head to the side and back, indicating where the High Council sat, "have not broached me on the subject. I told them you will make the right decision for our people, as you always have."

Sudden rage boiled within Stefan. Fists clenched, he

gazed toward the High Council. These men and women, most of whom he did not know, dared ask such a thing? His gaze met Cerny's. The Knight General gave him a smile and a nod. Stefan scowled. In response, Cerny shrugged. To resist the urge to charge up the stairs and separate Cerny's head from his shoulders, Stefan shifted his attention to the King. "Was it his doing?"

"Cerny? Who knows? He is as crafty as any in terms of political maneuvering and he has eyes in the unlikeliest of places. Anyway, enough talk about that for now. Our food is here."

Still seething, Stefan made to say more, but he stopped himself. He needed time to think. Not to mention the King's dismissal meant any further discussion would either go ignored or spark the King's ire.

Five servants brought the food to the table. Heaped on silver platters were an array of fruits, cheeses, breads, and meats. Stefan spied corn and various ground provisions covered in a creamy sauces. Two more servants arrived with several flagons. The mix of scents varied from peppery, to hints of mint, to outright sweetness. Despite his temperament and the concerns clouding his mind, Stefan's mouth watered and his stomach's rumbles reminded him of his hunger.

After they placed the feast on the table, the servants hurried away. The King stood, took a plate, and set about piling on food. With a smile on his face, Stefan followed his lead. Soon they were both eating and drinking wine while taking in the sights within the arena.

The first fights between the dartans ended. Slaves with spears and whips led away the surviving beasts. Several others dragged the prone and torn forms of the dead dartans onto drays and rolled them out through the arena's gates. A buzz of anticipation thrummed through the patrons. Horns blared. The announcer called out the next event.

A game of Senjin.

"Your favorite sport in honor of you," Nerian called amid the people's applause. He held up a ball a foot long and half as wide made from layered leather. "Wait until you get a taste of the twist."

Two flags, set opposite each other across the arena's width, marked the middle of the playing field. Red paint on the walls divided the two halves into thirds. At the far end of each side, white sand covered the ground in an area roughly twenty feet across and ten feet wide. If lines were drawn across each section, they would divide the playing field into eight parts, four per side—scoring zone, rear, mid and forward.

The players filed out the gates. From the east, they were dressed in gold. For these men, the crowd cheered. When the ones from the west entered wearing white, the spectators jeered and threw food. The ebony skin of the men in white stood out. Squinting, Stefan made out the slits on the sides of their necks.

"Astocans?"

"The officers that escaped into the Sang Reaches to be exact," Nerian said.

"Against Banai?" Stefan guessed, from the baldheads and wiry frames of the Astocans' opponents. "A Senjin match to the death?" The Banai and Astocans were mortal enemies. The game could end no other way.

"Oh, that is only a part of it. Wait until you see the stoppers."

As the players took positions facing each other on the field, the gates opened once more. On lengths of chain, slaves led two dartans, one mottled green, and the other a dusty brown, toward the scoring areas marked by the white sand.

"Oooo," the crowd cooed, their excitement near palpable.

The stoppers were slaves? Even as the question crossed Stefan's mind, the slaves fastened the chains to steel rivets on the wall a few steps behind the sand. They turned, bowed to the crowd and left. As he understood, Stefan's eyes widened. The dartans were the stoppers.

Nerian laughed. "You should see the look on your face. This makes the game so much more interesting. You have to risk your life to score."

"What if they choose not to?"

"That is the beauty of it. They are condemned to death anyway. If they do not score, they die. We start with the shielders if the teams hesitate to give a full effort."

Stefan was speechless. He hadn't played Senjin in years, but the positions and rules returned to him as if his last game was yesterday. Shielders played in the section closest to the stoppers. They were not allowed to cross into other areas like the supporters and assaulters, but they defended all the way to their scoring zone. Removing them placed a team at a severe disadvantage. It didn't matter that the supporters were limited to the middle and forward areas, because assaulters traversed the playing field at will except for their own defensive zone. If Nerian had a team's shielders removed, that team's lone stopper would face two opposing assaulters. In such a case, preventing a score was near impossible.

A normal game of Senjin was simply a sport—winners get the bragging rights, the ladies' affections, the people's admiration, and of course the pride, fame, and riches if the games were within tournaments. In the arena, losing a game meant extra shifts at the mines, less food, and for some, a beating. Death, though, added a new element.

King Nerian stood amid growing cheers. The shouts dwindled. He held the ball up in one hand, high over his head.

With a flick of his hand, Nerian sent the ball flying down into the arena. The spectators' roars shook the stadium.

As if caught by some invisible hand, the ball stopped in midair between the central flags. A collective 'Oh' sighed through the arena. The ball drifted down toward the exact center of the playing field like thistledown caught in the wind.

Then it fell.

In the same instant, the assaulters charged each other. A flurry of blows ensued, too fast for any but an experienced eye to follow. The men attacked with kicks, punches, throws and an array of fighting moves. Blood flew. The crowd's frenzy grew whenever a blow landed.

The teams countered each other—the Banai relying on their speed while the Astocans used their greater strength. Soon the supporters joined the fray, the ball forgotten as each team tried to secure the upper hand by disabling at least one man. These men were all once soldiers, so they relied on sheer brutality rather than tactics.

Experienced Senjin players knew to maneuver themselves to acquire the ball as soon as possible. After all, those who scored first often won since it required only three scores to earn a victory. A veteran team, when they got the ball, dropped back into the zone with their supporters. From there, they kept the ball between them, passing it from one to the other with a series of throws or handoffs. They advanced while defending the ones carrying the ball until they reached the end of the opposition's midfield. Once there, the assaulters crossed into the defensive area, faced off against the shielders and stopper. If they managed to defeat them, they scored. At that point, the supporters needed to drop back to the safety or their own area before the opposing teams members overwhelmed them and prepared for the next sally.

However, either due to them being soldiers or more the fact the Banai and Astocans hated each other, there were no such tactics deployed. This was an outright fight to the death from the start. The Banai appeared to be losing, until one of their assaulters dashed for the ball, snatched it up, and ran. The Astocans disengaged from the fight to give chase.

Stefan found himself on his feet. If the Banai assaulter gained the Astocan defensive area, he and his partner would face the shielders, if in turn, his fellow assaulter made it past the four Astocans.

Blood flowing from a gash to his head, his counterpart obviously knew this because he was already sprinting down the far side of the field. So intent were the four Astocans on the Banai with the ball, they ignored the other. Their shielders were waving wildly to show them their error, but the men paid no heed. The crowds' yells pitched even higher as they too realized what was unfolding.

As the Banai grew closer to their defensive zone, the Astocans understood their mistake too late. The other assaulter crossed.

Maybe thinking he had no other option, the closest shielder charged the Banai with the ball. The Banai made no attempt to fight him, and already travelling incredibly fast, he spun to one side and raised his arm to throw. The opposing shielder must have expected the move because he leapt into the air ready to block the throw and catch the ball.

But it was a feint.

The Banai flung the ball on the ground instead, spun, and crashed into the Astocan shielder nearest him.

His partner snatched the ball after it skidded and rolled to him. Caught by surprise, the second shielder could only bellow his frustration as the Banai headed toward the scoring zone.

If the crowd noise before was thunderous, now it seemed as if the noise would bring the amphitheater crashing down.

Then, a strange thing happened. At edge of the scoring zone and several feet from the dartan's reach, the Banai stopped. The crowd shouted at the man, goading him on as the Astocan bore down behind him. Aroused by the smell of blood streaming down the man's face, the dartan went berserk, thrashing against its chains, mewling as it strained to attack the assaulter.

Undaunted, the Banai took several steps forward until he stood within a foot of the frenzied beast and began to sway. Stefan couldn't believe his eyes. The man was dancing. The dartan's neck swung from side to side, and slowly, its movement matched the Banai's.

In that moment, the Astocan shielder, now within range, leaped at the Banai assaulter. As if he had eyes in the back of his head, the Banai sidestepped. The Astocan flew by him.

The dartan's sway stopped. In a strike too fast for Stefan's eyes to follow, the beast snatched the Astocan from the air. Tossing him like a toy, the dartan tore into the man. He managed to wail once before the animal's maw closed on his head, cutting off the cry.

While the beast was busy devouring the Astocan, the assaulter sauntered into the scoring zone and raised his hand into the air. The spectators greeted him with triumphant cheers.

"Fools," Nerian said from beside Stefan. "So predictable."

The anger in the King's voice made Stefan glance up.

Gaze locked on something across the arena, Nerian waved his hand. A blur of motion streaking across the distance resolved into arrows. Several platters flew up from the table to intercept them. Food and sauce spattered Stefan's clothing.

A burning sensation scoured Stefan's chest. He snapped a hand up to his jacket and came away with his fingers wet and red. The cloying odor of blood filled his nostrils. From the corner of his eye, he caught a flash of silver. A sword swung down and slashed an arrow intended for the King out of the air.

Before Stefan could discern the weapon's owner, a resounding thud and clang of metal on stone made him whip his head around to the other side. One of the Royal Guard now stood on the table. Four arrows protruded from his breastplate. Blood bubbling from his lips, the soldier keeled over, grasping at the shafts and fell off the table with a crash.

High—pitched screams echoed from all around. The games erupted into chaos.

CHAPTER 13

The stampeding crowd shook the stonework. Dust and pebbles dropped from parts of the walls. Across the arena, a space cleared around a lone man who stood with a bow pointed in Nerian's direction. The Royal Guards streamed out from the doorways near the attacker. They also rushed out from the passages close to the King's throne. People were screaming and pointing to the left. Stefan turned his head. Less than forty feet away, another man dressed like a typical commoner, held a bow also aimed at the King. The crowd cowered away from him. Some sought to leave, but guards at the exits prevented them from fleeing.

"Be calm, my people." Nerian's voice, deep yet serene, carried above the panicked cries.

Kahar stood beside the King, sword in hand. The milling mass of people attempting to escape slowed and then stopped altogether.

Palm facing outward, Nerian kept his outstretched arm raised. Face an unreadable mask, he said, "Take your seats again, but leave space for me to deal with those who would harm your King."

The spectators complied with his wishes despite the nervous mutters buzzing amongst them. Twenty feet of empty seats separated them from each attacker. The effect of Nerian's voice and demeanor made Stefan want to sit and relax, but he fought against the urge and remained standing. He studied his chest. A ragged gash marred his jacket from one side of his chest to the other. Frayed ends of satin and linen waved in the breeze. The wound stung, and the blood stained the blue to give it a purplish color. The sight of how close he'd come to death and the assassins' attempt on his King's life brought a wave of anger bubbling up inside him.

"Empty the arena and prepare for the main entertainment," Nerian ordered. Perspiration beaded the King's forehead, but his face was stoic.

Stefan frowned. In all his years, he did not remember seeing Nerian sweat, not even on the hottest days in the armor he always seemed to wear. The clank of gates drew the Knight Commander's attention below. Guards entered the arena and herded the players from the field. The dartan handlers came next and led the beasts away.

As he worked to calm himself, Stefan wondered why the would–be assassins didn't fire. The answer came as Nerian gave a slight wave of his hand as if directing a band at a ball. Frozen in the act of shooting, the two attackers rose into the air and floated several feet above the arena. A squeeze of Nerian's hand into a fist and the men fell to the ground.

Arms flailing, they cried out and dropped their weapons. They landed hard despite trying to roll. One managed to scramble to his feet. The other man's leg was bent at a crooked angle. He groaned as he struggled to stand. His accomplice rushed to his side and gave him a hand. Together they faced the King.

"My dear subjects," Nerian began, "what we have here are elite assassins sent by the Tribunal. Two Raijin to be exact."

Awed murmurs rippled through the crowds. Stefan stared. The Raijin were nothing like he expected. He always pictured them being similar to the Pathfinders, moving with a deadly grace in all they did. These two men seemed normal and unimpressive, but he knew better than to judge them by their appearance. Raijin were among the deadliest swordsmen and Matii within the Tribunal. They were supposed to be worth any five experienced fighters in a battle. Their ability for stealth and infiltration were second to no one's.

"You had a good plan," Nerian said to the two men. "Not Forging so I would be unable to spot you beforehand. Using *divya* arrows to penetrate any Forge I might use or my armor. Too bad you forgot that something as simple as a dish, a piece of stone, or a normal blade has the ability to intercept an imbued weapon when used correctly." The King gave a sly grin. "I am not above using the mundane."

"You knew of this?" Stefan whispered.

Nerian shrugged. He gestured to the Raijin. "Now that you have given up the one chance you had to use the elements, what will you do? Wait, I know. You will fight for your lives."

Shock ran through the spectators at the King's proposal. They understood what killing Tribunal Matii meant.

War.

Despite his urge to retaliate against the Raijin, a sense of dread knotted in Stefan's gut. To talk of campaigning against the Tribunal was one thing. Committing an act that without doubt would start the conflict was another. "Are you certain you want to do this?" he asked.

"They did this, not I," Nerian snapped. Not once did his or Kahar's attention waver from the Raijin. "They attacked us first. What are we supposed to do? Cower? Hide? Not respond? The Tribunal made the first move and played their hand. Now, it is time to play mine."

"We're not ready for this."

"Fortune waits for no one." This time Nerian's voice did not rise over the nervous murmurs of the people. "More often than not, you must take what is handed to you and fashion it into what you need."

"But—"

"In this, there are no buts, Stefan." Nerian pointed to the expectant crowd. "Seti needs you. Your men will need you."

Stefan almost said more, but this wasn't the place to argue. Regardless, Nerian wouldn't be swayed. In ways, he didn't blame the King. If the assassins were anyone else but Raijin, he would have killed them himself. The Knight Commander bowed. He hoped the King was making the right choice.

"My people, I know you have your doubts as I would if I were in your place. The Tribunal has done much to help our people and Ostania as a whole in the days when the shadelings were slaughtering and converting all before them in the name of their god." A murmur of agreement issued from the crowd. "But those days are done—long gone. As a people, we did our part too. Countless thousands sacrificed themselves in those wars. The Nagels, the Abenderoths, the Durrs, the Engels, the Jungs, the Kalbs." Nerian continued with a long list of family names. With each name called out, the whispers grew to crying and wails as people remembered those they had lost. Finally, he said, "the Dorns."

Stefan's chest heaved. His ancestors had been involved in every major war in the last several hundred years in Seti. There were few left in the Dorn lineage.

"You can trace our loss in the bloodline of ANY Setian family," Nerian shouted, voice mired in passion. Then his tone softened. "We lost much … not only lives but also our standing as being foremost in Denestia. Most of all, we lost our freedom as a people. For too many years we have … no I have … subjected us to the Tribunal's whims under the guidance of their High Ashishin. Their Shin were treated better than our own Alzari." The King paused as several people shouted that the Alzari deserved better.

"I agree," Nerian said. "For that I am sorry. I allowed them such a pedestal. But no more. After all, what is the difference between them and us besides the types of elements they can call upon? None. What makes the Shins superior? Nothing." An expression of regret crossed Nerian's face. "Sometimes a King must make a choice to see his people survive, no matter how detestable the decision may be."

Stefan took in the many nods among the spectators. Where doubt and questions once existed, the people now clung to the King's every word.

"Now …" Nerian shook his head as if in resignation, "months after I told the Tribunal we no longer required the services of their Shins … and that in fact, we wished to stand alone as a people to rebuild Seti and Ostania to its former glory," he gestured to the Raijin, "they sent their answer. Death to me because I want more for you, for us, as a people."

This time, the mutters spreading through the amphitheater carried hints of anger.

"Tell me what I should do? Should I return these assassins to their rightful owners, apologize, and inform the Tribunal I will do whatever they want? We hold all of Ostania except for Felan and Harna. Should we now give all we own, all we have paid for in blood to the Tribunal? Should I forgive this act, this attempted assassination? Better yet, do you wish to ignore that they almost killed General Dorn, the man who has brought us victory after victory and ensured most of your loved ones came home safely?"

Resounding echoes of 'No' rang through the amphitheater. People screamed their outrage.

"Well, Lord Dorn," Nerian said without facing Stefan, "What do you say? Fight or not to fight."

As he took in the expectant faces and the boisterous masses Stefan's shoulders slumped. Nerian had trapped him. The promise he made to his men echoed in his head as he said, "Fight."

The people's jubilant roars drowned out his thoughts.

"So be it," the King shouted, his voice joining the crescendo. "Deploy the Zar."

All around the amphitheater, Alzari dressed in their green and gold uniforms appeared at the entrances to the stands. They took places overlooking the arena. Stefan lost count after a hundred.

"Today, I will show you why we have nothing to fear from the Tribunal's Matii. You will learn that our own are as strong if not stronger." Nervous rumblings rolled through the crowd at what Nerian said. Some attempted to get as far away as possible from the sides of the arena. "Be brave, my people, the Alzari you see shall keep you from harm."

Eyes narrowing at the King's words, Stefan opened his Matersense. He gasped. Although neither he nor any other Dagodin could Forge Mater, Thania had been adamant in teaching him how to read what other Matii were doing with the elements.

Hardened by the Alzari's strength, which lay in manipulating the essences of earth, a shield made primarily of their weakest essence—air—encircled the arena. The shield rose up to form a dome. To the naked eye, the air was clear, but to any Matii capable of reading Forgings, the Alzari had used earth essences to darken their work. By doing so, they limited the essence the Ashishin were strongest at manipulating—Light.

What fascinated Stefan even more was what the King himself did. Stefan knew Nerian's power ranked him with at least a High Shin or High Zar, but he'd never noticed any particularly strong Forge done by the King until now.

For several hundred feet around the two Raijin, the King had Warped Mater. The essences within the area were so distorted they would feel like oil sliding through one's hand. The Raijin would not be able to Forge until the effect ended. Stefan took in the soldier's corpse at his feet. Now he understood. The man's act had been twofold. Not only had he sacrificed himself for his King, but his death had given Nerian the necessary essences to draw upon to create the Warping. Essences that could only be garnered when something died.

But how long could Nerian maintain the Warping? The King's face bore the answer. His eyes showed strain, and sweat rolled down his forehead.

"Now to introduce our champion," the King shouted. "Cerny."

CHAPTER 14

S tefan snapped his head around to where he'd last seen the Knight General, but Cerny was no longer there. A cheer drew his attention back to the arena. The gates slid up, a hole the size and shape of a doorway appeared in the shield, and Cerny stepped through.

At the same moment, Nerian released his Warping. The King took in several heavy breaths.

In the arena, the two Raijin glanced around. The wounded one reached down and twisted his leg into place. A yell escaped his lips. Moments passed as his chest heaved then he stood and flexed his leg.

Stefan expected Cerny to press the advantage, but the Knight General didn't. A devilish smile on his face, green uniform pristine with its three golden knots standing out chest–high, he strolled toward the Raijin.

A hush fell over the amphitheater.

The two Raijin took in Cerny's leisurely approach before nodding to each other and splitting apart. The entire scene felt surreal to Stefan as the shield not only prevented anyone from entering or leaving, but it also kept in all sound. In the silence, he heard his and King Nerian's breathing.

There was a sudden blur of movement as both the assassins thrust their hands in Cerny's direction. Bars of solid white light bright enough to sear one's vision shot across the distance. A solid slab of earth grew up from the ground in front of Cerny. The bars of light struck it and sent dirt and rock showering into the air.

The earth within the arena heaved and rolled in a wave toward the Raijin. Both men dived out of its path. It slammed into the edge of the shield with an impact that shook the amphitheater.

The crowd cheered. Stefan blocked them out as he watched.

When the two assassins gained their feet, they looked around frantically then their gazes focused on the sky for a moment. Stefan shook his head as they now realized their plight.

They sprinted, throwing their hands out, streaks of lightning and light bars shooting out from them toward Cerny as they attempted to overwhelm him. Cerny simply stopped. The constant protection of earth rose around him, blocking whatever they did. The Raijin continued firing, their attacks growing from streaking bars and bolts to small balls as their power waned.

Then, the earthen shield broke apart into a thousand pieces. As it did so, several balls of incandescent light shot through. Cerny raised a hand. Something flashed into shape around his arm, almost like armor, and he swatted the balls away.

A breath hissed from Stefan's lips. He did not recognize any of the essences Cerny had used to block the attack. For a moment, he thought he spotted slight mixes of shade among them.

In the same instant, the pieces of earth, still floating, shot toward the Raijin like a thousand arrows. The men had no time to react. Stone and earth ripped through their bodies. Blood spattered the sides of the dome behind them. In silence, they fell to the ground dead.

Cerny strode from the arena.

"And as simple as that, the Raijin fall," King Nerian said, a satisfied smile on his face. "Proof they can be defeated."

The crowd's jubilation rose to a crescendo.

"Stefan." Nerian's voice dropped several notches. "Now you know one of the reasons Cerny will take your place if you refuse to lead the men." The King kept his gaze fixed on the people. "He does not hesitate to kill."

"I would ask what of the Tribunal's response, but now I understand why you wanted me to be here and why you wanted this as a public display."

"Oh?" Nerian's amused expression didn't change. "I expected nothing less, but go ahead and tell me."

"The word will get out about what happened here," Stefan said. "Killing two Rajin this easily will make the Tribunal plan before risking open war. You showed them a strength they didn't anticipate."

"Yes," the King agreed. "I have also given you time to consider the decision before you." He no longer smiled. "It has been a pleasure spending time with you again, despite all this … but I have kept you long enough. Besides," the King's gaze shifted to the steps above them, "the High Council has been clamoring for my attention. The time has come for me to reveal some of my plans to them."

A seemingly heated debate was taking place between several members of the Council. Normally it was Stefan who handled such issues before presenting the Council's concerns to the King, but because he'd kept himself apart since returning and with his absence on the campaigns, the role apparently now belonged to Cerny. The Knight General stood to one side having a conversation with Renaida and Senden. By their gestures and faces, neither of the older men were pleased. Every so often, they peered toward the King and Stefan.

"Send my well wishes to Thania and the children," the King said. "I look forward to hearing from you soon. Now, go spend some quality time with your family."

"I will and you shall. Until then, sire." Stefan bowed from the waist and left.

As he strode through the throngs in the amphitheater, the day's events nagged at him. He couldn't blame Nerian for his decision, not after the assassination attempt, but the Tribunal's potential reaction still worried him. The King was gambling with lives. If they decided to retaliate, he was uncertain whether Seti could handle an immediate attack. At the same time, he knew Nerian for the shrewd, calculating King he was. The King wouldn't have made this move unless he thought his armies were ready. That, in itself, bothered Stefan the most. How did Nerian plan to deal with the Alzari's instability? The few High Alzari they used to monitor their own Matii would not be enough. Stefan nodded absently. *The King knows everything you do and more. He's thought of this already.* But no matter how he tried, he couldn't shake his doubts.

Stefan sniffed and stopped. *What was that awful smell?*

The thud of marching boots echoed from nearby. Without realizing, he'd made his way below the amphitheater where they kept the prisoners in addition to a barracks. Several thousand soldiers were in process of forming up. Stefan frowned. The men were preparing to leave.

The Knight Commander strode over to a man who stood a few feet away from them. The single golden knot on his breast identified him as a Knight Captain, or he would have been one if not for the King changing the titles within the ranks. "Captain." Stefan made certain to use the King's new titles. "These men have been reassigned?"

The soldier took one look at Stefan and immediately straightened his posture. "Yes, sir."

"By whom and to where?"

"Lieutenant Cerny's orders, sir. We are being sent with Lieutenants Senden and Renaida as part of an advanced party to gather information on the Erastonians."

"Ah," Stefan said. "Carry on." He strode away.

So Cerny is effectively doing away with ones who voiced opposition to the King's plans. Stefan nodded. Despite his dislike for the man, he appreciated his cleverness.

Several mewls broke Stefan from his thoughts. Over to one side was a dartan pen. His musings had drawn him in so much he'd automatically found his way downstairs for something else that had caught his attention and niggled at the back of his mind. The pungent odor from earlier returned stronger than ever. It was from dartan shit and old rotting meat within the pens.

Dressed in silks, Merchant Vencel was poring over a ledger of some sort and writing information down as he inspected the animals. The beast with the saddle carved into the shell stood alone in another enclosure.

"Merchant Vencel," Stefan called as he took in the docile way in which Vencel's strange mount eyed him. "Just the man I wanted to see." Now, all he needed to do was find the Banai.

CHAPTER 15

Eyes shifting from side to side, Stefan studied the seven men who circled him in the training room. Nine months had gone by since he returned to Benez. Every day since that fateful night, he practiced the sword and spent time with his children. Sweat beaded his forehead, but he resisted the temptation to wipe it away. Instead, he kept his focus trained on Knight Carim and his friends. Shirtless, Stefan pivoted from foot to foot, ears straining for the telltale scuff of a boot, the kiss of a breeze where there should be none, the reflection in an opponent's eye, or the twitch of an eyelid. Any such move would reveal a threat.

A scuff. Stefan spun, bringing his sword up to parry the attack from his left. His foot snaked out to the trip the man. As the attacker fell, the Knight Commander followed through, the hilt of his sword connecting with a jaw and driving his attacker into the ground.

The faint whistle of a blade slicing air. With a slight shift of his head, Stefan dodged the blow. The attacker's arm flew by him. He gripped it and yanked. Already off–balance, the second man's body shot forward as Stefan twisted and brought his knee up into his assailant's unprotected stomach. The man crumpled with a grunt.

Two down.

Frustrated glares met Stefan's smile. He waggled his weapon at Carim. A good taunt often drove youngsters to attack callously. Not Carim though. The youth had learned his lesson the hard way.

Marveling at his seemingly endless energy, Stefan allowed his chest to heave as if he'd exhausted himself in the brief exchange. The first session when he'd used his sword, he thought it was his imagination that he was faster, stronger, lighter on his feet. Now, he knew it *did* have such an effect brandishing the *divya*. Out of curiosity, he allowed Kasimir to wield it a few times. His friend said he felt nothing unusual.

Carim's eyes flickered. Motion from behind reflected in the silversteel surface of the Stefan's blade. They were attacking as one.

Immediately, he drifted into the Shunyata—the deep place inside the mind Matii used when they touched Mater or when they fought—for stability and control. Whereas, when he first received his *divya*, he thought it *felt* as if he and the sword were one, when inside the Shunyata, they *became* one. The weapon was an extension of his will.

He spun, caught the attack of the man from behind on his blade, and turned it aside. Without trying to counter, he ducked Carim's stroke and rolled. The move brought him in close to the next attacker, and Stefan kicked out, forcing him to leap away.

Back now to a wall, Stefan struck a pose in one of the Stances based on the formlessness of the Flows of Mater. Within the Shunyata he no longer needed to wait for them to attack. The initiative was his. He discerned their patterns, their intentions, as clear as a cloudless sky at noon. They were his partners at a ball, their movements a simple two step dance, an obvious synchronization. His was a glide into a saltation of Styles and Stances to music only he could hear.

Stefan charged.

Into their midst he flew. His sword flashed up, down, left, right, and diagonal in Aeoli's Hand, The God's Way, imitating the thirty–two directions of the wind. Like the god of air, he was a storm of movement, unending, unrelenting.

A thud of the flat of his blade to the back of a head. The quick lick of a slice against flesh. A groan, a moan, an anguished cry. The breeze of a blow missing him by a hair. Parrying a cut, the impact more like a feathery touch than steel on steel. The clink of metal and the imperceptible squeal of edge striking edge. Foot lashing out to a groin, spin, then drop. The Knight Commander flipped up from his back as the next attack missed him. The series was surreal, a dream. His sword clashed with the last man standing in a steel on steel embrace.

Carim.

Stefan flicked the young Knight's sword aside. With his next step, his weapon rested an inch from Carim's neck. Stefan smiled. "Yield?"

"A draw I'd say."

Frowning, Stefan looked down at the tap against his ribs. A dagger in Carim's hand beat time on the Knight Commander's sweaty skin.

"You always teach overconfidence can be the downfall of the best swordsman," Carim said, perspiration trickling down his lips onto his chin as he smiled.

Stefan nodded and sheathed his sword. "A draw indeed. You're right about overconfidence too. I guess even us Knight Commanders tend to forget what we teach sometimes."

"General, you mean?"

"Or that," Stefan shrugged, "but I would rather Knight Commander when you're in the confines of my home." *A man must maintain some semblance of control even when certain events are out of his hands.*

The other Knights struggled to their feet amid moans and gritted teeth.

"Take your men to the menders, Carim. Good fight. Pay each of them a gold eagle." Stefan smiled at the open mouths and grins from his soldiers. The reward was enough money to keep them going for several weeks of drink and women. They deserved it; their time here in Benez was almost at an end.

Stefan waved to Kasimir and Garrick to join him as the

young Knights shuffled off with the help of their counterparts. Both with the new pins and stripes of their rank on display, the two Knight Generals arrived at his side by the time he pulled his tunic on and buttoned up his shirt.

"Aren't you supposed to get slower with age, Stefan?" Kasimir asked.

"And weaker?" Garrick added with a shake of his head.

"Must be my wife's cooking." Stefan grinned as a servant brought over a cup filled with kinai wine.

A thoughtful expression crossed Garrick's face as he twirled his mustache. The corner of his lip twitched.

Cup in hand, Stefan chuckled. "No, you can't twist my words to make Thania think I spoke ill of her culinary skills."

With a shrug, Garrick said, "Was worth a try."

Stefan took a deep gulp from the cup, swilled the wine around, and then swallowed. The liquor coursed down his gullet in a trail of fire. Moments later, he felt as if he could fight a dozen battles. After he emptied the cup, he led the way out the oak doors and into the stairwell.

"How's the training and recruitment gone?" Stefan asked as they headed up the steps.

"Both have been exceptional," Kasimir said.

Garrick nodded his agreement.

"Numbers?"

"We replaced a third of our normal legions with new recruits," Kasimir said. "They took well to the rigors of our training regimen. You can thank Garrick for that."

The bear of a Knight General smiled. "Someone had to push them. The others who aren't joining us this campaign were only too happy to help."

Glad he would at least hold up his promise of peace for some of his older warriors and for those who wished to be with their family, Stefan issued a silent prayer to Ilumni. "Good," he said. "Just in time too. The King has summoned me today. There's no doubt our forces will march within the next few hours."

"Knight Commander?"

"Yes?" Stefan frowned at Kasimir's tone and grim expression.

"What are we going to do about the Erastonians? We know nothing of how they fight."

"Not even from the Scouts?"

"No, sir," Garrick answered. "The Heralds have not received word from any of the Scouts. Every party we sent into Everland disappeared without a trace."

Stefan stroked his chin. This wasn't much different from what they'd faced against the Astocans until they actually met them in their first battle. *So why do I have these nervous flutters?* "We'll improvise if we should have a need. Use the same formations if we can. It's a few months march from here into Everland. By then we should have some reports." Stefan hoped he sounded more confident than he felt. "Garrick, you let the men know to prepare. Kasimir, when you get a chance, check on Merchant Vencel."

"Yes, sir," both men said together.

They spent the rest of their time discussing family and the enjoyment of their break without the rigors of war. It was good to see his men in such high spirits considering they would again be leaving on a campaign. Stefan thought about visiting Anton and Celina before his trip to the Royal Palace, but decided to wait. He led Garrick and Kasimir out to their mounts.

The dying sun pricked the horizon as they said their goodbyes and departed. The two Knight Generals rode off toward the west where they could prepare the army for their long march at the entrances to the Travelshafts.

The onset of summer meant the celebration of Soltide. It signaled another successful harvest season for Seti's bustling economy. The festival lasted weeks. Accompanied by tumblers, jugglers, and musicians, the revelers in costumes featuring outlandish colors and bits of lace that left little to the imagination, danced along the avenues. At least the nobles had on that much. Stefan could only imagine what the more free–willed common folk wore or didn't wear.

Two stagings—one of the more expensive types of costumes—set on drays pulled by Cardian slaves, rumbled along behind the procession. The first staging was a woman covered in the plumages of several birds, their colors even more beautiful in the evening sunlight. The second was a representation of the god Humelen. This one was a man with mountains and forests painted onto his skin along with imitations of precious metals stuck to his body. Earth, wood, and metal—the solid essences that made up the element of Forms belonging to that god.

Original. Stefan nodded, quite impressed by the creativity. The staging of the god was sure to win a prize at the contests later in the evening.

Stefan rolled his eyes at the blocked streets ahead and turned down one of the side lanes. This one wasn't as crowded, but he needed to make another detour as it became more congested. Soon, he gave up riding altogether, choosing instead to dismount. After a bit, he left his horse at one of the few stables still open during the festivities. Weaving his way through the throngs became easier, and as he drew nearer to the Palace, the crowds lessened.

Lamps and torches lit the streets now as the sun had fled the sky leaving the pallid light of Denestia's twin moons as the night's herald. Up ahead, a staging blocked off an avenue. Rather annoyed now, Stefan cut down one of the few small alleys in the Upper City. Save for four inebriated revelers cavorting down the road, the alley was conspicuously empty. The three men and one woman waved to Stefan, laughing and singing in god–awful tones.

The revelers were within six feet of him when his sword gave off a subtle vibration. He frowned and touched the weapon's hilt to make sure of the sensation. An attempt to remember where he experienced it before proved fruitless. In the next two steps, the sword thrummed against his palm so hard that he swore it wanted to leap from the scabbard of its own volition.

A scuff of a boot moving stealthily. The sound was too purposeful for a bunch of drunks. By instinct, he ducked. A blade sliced the air vacated by his head.

"Do not allow him to draw," a guttural voice said.

The words were like a gargle of spittle deep within a throat, more growl than speech. A hand clamped onto Stefan's wrist with frightening power. Stefan stared down into a chiseled face with glittering coals for eyes. The man grinned. Stefan's nose twitched at the fetid stench rolling off the would–be assassin.

Aided by the speed and strength from his touch on the *divya*, Stefan's hand darted to his left hip. He whipped out his dagger from its sheath. In the same motion, he sliced down and across the hand restraining his own. There was a surprised yip, followed by a snarl. The man's grip loosened.

The sword still vibrated like a madly beating heart. Stefan whipped his hand out and spun as the other three attackers attempted to assist their accomplice. Instead of whirling to escape, he used his momentum to bring himself into the first man. Eyes widening in surprise, the chisel–faced man didn't have a chance to move as Stefan stabbed. The sword punctured his assailant's gut. Stefan ripped up. Warm bowels gushed onto his hand and uniform.

The man grunted and a dying breath hissed from between clenched teeth. Stefan kicked him off and stumbled backward to make space for the other three assassins.

A choked howl issued from the man he'd gutted. Stefan's gaze flitted from the three accomplices to the form thrashing on the cobbles, fluids leaking from the gashed stomach. The man's eyes changed to a glowing, feral green.

What in Amuni's name?

The stench hit Stefan more powerfully then, rolling in waves. Rot. Decay. Moldy fur. The pungent smell of a wraithwolf.

Shadelings? Here in Benez?

Around his twisted face, the dying man's flesh sloughed off. Black fur replaced tan skin. His clothes writhed and stretched. The assassin was changing, growing, transforming. Ripping cloth accompanied bulging muscles as shirt and tunic tore. Gangly arms stretched down past the knees, ending in black–nailed claws twice the span of a normal man's hand. The mouth and nose elongated into a dark muzzle lined with canines. The head thrashed once more, a puppy–like whimper escaped the beast's jaws, and then it lay still.

Paralyzed by the transformation, Stefan stared openmouthed at the prone form of the seven–foot wraithwolf. From the corner of his eye came a flash of movement.

A fist crashed into his face with a force akin to someone picking up a flagstone and slamming it into his jaw. Something cracked. Lights danced across his vision. Blood filled his mouth with a bitter taste. Stefan stumbled to one side, swinging his sword wildly before him.

A growl rumbled from a few feet away, sending chills down his spine. He shook his head in an attempt to clear his sight. Vision still blurry, he picked out the shadowy forms of his six … no … nine … no …. The images merged into the three remaining assailants before doubling and tripling then becoming one again.

One hand on his broken, throbbing jaw, blood a roar in his ears, Stefan retreated until he rested against a wall. In front, two of the assassins snapped their heads back and howled. With that action, their clothes tore from their bodies to reveal fur instead of skin. Wraithwolves' leering muzzles replaced human faces. The nauseating stink of death and corruption accompanied the transformations.

Desperately, Stefan sought the Shunyata. If he was going to die, he would do so fighting and take some of the beasts with him. Even as the thought crossed his mind, he gained the Shunyata's calm deep inside himself and frowned. *Why hadn't the woman changed?*

Obsidian fur rippling, eyes malignant green pools, the two wraithwolves stalked to each side as if they had all the time in the world. Stefan's sword vibrated so hard, it jarred his palm. The woman, face painted in reds and yellows, dimly highlighted by one of the two lamps at the alley's entrance, raised her hand slowly.

The air around Stefan grew heavy, thick, and constrictive.

He gagged, suddenly finding himself short of breath. His weapon felt as if it weighed a hundred pounds.

The woman was a Matus. A Forger.

"Before you die," she said with an air of nonchalance. "You will reveal to me how you came to possess your sword. You will release it to me and tell me what you know of the Chronicle of Undeath. Resist and your wife and children will suffer."

Stefan opened his mouth to speak, but words fled him. Throat and lips dry, he squeezed his eyes shut and strained for all he was worth against her Forging. *Dear Ilumni, help me. Please.* But he knew his efforts were futile. Still, he tried again and again, begging the gods for some kind of strength. His prayers went unanswered. He was going to die and so was his family. Images of Thania and the children ravaged by the savage beasts, souls torn and bodies transformed, brought tears to his eyes. If he could have wept at his helplessness, he would have.

Against his palm, the sword vibrated even more intensely. Heat throbbed through him, scouring his insides. Gritting his teeth against the weight suffocating him and stopping his movement, Stefan willed his sword arm to move. His fingers gave a twitch, his wrist turned and the weapon with it. Such a slight effect brought him a flutter of hope.

Somehow, he knew he would not die. He would be with Thania again. He would spend time with his children again. It was his will, and it would be so.

Stefan opened his mouth in a wordless scream. A tiny concussion rocked his arm, emanating from the sword. The pressure holding him eased.

The Matus' eyes grew wide.

In a quick motion, the foremost wraithwolf sniffed the air then whirled to scan the rooftops. Its counterpart did the same.

"What—"

Hooded cloak billowing, a man–shaped form appeared in front the Matus. Flames streaked from her hand toward the newcomer. The cloak swirled, and the fire simply dissipated as if gobbled up by the fabric. Before the she Forged again, the shadowy form took a step forward, and sheared her head from her shoulders with a slice of a sword so fast it seemed almost casual.

Completely free of her power, Stefan charged the closest wraithwolf, but his savior was faster still. In a blur of motion, both creatures suffered the woman's fate. Unlike her, the beasts didn't fall with blood spraying from the stumps of their necks, they crumpled to black ash which the chilly breeze swept away.

Stefan brought his sword up into a defensive position. The man eased off his hood. Mind partially preoccupied by the weapon's reaction, the sheer power it had unleashed, the Knight Commander squinted. A gasp escaped his lips when the stranger's hood dropped to his shoulders.

Kahar, the King's bodyguard, regarded him with those strange green and silver eyes of his. His face was a blank mask.

In the city, bells began to toll.

"Thania and the children," Stefan said in a labored breath. "They're in danger."

"The King has already dispatched several Alzari to your home." Kahar bent and wiped his sword on the dead Matus' tunic.

A weight lifted from Stefan's chest. "Still, I have to get to them. They need me."

"No. King Nerian needs you." Kahar stared off in the direction of Stefan's home. "Your family is fine. The Alzari have already arrived."

How could he know this? Stefan opened his mouth to ask, but the expression on Kahar's face was one of such unflinching certainty he nodded instead. "Do you know her?" He inclined his head toward the dead Matus.

"No, but ..." Kahar bent and ripped the woman's tunic from her shoulder to her breast, exposing a tattoo of a fist enclosed around a lightning bolt. "The Searing Fist. An Erastonian."

"An Erastonian Matus working with shadelings? Why

would they do such a thing?"

"It is man's tendency to do the unexpected and err toward his own interests. Come, we must leave. When the bells finish, anyone found outside will be considered an enemy and struck down."

"What? Since when—"

"Since assassins have been trying to kill the King."

"Lead on," Stefan said.

Cloak flapping behind him, Kahar set off at a jog, his effortless movements making him appear to glide. Thoughts swirling, Stefan followed. A craving for revenge bubbled into him as he repeated the scene and the insignia in his head.

They emerged from the alley to find streets once filled with revelers now desolate. The occasional person who was still fleeing the warning bells kept their heads down as Kahar and Stefan passed. Kahar stopped a pair of green and gold clad Alzari, instructing them on where to find the bodies and to guard them until the King sent one of the Captains. Accompanied by silver–blue moonlight, they continued along the lamp–lit avenues until they reached the palace.

The need to make the Erastonians pay grew stronger.

CHAPTER 16

"They dare to strike at me in my palace?" Dressed in ebony armor to match his braids, King Nerian paced across the marble floors before his huge throne. The gold and silver monstrosity would have dwarfed the body of a normal sized man, but with Nerian's giant frame, the throne fit.

"Sire," Kahar said, "I believe they had no other choice given their other attempts failed so miserably."

"It's possible," Nerian stopped, his eyes ablaze, "but they had to know they would suffer the same fate. Why not hire some mercenary Matii? An Ashishin, a disgruntled Alzari, an Astocan or Cardian Namazzi or one of those crazed Felani Deathbringers. Why use one of their own? Not that any would have succeeded. Why expose that they work with the shade?"

"Boldness? Desperation?" Stefan rubbed at his jaw, which still throbbed even after the mending by the King's High Alzari.

"This was well coordinated." Nerian turned to regard Stefan. "They struck at all my Generals. Renaida and Senden are dead. I suppose they thought to stop my invasion before it began, or at least stall it. Yes, Pilar?"

Stefan turned to the muffled footfalls on the carpet that ran down the room's center. Head down, Pilar, one of the King's

High Alzari, shuffled past the ruddy glow of several braziers positioned next to the carved pillars lining the hundred–foot walkway. Flames crackled in one of the three hearths along the walls. Pilar stopped at the semicircular steps and dais before the throne and bowed.

"A–A report from High Zar Galiana, sire." Gaze shifting from side to side, but not meeting the King's, Pilar's head bobbed several times. He dabbed at his forehead with a cloth.

"Go on." Nerian gave a nonchalant wave.

"A–Ashishin, sire." Pilar kept his head down.

Stefan perked up. The King's brow knitted.

"Look at me. What do you mean by Ashishin? I sent them all back to the Tribunal."

Pilar's head rose slowly. Licking his lips, he shot a nervous glance Stefan's way. "At General Dorn's home, Your Majesty. They were Ashishin. Four of them. Our High Alzari managed to kill three, but one escaped."

"So, again," Nerian sounded calm, but the tightness around his eyes told of a seething anger, "the Tribunal shows their true hand. Still, I can understand them wanting to kill my Generals to hinder my plans, or for revenge, but to send four High Ashishin, three shadelings and an Erastonian Forger for a mere Dagodin?" His brow knitted as he regarded Stefan. "Why?"

Stefan wrinkled his brow at the King's inclusion of the Erastonians and the shadeling with the Tribunal. The suggestion of Ashishin allying with the shade was akin to blasphemy. He thought about asking the King why he thought they were all working together but decided against it. Nerian was already in a bad mood.

"Any ideas, General?"

"Oh, sorry, sire … I was thinking," Stefan said. The Erastonian's words ran through his mind anew, but the sword was something he still wished to keep from the King. "Maybe, my reputation as Stefan the Undefeated, leader of the Unvanquished? Not to mention my wife is as strong as any High Shin and was once a part of the Tribunal."

"Ah, yes, there is that. How could I forget?" Nerian's jaw worked as he ground his teeth. Brows drawn together, the King turned to face the stained glass windows at the throne room's rear.

Pictures drawn on the surface of the twenty–foot panes displayed the gods of Streams, Flows, and Forms in a massive battle against each other and a formless, multi–colored force. The colorful waves surrounding the nine deities reminded Stefan of the essences within the three elements of Mater those same gods represented. Nights like tonight when he faced powerful Forgers often made him wish he could do more than sense Mater. Whenever his thoughts leaned that way, he remembered the fates of such men and women: Death, insanity, or both, brought about by the power they wielded.

"GENERAL STEFAN!" King Nerian bellowed.

Stefan started. "Yes, Your Majesty?"

Face dark, the King stared at him, his lips curled and his eyes steely. "Did you not hear my question?"

Stefan bowed his head as he spoke. "I apologize again, Your Majesty. No. I'm afraid I didn't hear you … I was thinking about my family." Stefan waited expectantly, but he knew the King would not repeat himself. In these moods, he never did.

"The King asked if your men are prepared to march," Kahar said.

"Yes, they are," Stefan replied.

"Good," Nerian said, "you leave in the morning."

"Yes, sire. What of the plan to find a way into Everland without discovery?"

"The Scouts have proved that to be impossible, Stefan," Nerian said. "The entire range of mountains between Harnan lands and the Vallum of Light are guarded. Regardless, after tonight, I want them to know we are attacking and when. I want them to know they can do nothing about it."

A bold maneuver that has worked many a time, Stefan thought. Yet, he could not shake the uneasiness clawing at him. Initially, he attributed it to him not wanting to be a part of this campaign.

Now, seeing that the Erastonians employed shadelings and Forgers made him wonder if they used either in battle. It would only make sense if they did, and he wasn't sure if his men were ready for that kind of a fight. Preparation and foreknowledge won battles. He preferred more time to plan and discover the strategies of his enemy, but the attack against him and his family deserved a punishment. Besides, once angered the King would not relent until they defeated the Erastonians. If indeed the Tribunal had taken part in this action, they too would pay a price for incurring his wrath.

"I'd like to take at least one Alzari cohort with me for our first crossing into Everland," Stefan said.

"You? Taking Matii other than Dagodin?" Nerian smirked. "The man who always rails against, what did you call it again? A Forger's instability on a battlefield?"

"My concerns were correct on more than one occasion in the past," Stefan said. "The massacre at the Sands of the Abandoned for example."

"Yet, without them, our land would not only be in chaos but under the shade's influence," the King countered.

Stefan almost reminded Nerian that according to history, Denestia had become the way it was—a land almost thrown into dark ages—because of Matii, but belaboring the point might lead to another argument.

"Nothing to add?"

"If the Erastonians are as desperate as they seem, it makes sense to take Alzari, sire."

Nerian smiled. "'Attack with what and how they expect, and at the most opportune moment, when they have settled on your predictability, strike in a way they cannot anticipate.'"

"Yes, sire." Stefan matched the King's smile with one of his own, but his uneasiness about the coming battle made him think more in terms of defense and survival.

Several hours later, after he discussed further strategy with Garrick and Kasimir, Stefan made his way home with an

Alzari escort. The manicured gardens to one side of his home were trampled and blackened. Several soldiers with torches patrolled the perimeter, snapping to attention when he passed. He bid his guardians goodnight and trudged up the stairs. This would be the last night with his family for some time, maybe five to ten years. He let out a deep sigh.

The door opened and instead of Perta, Thania greeted him. She was wearing a pink nightgown with lace on the most revealing areas. Not waiting for her to say a word, he snatched her up into his arms and kissed her. When he let her up for a breath, a tear trickled down his face.

"How are the children?" he asked.

"Fine. Asleep. They didn't see what happened outside."

"Good," he replied, wiping at his face.

You're leaving aren't you?" Thania's eyes glistened.

"Yes."

"When."

"At dawn."

"That doesn't give us much time," she whispered, pulling him closer and kissing him once again.

The heat of her body radiated through his uniform. His responded with warmth of its own.

The kiss ended, and Thania stroked his face tenderly, fingers soft and supple. "Well, the kids *are* asleep, but there's another issue you need to address first."

Stefan frowned.

"Galiana is here in the training room."

He let out an exasperated breath and straightened. "How long now?"

"Ever since she and the Alzari fought the Ashishin outside."

"Wait for me upstairs," Stefan said.

Thania nodded, and he reluctantly released her hand. She strutted away from him in that seductive, swaying walk of hers. "I'll be waiting," she said with one last look back at him as she reached the stairs.

Taking a deep breath, he headed downstairs. The night's events made him suspect a few things about Galiana, but first he wanted to hear her explain why Ashishin were at his home. He touched his sword's hilt. When he stepped into the training room, Galiana was waiting near its center apparently lost in thought.

"Shouldn't you be outside keeping watch?"

"No need," Galiana answered. "They won't return."

"How do you—." Stefan stopped himself. "No, don't answer. You have been playing both sides. You're actually working with the Tribunal, aren't you?"

"Yes and no," she said.

"Explain." For a moment, Stefan was tempted to unsheathe his sword and attack. The power it released earlier added to his confidence, but until he understood more, he figured it was best to act normal. Over the past year, Galiana had many chances to kill him if she wanted him dead. Added to that, not only had she given him the sword, but she'd also revealed Nerian's plans since. *What was the woman up to?*

"I am using the Tribunal so our people can have a place of safety when this is all done, but I do not support Nerian or them."

"And the Erastonians and the sha—"

"Do not be a fool," Galiana snapped. "I had nothing to do with their assault."

"Did the Tribunal?"

"I am not certain. There are several opposing factions within the Tribunal. One of which I am sure has a following of cultists who worship Amuni."

Stefan raised an eyebrow. *Ashishin who worshipped the god of shade?* Streamean worship supported unity of the gods, and shade was an essence of the Streams, but did it include Amuni's malevolence?

"I see the surprise on your face," Galiana said. "I felt the same way. That faction is a well–kept secret. I happened to stumble across it myself in an obscure tome in the Iluminus. I believe they were the ones who attacked your home tonight. They suspect I took the sword, but then they think so of a few other people as well. They will chase down any lead no matter the risk."

"The Erastonians know," Stefan said. "They recognized the sword."

Galiana's shoulders slumped, and she shook her head. "That is the last thing we needed."

"So what now?" Stefan asked. "I leave in the morning. Any special protection afforded to my family won't go unnoticed."

"We will manage," Galiana said confidently. "Thania is stronger than anyone suspects. With a few well–placed wards, she will be fine. I doubt the Erastonians or any of theirs will come after her. My worry is for you." She met his gaze. "One of the Ashishin was a plant by Nerian himself."

"Are you sure?"

Galiana nodded.

"Let me guess. The one that escaped?"

"Yes."

He scratched at his chin. "Do you think he knows about the sword?"

"No."

"Then the attack on my home could have been Cerny's doing. If so, chances are, things may we worse tomorrow."

"How so?"

"Well, you are already aware of Cerny's maneuvering. If he's willing to act as he did tonight in Benez, starting tomorrow, I'll be surrounded by several legions and a full cohort of Nerian's Alzari. Some of them probably belong to Cerny."

"Hmmm, that may be for the best," Galiana said. "You will have protection from the Erastonians and I will be able to slip a few of mine among them to thwart anything Cerny or Nerian tries."

"I still don't think Nerian has anything to with all this. He was as upset as anyone was tonight. Cerny, on the other hand, wasn't at the meeting."

Lips pursed Galiana shook her head but said nothing. Over the past few months, they argued several times about the matter. Stefan agreed Nerian was a bit unstable, but he believed Cerny was directing the King's actions. "So what's your plan from here?"

"To sneak as many of our people as we can to safety over the next few years," Galiana said. "Then bargain with the Tribunal for sanctuary in exchange for our help in defeating Nerian."

Stefan nodded. Allowing Galiana to think he was completely on her side was better than the alternative. The night's attack and Cerny's absence cast little doubt that the Knight General was responsible, but until he was certain of the man's influence on Nerian, he needed to keep his options open. *A good leader is adept in the art of deception.*

For the next hour, they decided on the best routes and methods to funnel people from the city, starting with the family members of his most loyal soldiers. This proved to be an agonizing process as Stefan realized he would lose many in this endeavor.

All their plans hinged on what the Tribunal would require in exchange for their help. Stefan put himself in their place. He would start by requesting easy access into Ostania. The problem there lay in the major ports closest to Granadia. With the Barrier Mountains blocking western Ostania, the closest harbors were in Felan. Not only had the Setian not been able to conquer or ally with the Felani, but the Felani secession from the Tribunal was still an area of contention. Sure, the Setian now controlled the Cardian ports, but those were thousands of miles east, past Felan. No smart captain risked sailing out into the Sea of Clouds in an effort to bypass the Felani coastline. Those who attempted to do so in the past never returned. He wished they could somehow gain Felani support. *If wishes had wings.*

"We could offer them total rule within the government," Galiana said.

Stefan shook his head. "They will have that anyway. When the Granadians assume control, the rest of Ostania will abandon us. There'll be civil unrest and the other kingdoms will marshal forces against us. We at least need the Felani. The Harnan would be a plus, but ..." He let the words die.

"True," Galiana said. "I believe I can convince the Felani that the only course of action left to them is to ally with the Tribunal and allow the Granadian forces to pass."

"You do?" Stefan strode to a map hanging on the wall. He pointed out the capital of Felan. "Surrounded by the Barrier Mountains and the ocean, Felan Mark's position is almost as impregnable as Harna and the City of Stone. In addition, since they're within the Vallum of Light, they have little to fear from the shade. The only way I can picture them agreeing is if Nerian wins against the Erastonians."

"By then it will be too late." Galiana let out a frustrated breath. "I will see how soon I can put my idea into place after I speak to the Tribunal."

They continued for a few minutes longer, rehashing what plans they had before they parted ways. Not wanting to wake any of the servants, Stefan let Galiana out the side entrance and headed upstairs.

Dim light from over a dozen candles suffused the bedroom in a warm glow. The sweet scent of bellflowers lit up the air. On the bed, in a diaphanous shift, lay Thania, her chest rising and falling expectantly, her hair spread in silky waves around her.

Trying his best to ignore her for the moment, but finding himself still sneaking a peek her way, he strode to the small bed in the corner where the children slept. He marveled at how much they resembled both him and his wife. *My children*. Without realizing, he found himself touching the pendant around his neck. It felt oddly warm. *My children*, he thought again. The words still seemed foreign, unbelievable as if murmured in a dream from which he would soon wake. He bent and gave each of them a tender kiss on the cheek.

"They're beautiful, aren't they?" Thania's arms snaked around his waist.

"Yes, very much so. Just like their mother."

Her face moved from where she'd snuggled against his

back to rest on the side of his arm. "No. They look more like you. My features help to smooth them out a bit. Celina has your nose."

"Maybe, but they both have your eyes. Well, your eyes before they changed."

"Hmmm," Thania said in agreement. "Anton already looks as if he's going to be as tall as you are."

"Runs in the family." Stefan unclasped her hands and faced her. "This first strike is more of a test before the main campaign begins. I intend to return to spend at least a little more time with you all. But—"

Thania placed a finger to his lips, cutting him off.

After kissing her finger, he gently removed it. "I need to say this." He stared into her golden eyes. "Teach them who and what they are. Never let them forget me even if I should be away for years. Above all, regardless of what happens, what Nerian does, do not leave them alone with him."

"The only way I will ever leave them is if I'm imprisoned or dead," Thania said. "Our pendants, the pieces of us I imbued into them, now also contain a part of the children's essences. The day you do not feel its warmth, our love, when within its presence is the day you will know something is amiss. But even then, there will be hope."

Stefan couldn't help his frown. The words seemed an odd thing to say. In ways, they reassured him, but the end sounded almost prophetic. Her hands stroking his face chased away the thoughts.

"Come, my love," she said, golden eyes shining, voice husky with need. She headed for the bed, hips swaying seductively.

A grin on his face, Stefan shed his clothes and followed. At dawn, he would spend some time with the children. But right now, all he wanted was to chase away his worries, all the plots, and make love to his wife.

CHAPTER 17

A relentless march past the Sands of the Abandoned then through the Everlast Mountains into Everland brought Stefan's forces to this rock–strewn pass. With Harnan territory due east of the Sands, this was the only route left to them. As usual, he'd made sure his soldiers feasted the night before. Men should not battle on an empty stomach. They needed their full vigor when they went to greet their gods. To either side, rock faces and slopes rose to sheer heights. His cape billowing behind him, Stefan surveyed the Erastonian army. Through a wavy haze of heat, black armor glinting, they spread below in an unmoving mass half the number of his forty thousand Unvanquished.

Stefan wiped sweat from his brow then raised the looking glass to his eye. The men of the Erastonian vanguard wore dark, shiny leather armor and bore short dual swords, one on each hip. Behind them stood infantry in black plate mail, either with two–handed great swords or tasseled polearms. Inside each helm, he made out faces so pasty white they gave the impression his men faced walking corpses.

Battle standards flapped above the Erastonian army, displaying a gray fist enclosed around a black lightning bolt— the Searing Fist. Against the backdrop of the valley and the mountains behind the enemy, a storm boiled. Lightning flickered among the gray clouds like some daemon's eye opening and closing quickly. With each flash in the puffed quilt, thunder rumbled. At a slow roll, Erastonian drums joined the bellows. Their trumpeters blared in unison. From over two thousand feet away, the enemy ranks rippled as they began their charge.

What do they hope to accomplish? They have no archers or cavalry, and we have the advantage of higher ground. This is going to be a slaughter. Still, something about the way they charged gave Stefan pause. He frowned, took the looking glass from his eye, and wiped away sweat once again. The Erastonian infantry appeared closer than they should be for men who ran. He scanned the field through the bronze tube. The Erastonians had covered over half the distance in moments. *In Ilumni's name, how is that possible?*

"Tell the men to fire the scorpios," Stefan yelled, hand clenched around the looking glass.

Both Kasimir and Garrick started at the order, but they passed it on. Trumpets along the Setian lines blew.

The Cardian slaves cranked the drays into position. Operators turned the loading mechanisms on the scorpios.

By the time Stefan brought the tube to his eye once more, the charging Erastonians were within five hundred feet. In a black avalanche, they swept down the pass, the rumble from twenty thousand boots shaking the ground. The absence of a single battle cry among them was more than disconcerting; it made Stefan's heart hammer. *Good gods, they're fast. Too fast.*

"Fire," Stefan shouted as he fought down the dread that threatened to become panic. "FIRE—Gods damn it—FIRE!"

Three thousand scorpios loosed their projectiles. The din of oncoming boots washed out the twang of the weapons' release. Through the looking glass, a nervous tingle rippling within him, Stefan followed the bolts' flight. Zipping sideways like rain showers whipped by the strong winds, the steel-tipped projectiles flew true.

Within a foot of striking their targets, the bolts rebounded as if they struck some unseen wall. They fell to the ground. Not one struck their intended targets.

Stefan gasped. Next to him, similar exclamations issued from Garrick and Kasimir. Shocked and awed murmurs rippled down the cavalry ranks to either side of them.

The scorpios reloaded and fired. Again, no effect.

The operators cranked the gears frantically now. Bolts flew and struck the same invisible wall.

A Forged shield, it had to be.

"Signal the pikemen to be ready." Even as he yelled the order, Stefan knew it was too late. He'd been too stunned by the infantry's speed and the failure of the scorpios. The Erastonians would slam into his men before they arranged their formation. "Cavalry, charge!" he cried.

Trumpets wailed as he kicked his mount into motion. A roar went up from his men as hooves began to drum on the hard earth. Sword out, heart thumping, Stefan leaned into his stallion's neck. The chances of saving his men seemed slim, but he had to try.

A scant few pikemen managed to set their spears forward before the Erastonians crashed into them in a boiling wave. A few of the enemy were impaled, which told Stefan the shield no longer protected them. Others leaped impossibly high and far over the extended pikes, landing behind the forward line of swordsmen and among the pikemen.

The slaughter of the Setian began.

Unable to drop their spears and unsheathe their short swords in time, the pikemen were cut down. Occupied by the enemy still pouring in, the defensive line of Setian swordsmen could do little to help. Those that did turn died to dual–wielding, white–faced Erastonians stabbing them in the weaknesses of their armor between torso and legs or at their necks. Blood spurted in gouts, painting silver armor red and made leather darker.

The second rank of pikemen did manage to draw their swords but found themselves outmatched by the faster, lightly armored Erastonians. Another enemy wave leaped over the milling mass of Setian battling along the front line to reinforce their other warriors. They hacked and slashed with merciless efficiency.

By now, the black plate wearing Erastonians gained the lines and began to lay about with their two–handed great swords, decimating all who stood before them. The Setian managed to strike down a few, but his men soon disappeared beneath the wave of black.

A trumpet sounded as his cavalry reached the rearmost infantry ranks. What remained of his men struggled mightily against the Erastonians to hold their own. Scorpios still tried to fire, and the ones that did loose were able to punch through a few of the enemy soldiers, nearly splitting them in half when they struck. But the quarters were too close. The Erastonians quickly focused on the scorpios, dropping slaves and operators in quick succession.

"Protect the scorpios," Stefan yelled. He dashed toward the closest ones, his warhorse knocking men from its path as he slashed left and right, carving a space around him.

His men, reacting to what he did, followed his lead, falling back to the scorpios to reinforce them. The battle boiled fiercest around the drays. Steadily, the Erastonians pressed on, fighting in small pockets, killing all before them.

Surrounded by one such group, Garrick roared as he chopped down one man after another. Then the black armored wave swept him under, stabbing and hacking. Stefan tried to head toward his friend, but Erastonians blocked the way.

Again, a trumpet blared.

Stefan peered down the pass. Another enemy wave appeared with more armored men. Behind them came cavalry. Among those on horseback were many dressed in black robes.

He was sure they had to be Matii—the ones responsible for the earlier shield.

"Retreat," yelled. "Cross behind the scorpios."

A few heard and tried to comply. He continued to fight on stabbing and slashing any enemy within reach as he tried to shepherd his forces across the threshold formed by the scorpio line. Locked in their many battles they couldn't move fast enough. Desperate he took a quick glance to where he'd hidden the Alzari cohort to their flanks above the pass. For a moment, he considered sending the signal that would have them bring the rocky walls crashing down, but too many of his remaining soldiers would be caught in the avalanche.

A small prickle of hope edged through him as he noticed now how his men rallied, not only around him, but ahead, fighting desperately. A Setian infantry wedge and cavalry formed and managed to hold the Erastonians at bay. The resistance would be short lived. Once those Matii gained a range where they could Forge again, the battle already lost, would become a complete massacre. They would leave none alive.

The earth heaved in a sudden lurch, almost knocking him from his mount. Whinnying, the horse reared up on its hind legs. A rumble and a tearing sound followed.

A chasm opened less than a hundred feet from where he stood fighting off a few white–faced Erastonians. The rift split the pass from one cliff line to the other. Animals, drays, Setian and Erastonians disappeared into the hole. Screams followed their plunge.

Dear Ilumni, what have they done. I didn't give the signal.

Throes wracked the earth again, but this time the accompanying rumble came from the surrounding slopes several thousand feet ahead. Boulders tumbled, and then the sheer rock faces on each side crumbled. The rubble filled the pass, cutting off Stefan's sight of the Erastonian army beyond.

Horns started a serenade behind him. A soft patter of rain began as the clouds above finally broke. He recognized the tune. Whirling, he could not believe what he saw as the horns continued to play.

Surrounded by several hundred of his Royal Guard and garbed in golden armor, cape flapping, was King Nerian.

A cheer went up from the remaining soldiers. The Knight Commander's shoulders slumped even as disbelief, quickly replaced by anger at the sacrifice of his men, swept through him.

He turned back to the ragged gash in earth ahead where nothing but silence greeted him. Here and there, his men finished off the few Erastonians left on this side of the barrier of rubble and the chasm.

If they were lucky, eight to ten thousand of his original forty thousand had survived. Today, they were no longer the Unvanquished.

CHAPTER 18

"You sacrificed nearly thirty thousand men," Stefan said quietly. Rage should have burned inside him, but somehow, it had sputtered out. A hollow formed in the pit of his stomach with the words. "My men. Men who trusted me to bring them home alive. Men I promised peace to, a chance to be with their families. You cost me a friend today." A growing sense of despair trickled through him. His hands shook.

At the table in the pavilion, not even bothering to look up from the map of Everland, Nerian shrugged. *"The Disciplines* warned you against making certain promises, did it not, General Dorn?"

Knight Commander Dorn, Stefan itched to say, but instead he bit his tongue and nodded. He'd failed to keep the one promise that meant so much to him and his men. The blame fell on his shoulders for his misplaced honor and arrogance in thinking he knew Nerian better than the man did himself.

"Anyway," the King continued, "the menders managed to save Garrick. He may yet be able to rejoin us if he recovers fully. It was a necessary sacrifice. The men believe in me now. They trust I will lead them to victory."

Stefan squeezed his eyes shut for a moment as he pictured the wounds hacked into Garrick's armor. He no longer recognized his friend when they removed the armor. When the Alzari were attempting to heal him, they said if he managed to live, Garrick would limp for the remainder of his life and have scars across his body and face. "All of those lives wasted for a ploy?" Stefan whispered.

"No, not wasted, used to attain the men's belief. They know now that they can rely on Matii to help them win battles the same as the Erastonians. They needed to experience the horror of an Erastonian attack and then see it turned back. You have been naÃ¯ve in this, Stefan, surprisingly so."

Eyes narrowing, Stefan said, "You knew how the Erastonians fought along. Why—"

"Of course I did. They defeated my Scout parties and other incursions."

"What? But you said no Scouts reported—."

"None did," Nerian interrupted.

The King was splitting hairs. "So how did you …"

"I watched when Renaida and Senden suffered defeat months ago."

Stefan frowned. *Then you had them killed before they revealed the Erastonian strategy. You are mad, aren't you?* "Why would you withhold that from me and cost us so many men."

"They were my men, to be used as I thought best. The same as I used you. Nothing must stand in the way of my triumph."

Stefan's hands clenched and unclenched. "Why? Why did you do this? Do their lives, their families, mean nothing to you?"

"Victory is everything, Stefan. I will use what I must, even fighting darkness with darkness if I have to."

"What do you mean by that?"

A slow smile spread across Nerian's face. "What pushed you over the edge to fight, to lead these men here, and to decide the Erastonians must be eradicated?"

Stefan tilted his head to one side, thinking for a moment. *No. He doesn't mean … does he?* "The shadeling and Erastonian Matus' attack in Benez."

"Exactly," Nerian confirmed.

"She wasn't an Erastonian, was she?"

"No, of course not." Nerian chuckled. "She was one of our own Alzari."

Stefan understood, now. *For me to commit, you gave me something I feared more than anything … a threat to my family from the supposed enemy. But that also means …* "The shadelings were yours." He gave an incredulous stare.

"Like I said, sometimes you must fight darkness with darkness."

"What have you done?" Stefan's words came out in a hoarse whisper.

"What I needed to ensure the Setian rise above the Tribunal to rule all of Granadia as we should," Nerian said.

Something else dawned on Stefan. He made an involuntary reach for his sword. Nerian's smug expression stopped him.

"Do not bother. I'm aware of the sword, but according to Kahar, it bonded to you. I can do nothing but wait to see if you possess the strength it needs. Afterward, you can pass its power onto me once you learn how to do so."

An onset of weakness almost overcame Stefan. If there was a chair nearby, he would have found a seat. "Power to do what?"

"Defeat the Tribunal. Undo whatever imprisons the shadelings within the Great Divide."

A gasp escaped Stefan's lips. "You would release their plague onto the world?"

Nerian smiled crookedly. "With their power and numbers added to mine, none can stop me."

"Who would stop them?"

"Why, me, of course."

"You really are mad," Stefan said, voice quaking.

"No. I simply understand what most do not. The wealth of information and power hidden within the Great Divide is there for the taking. Your sword, and the shade … no … Mater itself, are the keys. I simply need to unravel the process to control them all." A feverish gleam shone deep within Nerian's eyes. "Don't you understand? Remember the dreams we shared of making Ostania whole? We can achieve them together and so much more. Denestia will be mine with you as monarch under me. With this power I will become a god. It has already been written."

Stefan's insides writhed at what the words meant. All along, the King was already aware of the parts of the Chronicles Galiana thought she kept secret. He'd allowed her to deliver the sword. He deceived them all. '*A good leader is adept in the art of deception.*' The words from *the Disciplines* grated at Stefan.

Still, why didn't Nerian kill him and take the weapon? Unless he couldn't. Stefan thought back to the day he received the *divya* from Galiana. He added that to Nerian's mention of a bond. The tingling sensation that passed through him had not been his imagination nor how the *divya* felt as if he'd wielded it for centuries. Did the sword reject Nerian and now the only way left to gain its use was to have the bond voluntarily passed from another? He had to play this out correctly, use Nerian's own madness against him.

"What would you have me do?" Stefan asked in resignation.

A grin plastered on his face, Nerian strode over with his arms spread wide. Stefan allowed the King to hug him as if he were a long lost son returning to the fold. His expression a mask to hide his revulsion, Stefan returned the sentiment with a squeeze of his own.

"I knew you would understand eventually," Nerian said. He backed off and looked down into Stefan's face. "All I need is for you to help me defeat the Erastonians. Lead the men. After that, the Great Divide will be ours to gain its secrets. From there, the Tribunal will fall."

"What about those slaughtered by the shade?" Stefan looked away, unable to hold Nerian's gaze with the weight of the horror to come on his chest. "Those of our people who die during this campaign?"

"Sacrifices happen in war, Stefan. Their deaths shall pave the way for ultimate victory. Let today be the first day the Setian are remembered for all eternity, a day when a legend is born."

Yes, Stefan thought, *remembered in infamy and reviled for the cataclysm you will spawn upon the world.* Thinking back, he wished he'd accepted the Svenzar's offer. Now, it was too late. One thing remained without a doubt.

Nerian had to die.

CHAPTER 19

The return to Benez weighed on Stefan. He didn't deserve the outpouring of jubilation around him. The Setian were doomed, and he blamed himself.

Thania, at her usual position above the gates with Anton and Celina beside her, was the one thing remotely normal about the day. Seeing them made him smile for a moment, and he touched the pendant around his neck before melancholy crept in. Defeat occupied his mind, but the people still cheered. Along the roadside, out of their windows, perched on roofs, they waved handkerchiefs, tossed flowers, and screamed and yelled more than at any other victory celebration. *Don't they realize the Unvanquished have fallen? That thousands of men who defended their country died at Nerian's hands?*

The majority of his surviving men, especially the veterans, marched with their heads down, expressions grim. The newer recruits chattered excitedly among themselves. Others stared absently, forlorn expressions etched onto their faces.

A procession of wagons followed their group, carrying those who had lost limbs. Interspersed among his men were King Nerian's Dagodin and Alzari. At their head, surrounded by his Royal Guard, rode the King, broad shoulders appearing even more so in his armor, his figure an imposing one upon his huge warhorse.

"Hail King Nerian," someone shouted above the din of the crowds along the cobbled streets. "Savior of the Unvanquished!"

Stefan started. *So that's what they were calling the man?*

To Stefan's left Kasimir shook his head. "Been quite a few of those today."

As he listened closely, Stefan picked the names out: Nerian the Lightbearer, Nerian the Savior. The second title grated his insides more than any other. Carried by countless mouths, the name travelled along the avenue in a ripple with a power of its own. Eyes gleamed with fervor as they regarded the King. More than one person bowed their head in reverence as he rode by.

I lost thirty thousand men, Garrick still lies within death's grasp, and he makes them believe this was a victory. Stefan stared at Nerian's back, fingers caressing his sword hilt.

"There's nothing you can do," Kasimir said.

"Listen to your friend."

Stefan whirled at the soft–spoken voice at his other side. Next to him trotted Kahar. Stefan shivered as he gazed into the bodyguard's blank, silver–flecked eyes. Without another word, Kahar spurred his horse and rode toward the King.

Once they reached the Upper City, Stefan said to Kasimir, "Let the King know I won't be attending the feast. My family needs me."

"You sure?" Kasimir asked.

"Yes. He should understand. If he doesn't ..." Stefan shrugged. He nudged his horse through the crowd, onto one of the side lanes, and headed for home.

As expected, Thania had dismissed the servants for the day. She and the children were upstairs playing when Stefan made his way down to the training room.

"I wasn't expecting you to be here," he said to the form lingering in the shadows by the doorway across the room.

"Why is that?" Galiana stepped into a pool of lamplight.

"Because Nerian knows you gave me the sword, which means he knows about the parts of the Chronicles you kept from him."

"Yes. That is why I risked coming. To warn you. Nerian sent the shadelings. The Matus we thought to be an Erastonian was actually one of his Alzari."

Stefan nodded. "He revealed as much to me after our defeat."

"You lost?" Galiana's brow wrinkled. "All the reports we received said you won."

"Nerian did maybe, but the Erastonians defeated the Unvanquished."

"How?"

Stefan told her how the battle transpired.

Galiana's frown grew deeper. "Why would he send you into a battle without the information you needed?"

"It was something so simple it was genius." Stefan said. "By having the forces loyal to me destroyed, he got rid of his greatest possible threat. The best part is he never needed to raise a finger in attack. At the same time, he swayed any doubters to his side. Have you heard what they're calling him?"

Galiana shook her head.

"King Nerian the Savior." Stefan spat. "Please tell me you have better news from the Tribunal."

"Yes and no."

Stefan cocked his head expectantly.

"At first they refused to become involved, but after I translated more of the Chronicles, I had no choice but to take what I found to their Exalted."

A whistle escaped Stefan's lips. The Exalted ranked above even a High Ashishin in power. Rumored to be at least a millennium in age, they were supposedly the highest authority within the Tribunal, commanding from the shadows. They were legends whose existence Galiana's words confirmed. "What did you find?"

"Another passage referring to the future," Galiana

answered. "It read:

> *From Ostania's ashes and Erastonian blood, the Dosteri rise,*
> *Granadia will fall,*
> *Devout and all,*
> *As it was before*
> *So shall it be again*
> *World without end*
> *War without end*
> *When comes the appointed hour,*
> *Under the rule of the one with Etchings of Power,*
> *Stone will crumble,*
> *The void shall rumble,*
> *Clouds will grow,*
> *Water shall flow,*
> *Light and shade as one,*
> *Fire and ice as one,*
> *Denestia shall bend to its knee,*
> *Until the elements exist in harmony."*

The words made little sense to Stefan. His expression must have said the same to Galiana because she didn't wait for him to ask.

"It predicts the end of Ostania *and* Granadia," Galiana said softly. "A force or a race rising from the destruction of the Erastonians. The Dosteri, they are called. More than that, the passage tells of the release of essences and their combining, even light and shade, under the rule of one man."

"Nerian?"

Galiana nodded. "I–I think that's his intention. I thought convincing the Exalted of my translation would be near impossible, but they already knew. They expected something of this nature. They said if Nerian continues on this course, shadelings will be the least of our worries."

Something worse than shadelings? Stefan refused to believe his ears. He wracked his mind to come up with any possibilities but failed. "Did they say what?"

Galiana hesitated before she answered. "No, but the

information must be in the Chronicles somewhere. Regardless, they are willing to help by giving us a piece of land for those we can manage to save. They say the worst of what is to come may still be avoided if we can stop Nerian."

Her hesitation bothered Stefan, but he pushed it from his mind. The possibility gave him new hope. "What did they want in exchange? The sword?"

"No," Galiana said. "Actually, they gave you permission to keep it."

"They did? Why?"

Galiana shrugged. "They did not say, but they insisted that it was yours to keep. As for their price, they had several. The Alzari and Dagodin we do manage to save will be placed in schooling towns within Granadia. Mysteras, they called them. Their jobs will be to teach those who are born from any Matus bloodlines. Also, we will not be allowed to have all the survivors in one place. They must be divided and spread across Granadia."

"Makes sense," Stefan said. "Use our Matii to gain knowledge of Alzari Forges, while at the same time keeping us separated in case we consider betraying them." He frowned. "You're not finished, are you?"

"No," Galiana said. "Their other requirement was far worse." She took a deep breath. "They wish for the Alzari High Council to turn over the secret we have held for several thousand years. I ... I ... still do not know how I can tell them ..."

Brows drawing together even tighter, Stefan waited.

"They want the secret of our Forging that decreases aging among the Setian Matii."

Stefan's mind churned. The Exalted already outlived most or so he thought. "Why?"

"The Exalted are ancient withered things," Galiana said with a sigh. "Apparently, whatever Forge they themselves used to increase their life spans did not halt the aging process. It also involved killing many in order to use the dying person's essences to increase their own life. I have learned that the kingdom skirmishes in Granadia are fashioned by the Tribunal for this reason. It is partially why they involved themselves in our conflicts … to gain access to essences from the dying."

"No, that can't be true."

"It is. The Exalted take lives to lengthen theirs."

Stefan felt a weakness in his legs. He had thought he was doing the right thing; instead, he was leading his people from one monster to another. But what choice did he have? If the Chronicles were true, and he did not follow through with the plan, the Setian as a people would be no more. When he met Galiana's gaze, an overwhelming sadness reflected in her expression. "Is there something else?" he whispered, voice hoarse.

"Nothing." Galiana gave a slow shake of her head. She averted her eyes. "I–I will tell the Exalted we accept."

Somehow, he didn't believe her. She was keeping some other news hidden from him. At this point though, what they would be forced to do seemed terrible enough. If indeed there was more, he hoped Galiana told him eventually. He prayed she did so before time ran out. Reluctantly, he nodded.

Head down, Stefan left her. He trudged upstairs to share what he'd learned with Thania and spend some time with his children before the King summoned him once more. A solitary tear trickled down his face. He lacked the will to wipe his cheek.

War was coming. Death was coming.

"Dear Ilumni," he prayed. "Show me a way to survive."

PART 2

ALLEGIANCES, HOMECOMING, SANCTUARY

CHAPTER 20

Tobal had once been a prosperous Harnan town at the edge of the Mondros Forest. Now, the dead and scavengers inhabited its streets and rundown buildings. They hung out of windows, lay on the russet–splattered cobbles, perched on the roofs, or dug into their next meal. The stench of death overrode that of char, and the day's heat made it worse. The odor crawled up Stefan Dorn's nose and threatened to choke him. Covering his mouth with his hand, he fought down bile.

Crows and ravens pecked at bloated corpses. A lapra, its muzzle and body the size of a large dog, perched on four of its six legs as it tore flesh from a young girl's remains. The brown–furred beast ignored Stefan's approach. His arrow took the creature in the chest. The lapra keeled over. Their caws a chorus of protests, the scavenger birds took flight in a black ripple.

"This is all they leave behind," Elder Hurst said in a quiet voice. Near seven feet, like most Harnan, his shoulders slumped as he regarded the carnage. "May Humelen and the Forms embrace them," he prayed.

Behind the Harnan rode High Ashishin Clarice in her crimson robes with its silver sleeves. The dark–haired woman kept her face expressionless and back straight, but from her pallor, Stefan could tell she found the slaughter troubling.

This was not the first such town he'd seen after an Erastonian attack, nor was it the second or even the tenth. He'd witnessed too many massacres to count now. Most times the inhabitants were Setian. Since the day the Unvanquished had been defeated, almost fifteen years ago, the Erastonians proved to be an implacable enemy. They spared no one.

However, the dead within the town did not compare to what shadelings wrought. People who died to Erastonian swords were still able to see the gods. Shadelings took a person's life *and* their soul. They created more of their kind from death. That was the future if both the Erastonians and Nerian weren't stopped. The genocide was beginning with the Setian. Where it would end, Stefan wished he knew.

Since that first day, Nerian had not taken part in any further battles. He remained in Benez as the Erastonians countered his armies at every turn. Stefan was sick of defeat and his people's suffering, but before he could take on Nerian, he had to deal with the invaders.

"They can be turned aside," Stefan said. "But for that I will need help." He nodded to the High Shin. "From both of you."

"You bring this cataclysm down on our people and now you beg for assistance?" Elder Hurst shook his head, lips curled in disgust.

"I'm sorry for your loss," Stefan said, "but the Setian have lost more than anyone." Even as he said those last words, he regretted them.

Elder Hurst's face darkened with a rage so intense, Stefan thought the man might attempt to attack him. If not for the High Shin's presence as an intermediary, and the fact the Harnan followed Formist worship, which preached serenity, Stefan would have spurred his horse to avoid the Elder's possible strike. As it was, Hurst muttered a prayer and calmed himself.

"Words can't convey how I feel." Stefan hoped the man heard the sincerity in his voice. "This was never my intention.

If the choice had been mine, I wouldn't have ventured into Everland."

"There is always a choice," Clarice said.

"Simple enough to say when your family isn't about to die," Stefan said in bitter retort.

"Why should we help you?" Elder Hurst drew rein next to the piled remains of children. "You caused all of this. Why should we not call our people back to the Nevermore … to the safety of the Stone?"

Shuddering, Stefan averted his eyes from the corpses as a sudden picture of Anton and Celina among them formed in his head. He took a moment before he answered. When he did, he met the Elder's pitiless gaze. "The Erastonians won't stop until they suffer a defeat, but at least they are human. Retreating to the Nevermore will not save you. On the other hand, if Nerian wins," he gestured toward the bodies without looking at them, "things will get worse. We must act now while there's a chance to prevent further suffering for your people."

Elder Hurst peered all around him, a pained expression on his face. "Suppose I and my people agree, how do we win? We have been powerless to stop them and as yet the Svenzar have remained out of the conflict."

"We'll beat them by using something they cannot anticipate."

The Elder frowned.

"A good general doesn't give away any secrets," Stefan said. "Let's just say it's something no one has seen before."

"You expect me to believe this?"

"I'm asking you to trust me. I too have lost many in all of this, and I still stand to lose much more." Stefan stared Hurst in the eye. "What I propose is the only way."

"And that is?"

"Once we show the Erastonians we're capable of beating them, we then offer them an alliance against Nerian." Stefan prepared himself for the outburst that would follow.

To his surprise, Elder Hurst said, "Using the enemy of

your enemy ....” The Harnan's gaze swept toward the distant Nevermore Heights and the green slopes that appeared to bleed into the clouds. “Another man might seek only revenge, but I am not any other man, Lord Dorn. I understand the importance of survival.”

“Then you agree?”

Elder Hurst gave a long exhale. “Yes, but understand this ... you must secure the one victory to give our people hope before we commit everyone.”

“Praise Ilumni,” Stefan muttered under his breath.

“Where do we start?”

“Well,” Stefan nodded to High Shin Clarice, “that's one of the reasons we came here. High Shin, is he still following?”

“Yes,” Clarice said. “He crossed from the woods and is at the south end of town.”

The Knight Commander wheeled his mount and slapped his reins, sending the horse bolting down the main avenue to their south. Ravens and crows flapped from his path, cawing their annoyance. Hair streaming behind him, he swept by homes, many of them little more than burnt shells with their doors hanging askew.

Black flashed among the houses a few hundred feet away. It flitted between several structures before resolving into a man in the dark armor of an Erastonian. He was heading for the town's outskirts in a dead sprint. His legs ate up the ground faster than Stefan's horse galloped.

Stefan flapped his reins harder, but the distance between him and the scout did not close. It increased.

The Erastonian scout passed the last few homes and into the open field. Less than two hundred paces separated him from the towering evergreens of the Mondros Forest.

Perfect. The Knight Commander drew rein, bringing his stallion to a grinding halt. He leaped off the saddle, snatching his bow as he did so. As he sought the calm of the Shunyata, he took an arrow from the quiver on his back. He nocked it, aimed, drew, and fired.

Before the twang of the bowstring subsided, he shot again, several feet to the left. Then he loosed another arrow to the right.

Stefan didn't watch the arrows' flight. He kept his gaze fixed on the Erastonian. "Left or right," he said under his breath.

The scout made a sudden dodge to his left. The first arrow missed, but the second one punched through the back of his thigh. The man cried out as he pitched forward into the grass.

Knowing he had all the time in the world, Stefan slung his bow back onto his mount. From next to his saddle, he took a skinning knife. Torture wasn't one of his favorite things, but the scout had information he needed.

The Knight Commander took one more look at the corpses within Tobal. He took particular note of several flayed and nailed to the door of an inn. A tune called *The Bitter Onion* came to mind. It was a dark song that told of a man who sought revenge against those who took his family. Whenever he captured one, he set an onion beside them and peeled their skin from their bodies in imitation of the vegetable's many layers. Stefan whistled the rhythm as he strode toward where the wounded scout was dragging himself through the field.

Chapter 21

"You have done well, Vencel," Stefan said. "And you, Master Gavril." He nodded to the Banai. "This is better than I expected."

"Is least I could do," Gavril said. The bald-headed Banai spoke slowly in a garbled accent. He had a tendency to leave out some words. "You saved me from arena. Brought me home. I am in your debt."

Merchant Vencel shrugged. "Nerian ruined trade. Taxes are so high in Benez I don't go there anymore. The other major cities are almost as bad and he's taken a particular interest in the black market too. In times like these a man has to seek a new future."

Dressed in his usual silks, Vencel often made it seem riches were his only concern. Yet, he was more loyal and honorable than many soldiers.

"It good doing this," Gavril said. "Your men work long hours. They make good Banai."

Stefan laughed. Kasimir would cringe if he heard himself referred to as one of the short, bald-headed race. "Without you two, this wouldn't be possible. All these years of breeding and training raised this many."

The two men puffed up with pride.

"This day was a long time coming," the Knight Commander added as he took in the vast, lush plains with their abundant orchids. He sniffled, suppressing another sneeze from the perfumed scents. In the distance to the east rose the Ost Mountains. They had chosen this location for the abundance of dartans and its remoteness at the edge of Banai territory.

In the field below them was the focus of Stefan's enthusiasm, pride, and hope. Dartans. Thousands of them, all with the spaces cut into their shells to allow a rider. Each of them trained to be more docile by the use of shocksticks, the Banai beast–taming methods, and breeding. That day, back in Seti at the arena, a plethora of ideas had come to mind when he saw what he'd dreamed of long ago: a dartan under control and used as a mount. Not only were the beasts faster than the Erastonians by far, but he'd tested them against the sharpest swords, even *divya*. It was near impossible to penetrate their armored skin or the carapace on their back.

Swords slashing at imaginary foes, spears jabbing, Kasimir and six thousand of Stefan's men rode the animals, wheeling them in tight formations. Despite being twice or three times the size of a large horse, the beasts ran with speed and grace. Unlike riding a horse, there was no uncomfortable jounce. Their padded feet made little noise on the ground. In nondescript clothing, the soldiers hunkered down in the saddle within the cutout. The seat itself was a separate hump within the space to allow the men's legs to drop to the side with their feet resting on notches carved from the shell. It had taken Stefan several months to learn to ride the creatures, and he thought himself decent at the task. His men made him appear clumsy.

These dartans were the latest stock, not needing shocksticks to be controlled. He could picture a battle now, the dartans charging, barreling anyone from their path while their jaws tore into an enemy soldier's flesh. Precise attacks from the riders finished the job. Mastering weapons atop the mounts would take additional work, but his men already had a good grasp for the technique.

Stefan waved to Kasimir. The time had come to put their

new mounts to a test.

After days of hard riding northwest, that would have normally taken several weeks on horseback, they arrived at their destination—an encampment at a series of hills overlooking the meandering banks of the Tantua River where it split off to form the Kalin River. Moss hung like soggy, disheveled hair from the trees along the muddy banks of swampland. Stefan grimaced at the foul air's taste that managed to drown out the mustiness of his three thousand strong dartan cavalry. At this time of year, the water should be flowing freely, but the recent lack of rain made that near impossible. In the distance farther north, a wall of gigantic evergreen trees marked the border of the Mondros Forest and Harnan territory.

Banners depicting a mountain range ruffled in a breeze that did little to alleviate the day's humidity or the smell. The flags dotted the sprawling encampment. Tall, gangly soldiers dressed in leather and cloth armor blanketed the undulating hilltops. Each wielded a long–hafted greataxe. Between their hair color, which ranged from sandy brown to russet, their size, and their mahogany skin tones, the men could have been chopped from the same tree. The last time Stefan had seen this many Harnan Stoneguards was in his campaign against them.

One more battle standard stood out in the midst of the Harnan Stonewall banners: the Tribunal's Lightstorm. Three people, a female and two males, strode forward, separating themselves from the army. Stefan expected Elder Hurst and High Shin Clarice, but the last man was a surprise. Pathfinder Kaden's armor and deadly stride were unmistakable.

Stefan raised his hand as he slowed to a walk a few hundred feet from the army. Spreading to his sides and behind him, his cavalry followed his lead. "Stay a few steps behind, and no one speaks but me," he said. Without waiting for the reply, he set off at a trot toward the Harnan and the High Shin.

"Hail Elder Hurst and High Shin Clarice, Pathfinder Kaden,' Stefan called as he drew rein in front of them.

They acknowledged him with a slight tilt of their heads. Elder Hurst's gaze roved over Stefan's mount then shifted behind the Knight Commander. The Harnan's graying brows rose, and he gave an appreciative nod. High Shin Clarice's mouth hung open. After a moment, she snapped it shut. Kaden gave Stefan a respectful bow. The Knight Commander suppressed the urge to smile.

"How close is the Erastonian force?" Stefan asked.

"In a few moments, they will be topping the rise on the other side of the plains below," answered Elder Hurst as he turned and pointed up the hill past his army.

"And the Svenzar?"

A pained expression overcame Elder Hurst. "They will not come. They said you refused their offer once and made an enemy of them. You must prove yourself now."

"Fair enough." Stefan expected as much.

"A–Are you certain this will work?" High Shin Clarice still seemed distracted by the dartans.

Stefan kept his face expressionless, but smiled inwardly at her obvious nervousness concerning what he required of her and the other Ashishin. "When it does, will I have both your aid?"

"You have my word," Elder Hurst said without hesitation.

The High Shin eyes widened at the quick response, but she quickly masked her reaction and said, "And mine."

"Have your men make way," Stefan ordered. He snapped his reins and headed toward the hill's crest.

Crows and ravens darkened the sky, their caws masked by the thunder of boots and the blaring of war horns. A wave of Erastonians swept down the hill several thousand feet away. Their black armored mass seeped across the fields.

Stefan knew their strategy. First came the rush of light–armored infantry with greatswords and spears, protected by whatever Forging their Matii employed. Several other waves would follow, including the plate wearing troops, the cavalry, and the Forgers themselves.

Compared to the other armies he'd faced, this one was smaller, numbering maybe fifteen thousand. His men had already confirmed the information he pried from the Erastonian scout. The commander who led this force not only spoke Ostanian but was also said to be the greatest Erastonian war leader. Stefan had seen enough recounts of the man's exploits to believe in his skill. This battle needed to end swiftly.

Stefan kept his dartan cavalry out of sight, and he himself stood below the hilltop with only his head visible. Sword raised, he waited until the Erastonians reached the plains. As he expected, the next infantry rank crested the hilltop. He brought his sword down.

Dartans bounded up the hill, past him, and down the other side, padded feet making rhythmic thuds as they built their pace. The first five hundred of Stefan's cavalry galloped at about half speed. Moments later, the second wave, consisting of a thousand dartans began their charge, after giving the first rank time to gain distance. They would build to three quarters the dartan's speed.

The last cavalry rank came in two sections: the first one a thousand deep moving at a dead run. Behind them would come what made High Shin Clarice's eyes widen—dartans with two seats carved into their shells. One of Stefan's men occupied the front seat while an Ashishin sat in the rear. High Shin Clarice herself sat behind Stefan.

Below, the charging dartans mewled. The drums from the Erastonians beat faster as the two sides closed. From Stefan's vantage point, the impending clash resembled a black stream flowing down to swallow the grey trickle of the dartans. But his second wave was rapidly catching up to the first.

Stefan gave the signal and the third cavalry rank bolted. By the time their mounts gained the field, they were at full gallop. Clarice hissed as Stefan brought his sword up and down again to send his line into the charge.

The wind whipped at him as he bounded down the hill.

Ahead, the battle unfolded.

The first wave suddenly parted, peeling to either side moments before they could crash into the Erastonian infantry. Through the space sped the second wave, now at full speed.

When the two sides collided, gray slammed into black. The Erastonian line crumpled like dry parchment.

Stefan's first wave then joined the melee, swinging swords. Blood flew and Erastonians died. Dartans snatched black–armored men from the ground and flung them into the air. Armor tore under crushing jaws and piercing fangs.

By this time, the plate wearing Erastonians were charging across the field. Stefan's cavalry wheeled and turned away as if to flee. They charged back toward him in a tight line, keeping the final charge hidden. The heavy Erastonian infantry was close behind. At the last moment, they made a precise split.

In a wedge formation, Stefan's third rank tore into the Erastonians with the same devastating effect. His first and second lines wheeled around the sides and closed the trap. The milling mass of Erastonians at the front struggled to escape the dartans, impeding the progress of the ones behind.

A roar of voices announced the Harnan, who had used the riverbed to gain a flanking position, as they joined the attack. By the thousands, they streamed up from the moss–covered trees. The Pathfinders were among them, silver armor sullied by mud and grime. Where their *divya* blades struck, Erastonians perished.

Sweeping down the line of dartans, Stefan goaded his five hundred on, knowing they needed to act before the Erastonian Matii engaged. Sweat pouring down his forehead; he picked out the Erastonian cavalry riding down the distant hill. Men in armor galloped ahead of Matii in robes.

"Now," Stefan shouted to Galiana.

As his group rounded the edge of the battling mass, a bright light bloomed in the sky: the signal for the Ashishin to commence their attack.

Lightning scoured the distant hillside. The ground exploded with the impact, its roar washing away the clash of steel. Erastonians, horses, dirt and stone flew.

Loud thumps sounded behind Stefan. Balls of fire arched into the air and dropped among the enemy forces. The same attack repeated from every dartan carrying an Ashishin.

The Erastonian Matii countered, eventually erecting a shield. Lightning and fire peppered its surface.

Before the enemy Forgers began their attack, leather–clad Harnan Stoneguards appeared atop the hills behind them. They had come up from the Kalin River itself. They brought death with them.

"So," Stefan said to the Erastonian commander. "Guban, is it?"

Guban nodded. The man's hair was done in thick locks as if he once had braids he left untended. The same style coiled under his chin. Even without his armor, the Erastonian was twice as wide in the chest as Stefan and at least a foot taller. The fact he was on his knees made his appearance no less formidable.

"Tell me why I should listen to anything you have to say? Without you, your King loses much of his momentum, why should I release you?"

"I have a secret that is important to you," Guban said. His eyes carried a hint of defiance despite the purple and black bruises and the bloody gash across his face. One hand was missing a finger and several nails.

"I could have you tortured again."

"Ask your men how that has worked."

Stefan scowled. Not once had Guban cried out in pain or protested when put to the question. "What is so important about this secret?"

"It is a means to begin freeing your people from this dark King's grip."

"You have seen our new forces. We stand a better chance of beating you back now, or at least stopping your advance. With you gone, defeating Nerian is assured. Why would I give that up?"

"Your King is stronger than you think. Like me, you value your freedom and your people." Guban stared Stefan in the eye. "You are a man of honor. In this, we can help each other and ease the bloodshed. I have our King's ear. He will listen to anything I suggest. I cannot guarantee he will agree, but he will listen."

A part of Stefan distrusted the Erastonian, but something about the man, his eyes, or his willingness to suffer made Stefan want to hear he had to say. "Go ahead then, tell me."

As Guban began his story, Stefan's eyes widened.

CHAPTER 22

War horns ruptured the still, humid dawn in a long undulating bray. A cacophony of trumpets, barked orders, and frantic shouts echoed from outside Stefan's pavilion. Fifteen years of refining their plan and of plotting came down to what he began today.

Stefan sat up, grimacing at the poke of an offending sprig of grass through his blanket. Sleep gnawed at his restless bones as he struggled to his feet. The dying flame from the tent's sole lamp glimmered woefully, providing just enough light for him to find and pick up his sword belt and scabbard. He buckled it on and touched his hilt.

The weapon had saved him from shadeling assassins several times since the first night in Benez, alerting him to their presence with its vibrations. More often than not when he used the *divya*, he killed. He marveled at how he always sensed the sword. The caress at the back of his mind was a constant reminder of the bond.

With a sigh at the longing to be with his family, he ran his hands down his clothing to smooth the rumples of his uniform. Sparing a moment, he kissed the pendant of Thania. Then, with as brisk a stride as his tired legs could manage, he headed for the tent's slit for an exit. Waif–weak fingers of dawn's light greeted him as he ducked through the flaps and stepped outside.

The two Dagodin cadets appointed to guard his tent snapped to attention, shiny lances held high. Boots thudding in unison, soldiers were marching by in ordered formations, the Quaking Forest banners flying above them. Not far from those flew the Tribunal's Lightstorm. Forest green Setian uniforms and armor stained and dusty, the troops followed the commands of the Knight Captains yelling ahead of them. His men knuckled their foreheads when they became aware of his presence. He acknowledged them with a stiff nod. They continued to file by, the younger recruits' eyes shining with fervor; the veterans' expressions either blank or of ice–hearted resolve.

Shoulders sagging, Stefan expelled a breath. He didn't deserve the faith his men placed in him all these years. They would die. Eventually. He should have become numb to that certainty after witnessing well over a half century of war. Of death. Of destruction. Making friends only to see them perish; grieving when members of his family joined the legions and died in battles he himself led. But try as he might, he couldn't shake the pain in his heart, the melancholy surrender when he witnessed the butcher's bill. Not even after his most renowned victories.

All of this for what? The whim of a power hungry king? The need to expand borders? The craving to resurrect an empire long dead? The vanity of a man deluded by visions of grandeur? A man tainted by darkness? Well, no more. Nerian's schemes went beyond all moral standards and honor. *What is a man without his honor? An empty shell to be filled by corruption.* The plague eating at Nerian was blacker than a moonless night. Stefan was tired of watching men die, families shattered beyond repair for this cause, this abomination of an alliance Nerian had formed.

Fifteen years. He sighed. *Was it that long since I last saw Thania and the children? What does Anton look like now? Was he strapping and strong like me in my youth? Did the gods bless Celina with her mother's beauty?* Both would be eighteen now, a man and a woman grown. Would they even remember him? He'd given up what may have been his last chance at fatherhood for what? This? *No. You gave up that chance for your children's safety, for the freedom and livelihood of not only your men, but also your people.* He gazed out to the horizon and the distant Erastonian advance, his expression twisting into a scowl.

The dawn air brought no relief to the promise of another sweltering day of death. Pallid twilight pricked the sky where clouds massed like puffed mounds of gray ash, the occasional jolt of lightning illuminating their bloated underbellies. Heartbeats later, a distant peal of thunder followed. Stefan wiped at sweat already beading his forehead, his gaze following the rumble of tens of thousands of marching boots.

Beneath the roiling storm, rank after rank of Erastonians swarmed the undulating Crescent Hills south of the Kalin River at the edge of Setian territory. Black blotted out the once green fields, now as barren as a diseased womb. Stefan's forces had stripped them to keep supplied as well as to prevent the encroaching army from having any sustenance off the land they invaded. Every time lightning flashed, metal glinted amongst the advancing blackness. Above the horde, flags flew the gray fist enclosed around a black lightning bolt.

AWOOOOOOO! AWOOOOOOOO!

The Erastonian horns continued to bellow doom, followed by drums rumbling in the distance as if the buglers had called down the thunderstorms boiling behind them. Stefan's stomach knotted as he watched them slowly wash over the fields like a great wave of sewage. His recent victory over their forces did nothing to help. This army dwarfed that one.

He stifled the urge to call for an immediate retreat and turned away. Duty was a burden, but one didn't get to be Knight Commander without shouldering the load or by panicking. Today, his duty was more than any man should have to carry. Any sane man. Right now, two other concerns nattered for his attention.

The first was his growling stomach. The second … well the second he would deal with while he ate. He prayed Guban's information was wrong.

Stefan inhaled deeply, the faint whiff of food bringing another grumble of protest. He savored the sweet aroma from lingering cook fires before the stench of the waste pits drowned them. He hawked and spat. The phlegm spattered on the dry ground, appearing wet for a moment before the parched earth swallowed the moisture.

"Cadet Harvan, tell Knight General Kasimir to await my signal. Afterward, run fetch Knight General Garrick," Stefan ordered.

"Yes, sir." Harvan leaned his lance against the white canvas and ran off.

Stefan had been surprised to find Garrick, scarred face and all, with a full cohort when he returned from his victory over the Erastonians. Apparently, the King sent him to help with the upcoming battle. Garrick had shown open displeasure at High Shin Clarice and her Ashishin cohort, voicing his opinion several times. A time existed when Stefan might have dismissed the man's malcontent as part of his distrust for Forgers.

From the small incline near his tent, Stefan studied his forces as they maneuvered into formations below, spreading to the south, banners flapping in the breeze. Forty—one Setian cohorts in all—four legions—two consisting of heavy foot, one of light foot, and the other contained the dartan cavalry. Three quarters of their number were Dagodin. Not as many as he wanted, but enough for now. The others were regular soldiers. Today, he would make sure the majority survived.

A grimace passed across the Knight Commander's face at the single cohort of Ashishin standing to one side. *Use who and what you must.* Like the rest, they waited, four hundred strong, garbed in crimson tunics and pants with colored diagonal stripes down the front. Their matching, hooded cloaks hung deathly still. The Lightstorm insignia highlighted the back of each cloak. At their head were several High Shin and Pathfinders. While the other legions milled and fidgeted, this formation stood with an eerie, motionless silence.

Satisfied with the preparations, Stefan strode to a nearby

table laden with food. He heaped slices of quail breast, slabs of deer, and cheeses and fruits from bronze platters onto a plate. Then he poured himself a tin cup of watered kinai wine from one of several flagons. If he died today, he would do so with his belly full.

"May Ilumni keep me strong to lead my men this day and the next," he uttered in reverence, cup held up before him.

The Knight Commander threw his head back and emptied the cup's contents. Fire racing down his gullet, he scrunched up his face. Within moments, the slight weariness from days and nights with little sleep in preparation for this encounter seeped from his bones.

A strong vibration against his leg reminded him of his sword's presence and of the task ahead. His face curdled into an involuntary scowl before he casually rested his hand on the pommel. The vibration subsided until it became a near indiscernible thrum against his palm. Schooling his face to calm, he turned to the clink of armor.

Knight General Garrick Nagel stood behind him, his dark hair giving off a brighter than usual sheen, his chest an oak's trunk covered in silver armor filigreed with gold. Deep–set eyes of ebon steel stared back at Stefan in a scarred face hewn from granite. Garrick knuckled his forehead and bowed, but his eyes never strayed from the Knight Commander's own. He strode next to Stefan.

"Knight General Garrick," Stefan held out a cup, "any word from the Scouts or Envoys?"

Garrick's eyes narrowed at the title. Stefan suppressed a small smile.

"Not as yet, sir," Garrick answered, his voice a rumble as if he spoke from deep within his chest. He took the cup with a slight nod of gratitude.

Stefan poured the Knight General a drink from his flagon. "Have the men feasted as I asked?"

"Yes, sir."

"Kinai juice or wine?" Stefan's stomach growled again; a

reminder that he himself had not eaten in almost a full day.

"Juice, General. They'll have fervor and strength to spare." Garrick downed the kinai in two gulps, his eyes narrowing with the first swallow.

"Good, good." Stefan stroked the prickly stubble under his chin. "You know what I say: If a man's to die, he may as well do so on a full stomach. Better if he dies after making love to a woman. Unfortunately," he pointed at their surroundings, "there are never enough women soldiers to go around."

Garrick scowled at the mention of female soldiers. Like many, he considered fighting a man's job and women good only for tending home or bedding. "If you say so, sir."

The man had not always been a stoic one, but he became so ever since the day he almost died to the Erastonians. Garrick walked and talked but something else in him perished that day.

"Time's changing, Garrick," Stefan said. "Either we change with it or get swamped under by the likes of them and worse." Stefan gestured with his head toward the Erastonian army.

Garrick shrugged. "Maybe, but women aren't the answer."

"What's the answer then?" Stefan asked. "Having their women train and fight alongside them have worked for the Erastonians. They easily outnumber any other force and their fighting prowess cannot be denied. Why won't it work for us? How do we stop other kingdoms from following in their footsteps? The Astocans? The Cardians? We're losing because of our ways. If we don't explore every avenue, how do we win?"

"With fire and steel, not soft womanly wiles. That has always been the Setian way." Garrick spat to one side then gripped his sword hilt in a huge gauntleted fist. "Strike first and show no mercy. There's no greater advantage than surprise and fear."

"Sometimes, sometimes, indeed," Stefan said while stroking his beard, "but there has to be other ways that don't require killing. How long will we continue to ravage the land we intend to live in? What will we leave for our families?"

Garrick's lips curled. "This is war. You fight and you die. It's your kind of think—" He stopped mid-sentence as Stefan arched an eyebrow.

"It's fine." Stefan smiled, but didn't let the expression touch his eyes. "I know. It's my kind of thinking that's made the Setian and Ostania as a whole, soft. I have heard it before." Sword thrumming against his palm, he picked out a slab of quail with his other hand and began to chew, his gaze on Garrick.

The war horns blared again as if to remind them they still had a battle to fight. Drums rumbled their response. Out on the Crescent Hills, the Erastonians had finally drawn to a halt. They covered the plains completely, not a patch of brown earth showing among their ranks.

Stefan eyed his dartan cavalry as they wheeled into position. "I can give you one of the new mounts if your leg can handle riding."

Garrick flinched so slightly Stefan almost missed it. "No. They don't take to me or my men."

"Oh?"

Despite their location off to one side, the dartans swung their necks and kept their attention on Garrick's cohort. The animals' mewls were indiscernible from the drums, horns, marching feet, and jangle of armor, but their open mouths and swaying heads spoke of displeasure.

"I think they're too used to your men. Does the King know about them?" Garrick's brow wrinkled.

"Not yet," Stefan said. He licked grease from his finger. "I wanted to wait to see how they fared in a battle before I reported their use."

"And the Ashishin?" Garrick spat to the side again.

"Nerian won't be pleased, but we needed to try something new. Even he can understand that after so many losses."

Garrick grunted. "Do you wish to go over the plans with the Captains or address the men again, sir?"

"Neither," Stefan answered. "Like you said, this is war. We fight and we die. Even outnumbered five to one. No need to talk them to death is there?"

Gaze focused on the Erastonian horde, Garrick shrugged.

Delicately, now. Stefan tilted his cup. "Can you bring me another flagon, please?"

Garrick strode over to the pitchers of kinai wine at the table's far end.

"You should eat." Stefan picked up a slice of deer and tossed it into his mouth, chewing but not tasting. "After all, we might die today."

The look on the Knight General's face gave a subtle shift to confusion before he smoothed his features. He plunked down the flagon next to Stefan. "I'm not hungry, sir. I just want to get on with the battle. Wipe these arrogant fools from the world."

Stefan glanced out among his legions, noting the shift in Kasimir's troops. He finished the last of his deer then wiped his hand on his tunic before responding to Garrick. "You know my policy, Garrick. No man under my command fights on an empty stomach. Should they fall, I will have them go the gods well fed. So, is it that you aren't hungry or that you know you won't die today?"

Knight General Garrick stiffened. "I'm always prepared to die."

"Good. Then die." Stefan drew his sword and struck.

Garrick barely managed a half–choked shriek.

Stefan's blade, still vibrating, sliced through the Knight General's neck with a faint hiss. Blood spurted in a black geyser. Mouth agape, Garrick's head tumbled from his shoulders. The sword's vibration abruptly died.

As the head spun through the air, the illusion shattered, and a transformation began. Elongated lupine jaws, rows of sharp fangs, a lolling tongue, and stiff, black fur replaced Garrick's face.

The black–furred wraithwolf's head landed on the ground with a thud.

CHAPTER 23

A tear trickling down his face, Stefan spat on the corpse. "Burn the body." He gestured to Cadet Destin who stood with his mouth unhinged. "Now!"

Destin jumped before dropping his lance and running down the hill toward a line of torches at its base.

The clang of steel on steel followed by the cries and screams of the dying drew Stefan's attention to his men. Surrounded, the legion Knight General Garrick had commanded struggled against the other Setian.

Divya blades rose and fell in flashes. Kasimir had been able to arm every Dagodin loyal to their cause with the weapons.

The battle raged on. Shields parried and blocked. Swords stabbed and sliced. All moving in synchronous motions as they'd been taught. At this distance, to an untrained eye, the melee appeared more like chaos.

Behind the milling mass of Garrick's forward infantry, transformations took place. Green armor rippled and fell to the ground. In place of men were dark–furred wraithwolves, many reaching seven feet. They stood on two legs, threw their snouts to the sky, and released blood–chilling howls. Stefan wished he had scorpios.

Mingled between the beasts and those who were mere

men was another sort of creature. These flowed like black smoke made flesh. Blades darker than their billowing countenances sliced through the attacking soldiers as if their armor was wrought from paper instead of steel and iron. Stefan's eyes narrowed.

Darkwraiths. Gods be good.

Quickly, he dashed the kinai wine from the flagons onto the wraithwolf's corpse. *Where's Destin with the blasted light?* He whirled to the sound of approaching feet and snatched the torch from Destin's outstretched hand. As he tossed the firebrand at the remains, Stefan stepped back. A whoosh followed, and the black–furred body burst into flames. Heat spilled forth in a shimmering wave. Stefan shielded his face from the conflagration.

A trumpet blared—part of the plan he and Kasimir had devised. The dirge repeated.

The remaining Setian infantry fell back from the two types of shadelings and the soldiers who stood with them. A lull passed across the battlefield for the barest of seconds as the two opposing forces split apart, a space a few feet wide between them. Then a wraithwolf screeched—a skin crawling, high–pitched sound like metal squealing on metal—and its counterparts echoed the cry.

Stefan covered his nose and mouth from the stench of burnt hair and cooking flesh and peered toward the crimson–garbed Ashishin who moments before had stood unmoving and silent. They strode forward, shoulder to shoulder, in perfect, unnerving symmetry.

Gigantic balls of fire formed in front of them as if they'd ripped several suns from the sky. A moment later, the fireballs shot forward, blazing a trail as they flew to explode into the shadelings with a roar. At the same time, the earth came alive in a rolling wave of stone, tossing the beasts from their feet. The wails among them became plaintive cries.

Looking glass to his eye, Stefan licked his lips as the Ashishin, their faces furrowed with concentration, halted, gazes riveted on the traitors and the shadelings. He craved to reach out and open his Matersense as they Forged the essences around them, but he knew better. The very thought brought a shiver to his bones with the memory of the ethereal voices that seemed to call to him when he'd been in training so long ago.

A deafening rumble jarred him back to the present.

Where once there had been a stretch of plains occupied by the shade's minions, there was now a gaping rent in the earth like a mouth full of jagged teeth. Screams ensued. Above the lip of the gash, both darkwraiths and wraithwolves appeared in empty air, claws and shrouded hands grappling for purchase. They crashed into an unseen barrier before falling from sight.

Lightning flashed down from the ashen sky into the hole. First one, then two, then an incandescent flurry of bolts scoured the pit. No thunder followed, but there came another roar, this one muted. Flames spurted up from the crevasse, licking at its lips in hungry tongues. The blaze lit up the morning, burning away the earlier gloom.

Screeches and shrieks resounded in a cacophony of despair and death. Pillars of greasy smoke rose into the air, only to be swept away by a sudden gust of wind that also increased the pitch and length of the wails. The gale carried a stench akin to piles of cooking, rotten meat.

Then, all was silent.

AWOOOOOOOO! AWOOOOOOOOO!

The Erastonian war horns shattered the moment before a single Setian raised their sword in triumph or cheered. Out on the hilly plains, a full legion separated from the main enemy force. The obsidian line swept down the hill. Drums thudded in a beat to match the march of a few thousand booted feet.

Stefan's legions turned their backs to the pyre blazing not far from them. A trumpet blared again. This time only once. The Setian answered the call by reforming into precise cohorts as they marched to meet the Erastonian threat. His new cavalry detached itself from the position it had maintained well to the rear and began to trot forward—four thousand sets of padded feet noiseless on the ground.

"Bring me my mount," Stefan ordered without looking

at Destin. "The new one."

Slowly, the tempo of the drumbeats increased until they built into a fast–paced rhythm. The Erastonians disappeared below a dip in the land and moments later showed up at the crest. Stefan frowned at their numbers.

From this distance, they appeared to be advancing at a slow rate, but he knew better. Renowned for their stamina, the dark–skinned, sinewy Erastonians could run for miles nonstop, and under the influence of their *divya* armor, maintain a speed faster than any other race. These soldiers were doing just that, and from the ground they covered, they were charging in a dead sprint. *What was Guban playing at?*

The Setian cavalry's pace increased. The soldiers in the saddles carved into the shells of the beasts were a mere blot against the massive, humped forms that belied the speed at which they traveled.

A trumpet announced an advance.

Stefan's infantry moved as one in a slow jog, the clink of heavy armor accompanying their movement. Behind them, the Ashishin stood, cloaks swirling about them with the wind that suddenly rose in a howl.

Destin arrived leading the mount by its chain reins. Short tail swinging, the dartan bared pointed teeth and uttered a pitiful mewl in the direction of Garrick's charred remains. The beasts not only disliked shadelings but also possessed an ability to sense them. Its head swung around at a rumbling down on the battlefield.

Stefan followed its gaze to see the earth cave in on the death pit. Dirt and debris piled into the hole as if gigantic shovels dumped their contents. Wisps of smoke petered up followed by dusty bursts whenever a dirt mound spilled into the chasm.

Guarding against the possibility any shadeling survived, ten Ashishin stood sentinel near the hole while another twenty buried what was left of the slaughter. The remainder of their cohort followed behind Stefan's infantry. To either side of the foot rode the dartan cavalry in long lines, having split their legion in two. The silver armor of Stefan's Knight Generals and Knight Captains stood out as they crossed in front of the ranks, barking orders.

"Your mount, sir," Destin said, the reins held out in a shaky hand, sweat trickling down his face, his eyes wide as he regarded the dartan.

Stefan understood the man's fear. The dartan was twenty–two hands tall and its snake–like neck swung from side to side as it sniffed the air. It tried to take a step toward the wraithwolf's corpse, the smell of fresh meat no doubt drawing the beast. When Destin tugged on the reins to draw it back, the dartan showed its teeth and nipped at his hand. The Cadet snatched his arm away.

"I'll take it from here." Stefan took the reins and yanked them tight against the beast's jaws.

The dartan mewled once more and straightened.

"T–thank you, sir."

Stefan regarded the young man who averted his eyes. He remembered when he was young like Cadet Destin, aspiring to be greater than the sum of his parts with dreams of the glory of battle. Those dreams died during a campaign when he was one of the few who'd survived their foray into Banai lands. It had been their first encounter in Nerian's plan to build an empire. Here he was, years later, about to watch more men die. *Death's always simple. We spend our entire lives dying.* Wasn't that what King Nerian always said? Stefan clenched his fist at the thought of his former friend and King.

"Thank you, Cadet Destin." Stefan masked the strain of his voice for the Cadet's sake. "You have done well."

Destin gave a timid smile and bowed.

Reins in hand, Stefan used the handholds carved into the sides of the dartan's shell to climb up and slipped onto the seat cut into the shell. His insides twisting in knots, he flapped the chains and headed toward his army.

As he rode, *the Disciplines* came to mind. *Demand discipline by showing mastery of self. Demand they overcome after you prevail.*

Demand bravery by overcoming your fear. Demand strength by conquering your weakness.

Back straight and head held high as he schooled himself to calm, he jerked the beast into a gallop. The day was not yet done. There might yet be more death.

CHAPTER 24

Stefan caught up to his soldiers as they reached the hilltop overlooking the plains where the Erastonian army massed. Armor clinked and leather creaked as men saluted, their gazes following his path between their ranks. He tugged on his reins, bringing the dartan to a sharp halt ahead of the rest of the army and next to Knight General Kasimir.

"Sir." Kasimir gave a slight dip of his head. "Did he—"

"He's gone." Stefan sighed, fighting against the heaviness in his heart. They'd both lost a friend. "He's been dead ever since the massacre in Everland."

Expression grim and eyes watery, Kasimir nodded.

"Cavalry ready?" Stefan asked. He would show no more remorse in what he'd been forced to do. Those creatures were no longer his men.

"As ready as they'll ever be." Kasimir rapped a gauntleted fist on his dartan's shell.

"Good."

Several thousand feet and a few low hills ahead of the main force, the Erastonian cohort that had broken off stood in a motionless black snake of leather–armored men. The drums and horns stopped.

"You think they'll parley?"

Stefan grunted. "Their commander agreed to this. His example of good faith was the information on Garrick or rather, the shadelings that replaced Garrick and the others."

"Do you trust him? He might have told you anything to escape death."

"He didn't lie about Garrick, did he?"

"He wasn't doing us any favors," Kasimir said. "With the shadelings dead, their army won't have to face them in addition to us. Worse, by watching our skirmish, he no doubt realizes how many Matii we possess. We—"

"I made an agreement with the man."

"I know this isn't what you want to hear, but maybe we should have waited on killing the shadelings. Combined with our Ashishin—"

"No matter how dire things appear, I won't turn to the shade for help, Kasimir. The shade is to be destroyed, period."

Kasimir hesitated for a moment. "But we could have turned on the shadelings afterward. I mean, we're using Ashishin and Harnan now. Think of it the same way. The creatures would be another tool for us to use and discard. If what Guban said is true, and the King's with them, we could end this war or at least change the outcome."

Stefan allowed the Knight General's words to wash over him, resisting the urge to give in to his anger. "I'm not Nerian," he said softly."I won't throw away my honor or turn to the shade. You don't see the bigger picture, Kasimir. Who knows what adjustments they made to our small victory, but seeing the dartans will give them pause. Doubt is what we need."

"More reason to use every advantage," Kasimir implored, his dark skin shiny with the sheen of sweat.

Jaw grinding, Stefan glared at Kasimir until the Knight General averted his eyes.

"Fine. I understand not using the shadelings, but falling to the Erastonian horde may be just as bad. Towns littered with dead and slavery or worse for those they don't kill."

"At this point, I would take slavery." Stefan grimaced. "Kas, I need them to listen and come to an agreement. They have as much at stake as we do, because there's no bargaining with the shade. Our object here is to save as many Setian as possible.

Remember that. People are going to die, lose their souls, a great many of them, if Nerian isn't stopped."

"Are any less going to die if we don't stop the Erastonians?"

"Which would you rather, Kasimir?" Stefan arched an eyebrow. "To be mired in the darkness the shade brings or to be under Erastonian rule?"

"Neither."

"Exactly, but those are our choices right now, unless we do it this way."

"Surely the Granadian Tribunal won't allow Nerian's madness to continue?"

"They haven't done enough so far," Stefan said.

"I beg to differ." High Shin Clarice's voice came from a few steps behind them. Silver sleeves in stark contrast to the crimson of her robes, the dark–haired woman, rode up on a dartan.

Stefan scowled. "Disagree all you want, but you endorsed Nerian. I remember the boasts of him being the first Ostanian allowed in your ranks in five hundred years. What did it accomplish? He got his hands on the Chronicles."

"You speak as if you never supported him," she said, voice calm.

"That ended a long time ago."

The High Ashishin shrugged. "Not soon enough apparently. People tend to remember the worst of a person. For the Tribunal, it is bringing him among us. For you, the world will recall the wars you fought and won in his name." She glanced out toward the Erastonians. "And for the ones you lost."

"My intentions were always pure, High Shin Clarice." Stefan practically growled the words. "Given a choice to fight or fall to one of the other kingdoms or to the shade, I chose to lead my people's survival. I hope you never face a similar choice."

"Survival? Is that what you call it now?" Clarice smiled, showing perfect teeth. "Not once did you revel in the glory of battle? The pride of conquering all before you for his King? I seem to remember a name. Stefan the Steadfast, Stefan the Undefeated, wasn't it? A man so loyal to Nerian's ideals he could not be swayed either on or off the field."

Kasimir shifted uncomfortably in his saddle.

"He's dead," Stefan said, making his tone as icy as his expression.

"Good," Clarice replied, golden flecks flitting across the whites of her eyes. "He must remain so if your men and those you hold dear in Seti are to survive all this."

"Let me worry about who I am." Stefan turned from her to peer down at the Erastonians once more. "Are your Ashishin ready?"

"I will be the only one accompanying you."

Drawing his brows together in a tight frown, Stefan faced her. "Against them? Even after the way they defeated Nerian's Matii. Why—"

"Exactly. *Nerian's Matii.* Not the Tribunal's. Nerian is no fool. He sent his weakest, many of them not fully trained. He wanted those legions to fail, to die. A ploy so the remaining kingdoms continue to back him against this 'unstoppable' force. Sometimes, men only act when they are threatened. Often, others must see you deliver a victory for them to fall in line. *Demand they overcome after you prevail.*"

"*The Disciplines,*" Stefan whispered.

"Yes. Almost everyone is dancing to Nerian's tune, including you."

"I take it you discovered what he's after?"

"We have our suspicions, but we're not sure."

Stefan barked a laugh. "So many years spent 'enlightening' the masses yet you lack answers to what the man does."

"That is why we are here, why we agreed to help you in this endeavor. The Erastonians seem to know why Nerian turned to the shade and how. One thing is certain. All of Ostania will fall and feed the shade if he is not stopped."

"Yes, while Granadia hides behind its precious Vallum of Light, protected from the shade's reach." Stefan's lip curled. "Instead of crushing Nerian, his shadelings, *and* these Erastonians, you bide your time while my people die."

"Did we not help you ally with the Harnan and bring you a victory? Until your Councils agree to our requests, our help ended there."

Kasimir growled under his breath, his dark face growing darker. He opened his mouth to speak.

A look from Stefan stopped him. Inhaling deeply, Stefan deliberately moved his own hand away from his sword hilt. "You'll change your mind if whatever shadelings Nerian musters break through the Vallum."

"That," Clarice said with an air of finality, "will never happen. It will take more than shadelings to breach the Vallum."

"For your sake, I hope they don't. Come, Kasimir." Stefan flapped his reins, sending his dartan down the hill.

Stefan didn't want to admit it to himself, but Clarice was right. He could think of no way for the King to breach the Vallum of Light. On the other end, the Erastonians were steadily gobbling up Ostanian lands. Nerian was fighting a battle on two fronts and losing badly. *So why do I feel like there's something I'm not seeing?*

He touched the hilt of his sword for a sense of comfort. Except for that night in Benez, the *divya* had done nothing more over the years than grant him its speed and strength. *Was it really the key to what Nerian wanted to achieve?*

Gritting his teeth, Stefan urged his dartan on, the beast flitting across the faded brown grasses and empty fields in a gait so smooth it felt as if he flew. If not for the thoughts swirling through his mind, he would have thrown his head back and enjoyed the cooling breeze.

Ahead, the Erastonians shifted, three of them separating from the smaller force, black armor glinting in the meager sunlight struggling through the thunderheads above. The silence accompanying them was more disconcerting than if the drums and horns continued to beat and bray.

Stefan slowed, allowing Kasimir and High Shin Clarice

to draw abreast of him. Kasimir simply nodded, while Clarice's eyes blazed. Stefan smirked. High Ashishin had a habit of thinking they decided who should move and when. While that held true most of the time, he intended to deny the woman any satisfaction. He needed her angry enough to do her part.

A High Ashishin's power was something to fear, but it was no different to facing a skilled swordsman in battle. He was wise to be afraid of either, but he could never let the emotion show. *Showing fear, not fear itself, is a weakness. Fragility leads to death.* He had no immediate plans to die. Not even on a full stomach.

As they drew closer to the three Erastonians, Stefan frowned.

The men no longer wore their oversized helmets. Their pale, almost corpse–white faces contrasted immensely with their armor. Black, wooly locks wrapped their heads. Matching beards coiled beneath their chins. One stood ahead of the others, the large spaulder on one shoulder carved in the shape of a lion's head marking him as their King.

Behind him was Guban. Guban's gaze shifted from the King to one of the other men. Not once did he meet Stefan's eyes.

Something wasn't quite right. "You may get to prove how strong High Shin are after all, Clarice." Stefan eased his hand toward his sword.

Black leather rippling around his wide form, the King took a step back. The Erastonian soldier on his left strode forward, drew a short sword, and promptly slit his own throat. Blood spurted to the ground as he dropped to his knees, bent his back, and bowed in supplication facing the Setian.

A moment later, High Shin Clarice hissed. "I'm afraid I will be of little help. That one sacrificed himself so he could Warp the Mater around us. He has prevented me from Forging."

CHAPTER 25

S tefan hauled on his reins, bringing the dartan to a halt, its neck tossing and turning at the scent of blood. Beside him, Kasimir brandished his sword.

"They can't Forge either, correct?" Stefan kept his eyes trained on the two remaining Erastonians.

"Yes," Clarice said, her voice strained.

"Put away your weapon." Stefan didn't look, but the rasp of metal on leather confirmed Kasimir obeyed the order. "Stay here you two. Wait for my signal before you come to me. High Shin Clarice, at no time should you let them know you speak their tongue." He expected her to protest being ordered, but she rolled her eyes and nodded instead. A yank on his reins sent his dartan walking forward.

Guban stepped in front of his King, his gaze sliding from Kasimir to Clarice and back to Stefan. One hand rested on the hasp of the axe at his hip.

When Stefan came within six feet of the Erastonians, he made a spectacle of slowly raising his fist above his head. As he lowered his arm, he unfolded his index finger and pointed at Guban. In a sudden move, he brought his hand down across his body and up, imitating a quick slash.

A foot taller and heavier than Stefan by far, Guban flew to the side as if the wind snatched him up and flung him several feet. He hit the ground in a jumbled heap, dirt kicking up where he landed among the ploughed furrows of the field.

The Erastonian King's eyes widened then narrowed. His hand snaked down to the sword at his hip. He said something in his native tongue—a series of rolling yet harsh words. When he appeared to realize Stefan didn't understand or care, the King took two steps back and made to turn.

Stefan pointed at the King before clenching his fist and acting as if he lifted a heavy weight.

Caught in mid step, the King froze. He rose a foot off the ground and hung suspended.

Guban stumbled to his feet. "P–Peace, Lord Dorn."

"Now you beg for peace?" Stefan clenched his teeth against the urge to slay the commander.

"We meant no harm in what we did," Guban wheezed, blood dribbling from the corner of his lips, marring the white paint on his face. "King Jelani fears those such as she, as all the last of Everland's Dosteri do." He nodded toward Clarice. "We have seen the destruction when the madness takes their kind. In our land they are used up and disposed of quickly."

The name Dosteri sparked some familiarity in Stefan, but he pushed it from his mind. "Not in our land. Here you will treat them with respect."

"The King wanted to make sure she was no threat." Guban regained some measure of himself. His gaze darted from the King to Stefan's outstretched hand.

Words issued in a low growl from Jelani.

Guban started.

"What did he say?"

"The King ..." Guban eyes shifted uneasily. "The King apologizes for his misstep and begs for you to release him. He will make amends in any way you deem necessary."

Stefan sneered. He eyed Clarice who shook her head. Whatever the King actually said, maybe it was better he didn't know. Stefan needed to keep them off balance and fearful, thinking he Forged within a Warped area. He still had one last revelation to convince the King. "Tell him to signal the others hidden among the brush to the east. I came here in good faith, so should you. Didn't we prove ourselves against the shadelings?"

Guban translated, his words coming out in the harsh, guttural tongue of the Erastonians. The conversation went back and forth for a few moments before King Jelani nodded.

Out across the field to their east, several Erastonians, their garb a lighter brown to match their surroundings, stood and loped the way they'd come. They had split from the secondary force when the legion disappeared below the hill's crest. The slight change in numbers had been Stefan's clue.

Stefan waved then dropped his hand to his side.

The King crumpled to his knees. Guban hurried over to his liege and helped the man to his feet.

With a dip of his head, Stefan signaled for Kasimir and Clarice to approach. By the time they arrived, Jelani and Guban were standing straight. Guban's eyes were wary, but King Jelani's glittered angrily.

"High Shin Clarice, Knight General Kasimir, meet King Jelani and Commander Guban," Stefan said, resting his hand on his sword hilt.

Clarice and Kasimir nodded while Guban translated.

The King's lips curled at the mention of Clarice's title, and he asked a question.

"The King asks why they will not dismount."

"Well, in case you planned something else, they will return to our army before either of you can stop them. Warping doesn't affect us as you thought. So, in that case, we'll see if your horde can stand against a real Setian army." Stefan let his teeth show in a mirthless grin as he patted his dartan.

Guban passed the message on. The King blinked several times before responding.

"We bargain in good faith. Shall we begin?"

Stefan nodded.

After removing a parchment from a pouch at his waist, Guban squatted. He unrolled it to reveal a map of Ostania and placed a stone on each corner.

"In exchange for our help ridding you of your King, this Nerian, and saving your people, we will require a portion of your lands. We also want the people that inhabit them to do with as we will." Guban looked up.

No surprise there. Stefan nodded. He would agree for now, but no matter how long it took, he would eventually drive the Erastonians back into Everland. "What land do you require?"

Guban translated.

The King said a few words.

Guban drew a line with his finger starting from the Nevermore Heights in the north where they bordered Everland. The line continued south through Astocan and Cardian lands, all the way to the coast, cutting Ostania in half. "Everything to the east of this line."

A gasp escaped Kasimir. Clarice made a choking sound.

"You'll never get the Harnan out of the Nevermore," Stefan said. "Not with the Svenzar to support them. To fight them you must take on the mountains themselves."

"That is where you come in. You and your Ashishin will help us take the Nevermore."

"No." Expression stern, Clarice stepped forward. "We will partake in a battle to free the Setian from Nerian, but we will not help you take any other Ostanian lands."

"Then we have no deal."

"The Ashishin and the Tribunal might be hated in Ostania," Stefan said, "but if they offer to help free the land from both you and Nerian, all of Granadia will be at their disposal. With what Nerian has done, allying with shadelings, I'm certain more Ostanian kingdoms will side with the Tribunal. The Felani already have. The Harnan are with us, which means we also have the Svenzar. You suffered one defeat already by a small portion of our might. It's your choice."

"By refusing, Ostania will fall to the shade," Guban said, after translating.

Stefan gave the man a grim look. "Yes, and the Tribunal's

armies will simply return across the Vallum of Light, leaving you to battle the shade on your own. When you have been weakened …" He closed his fist.

Guban winced then relayed the words to the King who openly stared at High Shin Clarice. She shrugged.

"Here's what I propose." Stefan squatted, facing Guban. He drew a line south of the Nevermore Heights, starting below the Mondros Forest. "You can keep whatever you already claimed since you left Everland."

"Bah. This is nothing but deserts and mountains near the Everlast Mountains."

"Setian land nonetheless," Stefan countered. "We can help you claim these lands from the Astocans and Cardians. However, that will end at the southern coast, here." He indicated the Misted Cliffs. "We will never beat their combined might at sea where their strength lies." Stefan stood.

A long conversation ensued between Guban and Jelani. The King shook his head furiously several times and indicated the Nevermore Heights. Whatever it was, the man wanted something there in earnest. There was no way he would get what he coveted. Even if Stefan wanted to help, the Svenzar and the equally hardy Harnan were simply too strong when within the mountains. Finally, the King growled under his breath and gave a reluctant nod.

"The King asks what of this land to the east." Guban indicated Bana.

"No," Stefan said. "We owe the Banai much. If he presses the issue we can call this off now."

The two Erastonians spoke for a bit longer then Guban said, "We agree. He asks how do we know you will not turn on us after we deliver your city back to you."

"Faith," Stefan said folding his hand into a fist then releasing.

A slight flinch from the King brought a smile onto Stefan's lips. Stefan met the King's gaze, exaggerating his confidence in reminding the Erastonians of the power they feared he possessed.

After Guban translated, the King huffed and gave a slow nod.

As Stefan turned away from the two men, he held in a relieved sigh and mounted. Behind him, The King said a few words.

"We shall do our part and supply enough of our dead to keep up appearances of a deadly battle," Guban said. "The King asks how you will keep what happened here secret among your men."

"Tell him not to worry," Stefan said from atop his dartan. "All will be in place. A week from now you'll be able to strike Benez and help me free my people. High Shin Clarice will arrive when the attack is to commence."

A pained expression, quickly masked, fluttered across King Jelani's face before he nodded hesitantly.

"Until then, peace be with you, and may Ilumni guide you."

Guban started, before translating to the King, who frowned, then clasped his hands, and gave a slight bow of reverence.

Stefan returned the sentiment before yanking his reins to turn his dartan and trot away. When he was out of earshot of the Erastonians he finally let out the breath he held. "Well that went well."

"A little too much so," the High Shin said dryly. "Do you mind telling me how you managed to Forge where no other Matii should have been able to? King Jelani asked about what you did almost as much as he suggested killing you." She paused. "In fact, you cannot Forge, you're a Dagodin."

Stefan grinned. "I would say I do mind and leave you and yours to ponder the question from the next several years, but you would hound me down until you found your answers."

"Well?"

"First, I didn't Forge."

"But—"

"People believe what they think they see. Fear is a powerful thing."

"So what did you do?"

"Me? I did nothing besides wave my hand and look fancy, but he doesn't need to know that, does he?" Stefan waited for Clarice to understand.

Kasimir caught on first, sucking in a breath as he did so. "You had another Ashishin close by but out of range of the Warping."

Stefan rolled his hand in front of him and made a mock bow as if performing at a play.

"How ..." Clarice began. Her brows drew together. "She or he was Masked. Risky. Any slight move on their part would have revealed them."

"A worthy risk in this case."

"It's a wonder the Erastonians never suspected," Clarice said.

"Fear." Stefan shrugged. "I simply used their own plan against them and their emotions did the rest."

"Who was it?" The High Shin turned slightly, her eyes scanning the area behind them.

"You have your secrets and I have mine."

Clarice cocked her head to one side to regard Stefan. "Fair enough, but how did you know they would use a Warping?"

"I didn't, but if I was in their shoes, I would make sure I had some precautions against Matii. Accepting that nothing is beyond your opponent leaves you well prepared."

The High Shin nodded.

They continued riding, no one saying a word. The wind picked up, dry leaves and brush skittering across the ground before it, as the foremost part of the storm began to drift over. Behind them the Erastonian war horns blared twice, the drums thumped, and marching boots rumbled.

Kasimir broke their silence. "What I really want to know is how you plan to keep what happened here from reaching Nerian's ears."

"Easily." Stefan smiled at Kasimir's blank face. "We were defeated. Dead almost to a man. I alone will report our failure to Nerian, while you take what's left of the army into the Barrier Mountains. You'll await word from me there."

Kasimir gaped. "Sir, you can't do that. Or at least let me accompany you."

"I have no choice but to return, Kas. My family is still in Benez. Nerian has them watched day and night. Secreting the families of our men out of Seti over the years proved hard enough. There was no way I could do the same for mine without drawing more suspicion."

"I will have to agree," Clarice said. "It makes no sense risking more than necessary at this point. Besides, Nerian expected you to be defeated. Whether he will play this out seeing you as his old friend or simply another who failed against the Erastonians and deserves to be beheaded is another question altogether."

"I don't think I have anything to worry about there," Stefan said.

Nerian still wanted the sword after all.

CHAPTER 26

By the time they reached the encampment, the thunderstorm had swallowed their surroundings, turning late morning into dusk. The Erastonians had disappeared within the blinding sheets of rain, their drums, horns, and marching feet washed away by heaven's bellows. With Kasimir and Clarice following on his heels, Stefan entered the tent, happy to get out of the rain and the sucking slog of mud. Torchlight flickered within the pavilion's confines, throwing back the dimness the storm wrought. Outside, the wind's howls waxed and waned, and rain drummed an accordant percussion.

Deliberately not addressing her by title, Stefan said, "You know what's required, Clarice." He faced her and braced himself. "Get to it."

The High Shin's eyes glinted angrily, and her face flushed.

"I still don't agree—" Kasimir began.

The flick of Clarice's hand and Stefan's subsequent painful cry cut him off.

Heat spilled through Stefan in a rising wave, followed by stings and burning sensations all across his body. A final, agony–riddled surge ripped along his abdomen as if someone slashed his stomach with a sharp blade. His hand immediately went to the area. Blood spilled over his fingers. Fatigue attempted to suck him under as if he'd dueled a dozen foes.

Gasping, he uttered, "Enough."

Kasimir rushed to his side and steadied him. "He said

make it look good, not try to kill him."

"I hardly tried to kill him," Clarice said, her voice bearing a hint of satisfaction. "Anyone who inspects those wounds *will* think he's been in a deadly battle."

Stefan eased his eyes shut, gritting his teeth to quell the pain. "It's fine," he said in a raspy whisper. "If she went too easy, it would have been obvious." He sagged against Kasimir's arm.

"Maybe you should mend him a little."

"No. Any competent Forger will be able to tell."

"Don't do anything that wouldn't seem natural," Stefan said. Still clutching his side, he limped over to his table with Kasimir helping to keep him on his feet the entire way. "Here, this is where I need to go." He pointed north of a town named Karsten. "A Travelshaft is there at a main stationing point for our forces. They'll be able to mend me enough to get me home safely."

"I could simply take you near Benez," Clarice said.

Stefan frowned despite the pain. "I doubt you know the area well enough to Materialize me to the city. Even if you did, Nerian has wards placed all throughout the capital and its surroundings."

"So you are assuming I know this Karsten. You are also assuming I can manage to take you despite all the energy I already expended with my Forgings." Clarice shook her head. "I need more time to recover."

Stefan coughed. "I assume nothing. I didn't ask you to take me, did I?"

Clarice's eyes shot open. Immediately, she glanced around. "Your secret Ashishin is in here with us, isn't she?"

"Kasimir, show out our dear High Shin." Stefan lifted his arm from over Kasimir's and leaned against the table.

Kasimir bowed, touching fist to heart. "After you, High Shin," he said, hand on his sword hilt.

"You dare—"

"It's not what I dare, High Shin Clarice. I do what I must as you have learned by now. For this, I trust those closest to me.

I have already accepted the Tribunal's help in good faith. I even allowed you to know by what method I would return to Benez. That alone should suffice for you to show some faith in me. Accompany her to her tent."

Face a flushed mask, Clarice nodded. "As you wish." She spun on her heels and stalked out into the rain. Kasimir followed.

"Why didn't you let me do this?" High Shin Galiana Calestis' voice hissed from the height of Stefan's chest. From nothing, she appeared next to him, crimson robes bearing two more stripes than Clarice's. Concern clouded her golden eyes as she inspected his wounds.

Stefan braced a hand against her shoulder. "No. You or Kasimir would have went too easy on me. She took some goading, but I got the result I wanted. At the same time I kept her off balance."

"As you say. Ready?"

"Yes." He steeled himself.

Without another word, she raised her hand, palm facing outward.

There was a swish, like a blade cutting the wind. A jagged slice appeared before them as if a serrated blade punctured the air then sawed its way down. The slit opened into a convex shape much like an eye but with the corners at the top and bottom instead of left and right. Inside the opening was a dark surface. Through the portal, he barely made out the hills around Karsten. The view was akin to looking through the wavy haze of baking desert sands. To either side of the image, blackness beckoned.

Together, they stepped into the rift.

The world twisted. Stefan snapped his eyes shut against the inertia. The sensation imitated a leap from a vast height, spiraling into some unseen pit. His stomach dropped and heaved. Blood rushed to his head. Heartbeats later, solid ground caressed his feet. Rain and wind whipped at him. Thunder pealed.

"We are here," Galiana said.

Stefan opened his eyes. Sure enough, she had Materialized them within the hills north of Karsten. The rain, falling in lancing sheets, blotted out much of their surroundings.

"The mount." Stefan trembled against a bout of pain that wracked his body. "You had someone bring it right?"

"Of course. The dartan will appear as if it ran for days to get you here." She sloshed over to where the animal was chained against a tree.

He shambled after her, clutching his side, rain soaking through his already waterlogged uniform.

Galiana patted the beast where it hunched, now appearing half as formidable as earlier. She offered what help her diminutive body allowed as he mounted. Each movement was an exercise in pain for him, but he needed to bear the agony for a little longer.

"Goodbye, High Shin Galiana. I'll see you in Benez," Stefan said.

"Remember *the Disciplines*," she replied. "Persevere."

Stefan bowed once to his old teacher. With a grunt, he whipped the reins to send the dartan off toward the town, grateful that a jarring jounce did not accompany the splashing of its feet as it ran. In the growing dark, he lost track of time.

Body and wounds throbbing, the encampment at Karsten's outskirts abruptly loomed before him. Stefan almost fell from the saddle. He leaned listlessly, offering no protest as several rough hands helped him down.

"It's General Dorn," a voice yelled through a wavy haze. "Someone fetch the menders."

Blurred faces hovered above him. Grass or some other surface cushioned his back. Raindrops peppered his face. *When did I lie down?* Then the hands were whisking him away on the back of a wooden dray, wheels rumbling on cobbles. In several places, cool wind brushed against his exposed flesh. Above him, thunderclouds boiled in a gray quilt often punctuated by cyan lightning flashes. The dray stopped.

Hands again grasped him. They should have added to his pain when they dragged him out of the deluge, but he felt little. Torchlight greeted him, and he squinted against its glare.

Moments later, gentler fingers stripped his clothes from his body. Someone sucked in a breath.

"Within inches of his life," a female voice said.

"The work of a Matii." The second voice was a harsh, masculine hiss.

"And at least one or two swords."

Stefan wanted to smile, but the fingers slid down to the wound on his stomach and pried the edges apart. A spittle–filled gasp left his lips.

"Hold him down," said the first voice.

Someone gripped his arms and legs. Another held his face and slipped a thick cloth into his mouth.

"So you don't bite off your own tongue." The person above him was hazy, but he made out long hair. "This will hurt."

Searing heat tore through him. By comparison, the burning made what Clarice had done seem like hands warmed over a campfire. He tried to scream, but the cloth already opened his mouth as wide as it could go. All that came out was a muffled sound. His sight became nothing more than bright lights. As fast as this fire spread through him, freezing cold followed, chasing the heat. Kicking and thrashing, he arched his back, but the arms held him steady.

After a final spasm, he succumbed to blackness.

CHAPTER 27

"General Dorn," said the female voice he remembered.

Stefan eased his eyes open. The brightness of noon greeted him. He winced at the sudden exposure to light. Softness cushioned his back. The sweet scent of perfume or the soap she bathed with tickled his nostrils.

"Sorry." Footsteps drifted away from him, and the brightness lessened.

When the steps drew close once more, a young female's face accompanied them. Dark hair spilled about the shoulders of her green Alzari robes.

"How long have I been out?" Stefan sat up.

"A full day."

"A day?" Stefan's mind whirled. Enough time for Nerian's people to reach the battleground at the Crescent Hills. They would have found several thousand dead Erastonians and the pyre left by the Ashishin. The Erastonian habit of cremating corpses in any battle they won came in handy. With the enemy occupying the area and guarding the pyre, Nerian's spies could not have gotten close enough for a better inspection. Stefan pulled the sheet from over his body and stood before realizing he was still naked. The Alzari averted her eyes.

"Your new uniform is hanging in the corner. I'll inform Zar Ballard that you're awake. He'll want to make sure you're well enough to travel."

"No need. I feel as strong as an oak." His stomach growled. "And hungrier than a Harnan herder after a fast." His appetite didn't surprise him much. Mending took sustenance from the wounded as well as energy from the Matii doing the Forge. He strode over to where his uniform lay on a table.

"I'll send for food."

"Good and something to drink." Stefan paused. "Something strong."

"Yes, sir."

Almost as an afterthought, he added, "Have someone bring my dartan. Tell them to treat him as they would a bull if he's stubborn. Also, send word to the Travelshaft that I'll be on my way."

"Yes, sir."

Stefan listened for the swish of the tent's flaps lifting and her footsteps outside before he expelled a breath. The first part had gone well. He inspected the results of the mending. Where once he had gashes, his skin was now smooth and supple, unblemished, and a healthy tanned ginger color. Even the simulated slice and thrust of a sword through his side was unmarred. Prior scars on his chest and arms remained.

For a moment, his vision blurred as the exhaustion from the mending took its toll. The back of a nearby chair became his support. He yearned to lie down, but he'd lost enough time. After fumbling with his britches, he managed to get them on without tripping over himself. The buttons on the matching green shirt and embroidered coat proved a much harder challenge, but eventually he was buttoning up the coat. The day's heat didn't suit wearing the jacket, but the coming visit with King Nerian required formality. Anything to help dissuade suspicion. Stefan was sitting in the tent's lone chair tugging on his boots when the Alzari returned.

"General, I'm Zar Ballard," a man announced.

Stefan turned to the male voice he recognized from the night before. Today, the tone was smooth, confident. The man behind the voice was a reflection of that sound: chest up, back straight, hair slick with oil. His robes were pristine. The young, female Alzari stood behind him. Something about the man's demeanor annoyed Stefan.

"You need more rest. Delaying another day will not hurt," Ballard said, the words sounding more like a command than a suggestion.

Stefan stood slowly, drawing himself to his full height. "I'm sorry. Need? Did I miss when they appointed an Alzari above me? Delay? Are you sure that's what you want to tell the King concerning the news of our latest defeat and the Erastonian advance? The message was delayed?"

"T–That's not what I meant." Ballard stumbled over his words, swallowing several times.

Eyebrows rising ever so slightly, Stefan stared the man down.

"General," Zar Ballard added in response. He loosened his robes about his neck.

"I didn't think so," Stefan said. "Now, I thank you for saving my life, but our King won't care one way or another. Any other survivors reported from the Crescent Hills?"

"No, sir, not even our scouts returned."

Stefan shook his head in feigned grief, his hand on his forehead. "So many brave men," he whispered, his voice steeped in regret. "All dead. All because of me."

"It is not your fault, sir. How could anyone know the Erastonians would have such numbers or be this strong?"

"You don't understand, do you, Zar Ballard?"

Ballard seemed to mull over the words, but his eyes lacked recognition.

"Do you know what happens to those who fail of late?"

"General, I–I have heard stories, but surely ..."

"Have you ever seen anyone flayed?"

Ballard nodded numbly.

"Good." Stefan allowed his tone to take on a knife's edge. "Take care such a punishment doesn't happen to you should I suffer a second failure in not reaching the King in time."

The Alzari was speechless.

Stefan's stomach protested mightily. "Now, I distinctly remember asking for a meal."

"It should be here any moment, sir," the young female Ashishin said, a small smile playing across her lips that Stefan was sure came from witnessing the horror written on her superior's face.

"General," Ballard said tentatively. "You should rest at least another day. If you aren't fully mended and you take the Travelshaft, you risk—"

"I know the risks. Death using the Travelshaft to get the dire news I bring or death because I didn't deliver such news in a timely fashion is still death, Zar Ballard."

The Alzari bowed in quiet acquiescence.

A young cadet entered, carrying a tray heaped with food. What looked to be a roasted pheasant in a thick sauce, slices of bread, a blood orange, and several pink fleshberries. Next to them was a flagon and a cup. Peppery smells drifted from the dish, intermingled with the tantalizing scent of the fleshberries.

"I suggest the fleshberries first, sir," Ballard said. "They help with the mending process."

Stefan almost rolled his eyes, resisting the urge to inform the overbearing man this wasn't his first time being wounded and mended. Instead, he nodded and strode over to the table where the cadet placed the food before bowing, knuckling his forehead to Stefan and leaving.

After he muttered a brief prayer, Stefan pulled out a chair from the table and sat. He poured a cup of wine, popped a few fleshberries into his mouth, and washed them down. The kinai wine only added to the sweetness of the berries. Well distilled kinai at that, fermented in precise amounts. The taste was so familiar Stefan raised his cup, swirling around the contents, his brows drawing together in a lumpy frown. The quality of the drink was impressive. Not many knew the secrets of producing such a near perfect vintage.

The better the kinai wine or juice, the stronger the

restorative and energy inducing properties, or so Thania said. Only by picking the fist–sized, red fruit at the right hour, during early dawn or late dusk, could one be assured the essences were absorbed at their most potent. *Impressive indeed.* The liquor reminded Stefan of his wife's brew. He sighed and resisted the instinctive urge to reach for his pendant.

"You made this?" Stefan held up the cup to Zar Ballalrd.

"No, General. I brought it in from the capital. I only use this vintage on rare occasions such as this."

The wine might well be his wife's after all. Stefan nodded. To put the thoughts of Thania and the children out of his mind, he tore off a leg from the pheasant and chewed. Every time he sipped the kinai, memories flooded him: Thania in the kitchen, preparing lunch, little Anton running around a flowerbed with Celina giving chase.

Will I ever be given another chance to see children of mine grow up? Very few Matii had ever given birth to more than two children in their lifetime. A side effect of Setian longevity many said. In a different world, he would have surrendered his extended life span for a chance. He hoped what he was doing now meant a better life for Anton and Celina. He thought of nothing more horrific than a world overran by the shade, and people losing their souls to its taint.

Stefan tore into another piece of pheasant before pushing the remainder away, his appetite gone. "I dawdled long enough." He stood. "Is my mount ready?"

"Yes, sir," the female Alzari said.

"Lead the way then."

The two Alzari turned as one and headed outside.

Before he took a step to follow, a sudden bout of dizziness swept through him. He borrowed a moment to steady himself. Mouthing a silent prayer that Ballard hadn't stayed longer to witness his weakness, Stefan headed to the tent's exit. The Zar might be stupid enough to force the issue of his health and send someone else with a message to Nerian. Events were already on a precipice's edge, needing only a nudge or some mistake to come crumbling down.

Outside the tent, a dozen mounted Dagodin waited, silver armor gleaming. They snapped to attention at the sight of Stefan.

"An honor escort, sir," Zar Ballalrd said. "And protection should you have unwanted visitors in the Travelshaft."

Stefan almost groaned. Taking more men into Benez wasn't something he relished, but offering a protest wouldn't sit well. Not for who he used to be, and not with the Svenzar raiding the Travelshafts at their leisure. Head held straight, he stalked by the men.

At the end of the line, his dartan was snuffling at the some meaty carcass. The Dagodin's horses whinnied. His mount swung its head toward them and mewled. The horses pranced before the Dagodin brought them under control.

"He's been well fed," Zar Ballalrd said.

"Thank you." Stefan braced himself as he mounted, making sure he showed no weakness when he climbed into the saddle. Once he was secure, his shoulders reaching slightly above the front of the shell, he beckoned to the lead Dagodin whose pin and four tiny golden swords on his breast named him Captain. When the man reached him, Stefan said, "Keep your men close. If you see Svenzar, ignore them. We have no goods. I don't care what is being transported in the minor channels. The last thing I need is to lose men foolishly. Remind your men that they're safe as long as they stay within the central channel."

"Yes sir, General Dorn." He snapped his reins and returned to his men, addressing each one personally. When the Captain finished, he nodded to Stefan.

They set off at a trot, padding along a worn path toward Karsten's western outskirts. The backdrop of the town's stone edifices stood more than four stories high, poking above the surrounding walls. Guards dotted the bulwark and the occasional square tower. Outside town, Setian forces in tents occupied most of what had been farmland. Many of the soldiers watched as they rode by, some saluting to Stefan and the Captain, while others practiced formations, or lounged about as they awaited orders.

As Stefan expected, the central road itself was empty. Laborers and soldiers spread along the edge for the spectacle. Stefan waited for the Dagodin to draw next to him, six per side. He nodded and flapped his reins.

Head down, the dartan bounded forward. In moments, its speed surpassed any creature Stefan used before. Then it went faster still. His stomach lurched, threatening to spew its contents, but he fought down on the sensation.

The speed grew until those watching from the roadside melded with each other. In turn, the spectators became one with the tents and other fortifications. His clothes felt as if they wanted to rip from his body where they flapped, while in other places the cloth plastered itself to his skin. He huddled into the saddle as everything blurred into one unrecognizable stream.

CHAPTER 28

After the second rush of speed within the Travelshaft, Stefan cast a glance over his shoulder. The Dagodin were all with him, each appearing unaffected by their surroundings. He gave a satisfied nod toward the Captain.

Less than an hour into the trip, Stefan frowned. By now, there should have been travelers heading the opposite way on channel to his left. At least four or five caravans or nobles with their retinue. Not only the armies used the shafts, but also dignitaries, craftsmen, and other service providers like the menders or apothecaries. Anyone who could afford them and had the tiniest spark of Matersense took advantage of the Travelshafts. Wealthy merchants willing to pay the high price for quick delivery of goods for which they themselves charged a premium were among the most common facilitators. Their absence didn't bode well.

The answer to the mystery arrived in the clash of steel, cries of men, whinny of horses, and several great rumbles. A monstrous roar followed.

Eyes straining ahead, he tried to pick out the battle's participants. Slowly, the ethereal glow resolved into heavily armored, lance–wielding Setian infantrymen. They spread in a wedge formation with their backs to several wagons and coaches. On the ground, behind them and ahead of them, lay numerous wounded and dead men. A woman in rich clothing cradled a man's head in her lap. A wail ripped from her throat.

Standing over twenty–feet tall, a full–grown Svenzar was tearing into half a dozen wagons ahead of the retreating soldiers and fighting the remnants of the Setian cohort. If a mountain could lumber and had eyes, arms and legs, that would be the Svenzar.

Alongside the stoneform creature were at least a dozen Sven half its size. The Svenzar's young twins smashed into any soldiers who got close enough to be a threat. Among them skittered, the Svenzar's crab–like minions, the gerde. Steel flashed and stone thumped, the vibrations rocking the cavern as men and monsters battled.

Gerde darted back and forth on eight splayed legs, bodies to the ground, and carapaces often hardening to defend the strikes from soldiers. Their stony exteriors seemed to be a mixture of sediment. Maws wide and snarling, bodies the size of small ponies, they charged head first into what remained of the Setian ranks.

Men screamed and died. The smell of dirt and blood hung thick.

Twisted at inhuman angles, limbs missing, soldiers' bodies littered the ground. Half again as many gerde lay amongst them along with abandoned pieces of broken armor and cracked stone shells. Blood stained the earth red.

For the moment, the Setian held the enemy at bay thanks to two Alzari. Huge boulders ripped from the earth to slam into the gerde not engaged with any soldiers. Intermittent bolts of light stuck others, shearing rock from skin to expose pink flesh beneath. Gerde howled and screeched.

One of the Alzari focused on the Sven and Svenzar, but whatever he did proved ineffectual. Whether it was a light bolt or a rolling wave of earth and debris, the monolith of a creature flicked a hand, and instantly a wall of earth shot up to block the attacks. More often than not, the Sevnzar absorbed any rock or dirt that found a way through its defenses. Alzari strength resided in Forging essences of earth and wood, but in that, the Svenzar were stronger. When the Alzari switched to his meager skill in light or fire, his attacks failed.

Nearby, the Sven continued to defend against the last few soldiers who'd managed to sneak through. Stefan knew now they must be Dagodin. Whenever the Setian's blades or spears struck true, a Sven crumpled to a stony mound. Only *divya* produced such an effect.

Abruptly, one of the soldiers among the group turned and made an inhuman leap toward the closest Alzari. The Forger must have seen the movement from the corner of his eyes, because his hands swept toward the man. A huge fireball roiled to life in front of him before streaking up and catching the leaping soldier in the chest. The impact blew the man backward. When he landed with a smoking hole in his torso, a transformation began.

In the place of the Setian soldier was a dead Sven.

The Alzari spun to face the other Setian. He peered at them, hands outstretched, and then as if seeing whatever he sought, he turned back to the rock–armored gerde and began his attacks anew.

As Stefan watched, the boulders striking the gerde grew smaller and decreased in frequency. So did the bolts of light. The creatures began to ignore the bolts altogether, some not even bothering to screech when they were struck. Legs clicking on the metal and stone of the channel, they easily shifted from the path of incoming debris or slapped them to one side. One after another, the soldiers fell to the beasts until only six remained with the two Alzari.

The attacks on the Svenzar ceased altogether as the second Alzari now assisted his counterpart with his attempts to keep the gerde away. The Svenzar and Sven finished their demolition of the wagons and supplies and turned to the cohort's remnants.

Commotion near the wagons drew Stefan's attention. The doors to one of the coaches opened, and four children, two boys and two girls, ran over to the grieving woman. When they saw the man, they too burst into tears, falling to the ground, clawing at the man's tattered clothing and bloody face.

A roar echoed from the direction of the battle.

There, a glow suffusing his body, one of the Alzari raised his hands. The last of the Setian and the other Zar fled. The gerde closed in.

Luminescent sheets arched from the man's body like a hundred tiny, forked lightning bolts. They shot into the gerde, blowing limbs from bodies. Stone armor shattered as the blasts lifted the beasts off their feet and slammed them into the nearby wall. When the burst dissipated, the Alzari crumpled, his body a smoking ruin.

The last few gerde and the Sven and Svenzar advanced.

Despite the apparent hopelessness of the situation and ignoring his own warning, Stefan spurred his dartan the remainder of the distance. He could not sit by and allow these innocents, this woman and her children, to die like this. He glided across the central channel, through the luminescence separating it from the others and onto the same tracks as the retreating men.

"NO!" a voice screamed in a tone like a high–pitched musical note.

The word rocked Stefan to his core. It came from the Svenzar. Something about the voice seemed familiar, but he shook the sense off.

A massive arm stretched toward Stefan. All across the creature's body, almost the same color as its stone exterior, tattoo–like drawings writhed. Shaking off his surprise, Stefan whipped his reins and drew up next to the Alzari and his six fellows. He turned to the oncoming Svenzar.

His sword vibrated.

By pure instinct, Stefan snatched his weapon and whirled to face the Setian.

A howl echoed.

His escorts had no time to react before several wraithwolves tore from the body of the soldiers and leapt on their backs, jaws snapping and snarling. The lone Alzari's lips curled into a venomous smile, his eyes glittering as he regarded Stefan. Behind him, the same transformations were taking place not only among the other soldiers, but also from the woman herself and the four children.

The world slowed as the Alzari raised his hand.

The ground rumbled and shook. The earth heaved, causing his dartan to stumble to one side. A massive undulating lump roiled past Stefan. Yanking on his reins, he retreated.

The Alzari's mouth fell open as the mound pushed up from the earth, forming a head bigger than the size of a wagon. The form continued to pour up from the ground, stone and dirt spilling away as neck, shoulders, then torso and arms grew. Intricate tattoos covered the Svenzar's surface. They writhed around its body as if they wanted to tear from the creature's skin.

Stefan recognized the Svenzar. It was Kalvor.

Light lanced out from the Alzari, striking Kalvor's body, but not once did the Svenzar react.

"You helped save the Harnan," Kalvor said. "For that, we are in your debt. We can help your people but you must make Nerian create an opening."

"What are you—"

"Nerian is like a child, not knowing what he is doing, touching powers that lay dormant for years. One is holding him back. Your King must begin the process to unleash all he is. Only you and your weapon can provide what he needs."

"How?"

"Use your sense when the time comes."

Confused, Stefan opened his mouth to speak.

GO! NOW!" Kalvor commanded, towering into the cavern, his back to Stefan. "You will understand when you meet him."

A face grew on the Svenzar's back.

Stefan gasped. It was as if he was looking into a mirror at his own reflection, but several times bigger.

"Remember to trust what you feel, not what you see," the face said. "Begone."

Without waiting for another invitation, Stefan pulled on the reins and dashed to the central lane. A quick look over his shoulder revealed several wraithwolves trying to leap across. The ground shook again, but this time, Sven rippled up from the earth to block the creatures.

Turning his focus ahead, Stefan sped away from the clamor of battle.

CHAPTER 29

Hours later, Stefan arrived at the Travelshaft's exit. Not much of what happened made sense. Why would the Svenzar defend him? Not only that, he could have sworn it seemed as if Kalvor expected him to be there. The same as the time when the Svenzar met him in Astoca. He frowned as he tried to understand what Kalvor meant by the sword providing Nerian with what he needed. One thing was certain. He was not giving the *divya* to the King.

His mind drifted to the shadelings, and he considered if Nerian sent them. But that didn't make sense. Why not wait for him to come home? Unless Nerian assumed he was fleeing. He shook the thought off. Nerian knew he wouldn't abandon his family.

Head spinning, Stefan continued to ponder his dilemma. What if someone else was acting on their own accord? Cerny maybe? If he made the wrong choice, not only his family's lives, but those of the other men and women who now relied on him would be forfeit. With the thought, a hollow formed in his chest where the pendant of Thania rested. Whatever he decided, he had to proceed with the utmost care. One mistake and all would be lost.

A warning gong echoed. Ahead, the exit's white glow came into view. *Self–mastery*, he reminded himself. He spurred his dartan toward the light.

When he exited, the air here deep in Seti was much cooler than he'd experienced at the Crescent Hills or even Karsten. The weather carried the chilly nip of autumn. Lit up by the orange glow of late evening sun, the peaks of the Cogal Drin Mountains loomed, soaring sentinels guarding the valley in which Benez nestled beyond the hill ahead. The clamor of an army on the march and clinking armor greeted him along with the trundle of wagons and shouted orders. Soldiers accompanied by Alzari massed on other roads leading to the shaft. The smell of man, metal, pack animals, and mounts rode heavy on the air. Several people pointed or stared at his dartan. The beast eyed them, mewling its displeasure.

On the main causeway where the road to the Travelshaft ended, ten mounted Dagodin in red and blue waited—the King's Guard—their horses as stiff as the men themselves. General Cerny led them. Back straight and chest puffed out in his uniform with its crimson scrollwork running down the sleeves, the man was all smiles. A prickle ran through Stefan.

"Good to see you're safe. We had reports of an encounter with Svenzar within the Travelshafts," Cerny said as Stefan drew up in front of them. His horse whinnied and shied away from Stefan's dartan. With a deft move of his legs, Cerny brought his mount under control and threw Stefan a fur–lined cloak. A curious expression crossed his face as he took in Stefan's dartan.

"Thank you. Glad to be safe." Stefan attempted to sound as genuine as possible as he caught the garment and slung it over his shoulders. "The Svenzar were preoccupied with their raid. I was able to sneak by." He nodded toward the guards. The men did not acknowledge him. "I gather the King received word from Karsten?"

"Yes." Cerny peered at him over his bulbous nose. "An eagle arrived earlier today. The message said you reached Karsten near death … and alone." His eyebrows rose questioningly.

"I did." Stefan kept his face stoic but questions abounded. If the Cerny knew he left from Karsten, then he was aware of Stefan's Dagodin escort. *Why not ask after them?*

"Defeat then." Voice low but not quite a whisper, almost as if he was rolling the word around on his tongue, Cerny raised his hairless brows.

"Yes," Stefan said, allowing his shoulders to slump and holding his head down for a moment.

"I think the King may have expected it, as did I." Cerny's tone carried the hint of a gloat.

"I guess that explains the numbers Nerian appears to be sending to the front." Stefan wheeled his dartan to face the Travelshaft. He counted at least ten separate legions. Among them there were six made up entirely of Alzari. Several cohorts of men and women in flowing gold and green robes led them. The number of High Alzari was nothing less than astounding.

"He reacted a bit ... angrily to your apparent defeat in the field. I suggest you soothe his temper."

For the briefest moment, Stefan considered ignoring the man again. Instead, he said, "My ability to influence Nerian disappeared when I begged away from leading the first assaults into Erastonian territory."

"I'll pray to the gods for you then," Cerny said.

Brows raised, Stefan cocked his head to one side to regard the General. "Things are that bad?"

Cerny let out a deep breath and nodded. "Worse. One of my men overheard the King saying you should have died with your men."

And you tried to fulfill the King's wish by sending the assassins in the Travelshaft, didn't you? Stefan shrugged. "It won't be the first time he's threatened my life over the last few years. Certainly won't be the last."

"I guess." Cerny peered around as if gauging the distance between the King's Guard and them. "But," he whispered under his breath. "If you should need my help in securing a way—"

"I'll take my chances," Stefan said, cutting the man off.

"Don't worry. I'll keep your suggestion to myself."

Cerny gave Stefan a slight bow. "Then let's not keep the King waiting."

Smiling inwardly at Cerny's sullen expression, Stefan slapped his reins and sent the dartan trotting up the cobbled road. The King's Guard didn't need to clear a path for him as the sight of the dartan created ample room. He yearned to rush off and have his family start their exodus, but the King had given him little choice but to attend to him first. Somehow, he needed to get word to Thania. The chances of leaving Nerian's presence alive seemed more uncertain now than ever.

He crested the hill, pushing his chest out to make himself appear to ride with all the pomp necessary for a General, even a defeated one. The dartan's massive size added to the effect. Behind him, hooves drummed a constant dirge. The thought of Cerny's escort almost made his shoulders sag, but he refused to show any weakness. Part of him was still Stefan the Steadfast.

Across the wide valley, Benez's gray edifices rose before the soaring, black feldspar walls. From the small dwellings within the slums to the larger buildings, the city's structures wound their way up the valley and onto the mountainous slopes upon which the Royal Palace was built. The Palace itself sparkled with the evening sunlight. What may wait inside sent a chill through his bones.

Fifteen years.

Alongside the road, travelers pointed at Stefan and his escort. Others made way for their passage, keeping their heads down and eyes averted. Stefan frowned. The Setian he remembered were a proud, happy people, always walking with their heads up, pride for their soldiers evident. Even the ones who were lesser off. The expressions now were often grim, hateful. More than one person spat as they rode by. Many shuffled, backs bowing under the weight of belongings they carried. The wagons held up along the road were bursting to overflowing with both people and personal items. The press of unwashed bodies reeked. For the first time, Stefan noticed soldiers searching some of the wagons and at times carrying off the owners or walking away with young men under guard, their mothers wailing in protest.

Stefan slowed until he rode alongside Cerny. "What's happening?" He nodded toward the young men.

"The King needs recruits in order to take on the Erastonians. He recently passed a new law. Every able–bodied male must serve in the army."

"What?"

Cerny shrugged. "King's orders."

"Not everyone is born to fight, Cerny. What the King is doing is—"

"I understand," Cerny said, nodding, "but if I were you, I'd keep those thoughts to myself. Of course, I could pass on your sentiments if you would like?" His eyebrows rose inquisitively, and he rubbed at his nose, his lips twitching ever so slowly into a cruel smile.

"No, if I need to, I'll speak to him."

"Fine."

"Are all these people fleeing Benez?"

"They're trying to. Most aren't allowed to leave, at least not before inspection. The King believes the Erastonians have infiltrated among us. The dungeons overflow with suspects." Cerny sounded almost pleased by the prospect and the gleam in his eye said as much.

Stefan ground his teeth. Rumors had reached him of how bad life had become, but this was terrible. Something else drew his attention. There was tenseness to the air, a poised readiness, like a rockslide waiting for the one boulder, the one weakness to send the stones tumbling. While some people did appear cowed or resigned to whatever fate would befall them, others seemed ready to attack, fists clenched around anything resembling a weapon. Often it was their hands balled into fists, but that was the extent of their protests. The gestures gave him hope. There might be a way other than fleeing after all.

First, he had to convince Nerian only a few survived against the Erastonians and that Garrick's entire legion perished.

A tall order if there ever was one. The occasional vibration from his sword when some soldier passed close or the mewl of his dartan toward one person or another lent to his sense of dread.

For all intents, he'd known this trip might be a suicide mission.

CHAPTER 30

B y the time they reached the city's walls, evening sun
had given way to twilight and that had surrendered
to dusk. Denestia's twin moons had risen, shining sentinels so
large they gave the illusion they were within reach. Shadows
elongated, covering the land in creeping fingers. Stefan and
his escorts were the last allowed through the gates before the
enormous metal structures rumbled shut, black slamming on
black. The steady stream of people attempting to flee Benez had
continued until the gates closed and soldiers denied any further
passage. Travelers along the road bedded down wherever they
were, not giving up on their quest for freedom.

Torches lit the wide–cobbled King's Road, their light
pooling on the huddled forms of those who'd bundled up against
the night's chill. As was the norm, the temperature within the
valley, and in Seti in general, varied to one extreme or the other,
with daylight often bringing sweltering heat and the night, a
bone–chilling cold. For Stefan, his years away from Seti on the
campaign almost made him succumb to the change. He clenched
his jaw to combat the cold and give his body a chance to adjust.

Thoughts preoccupied by worry for his family, Stefan
studied his surroundings. The slums, he expected to be in disarray,
but they extended farther into the city than ever before. Garbage,
the stench of old feces, and clogged sewer drains permeated the

air. The city's neglect was shocking. Not only did refuse line the streets, and a god–awful reek filter from the sewage system, but many buildings were in disrepair. Once prosperous inns were shuttered and dark. What music tinkled through the night was muted and melancholy. If the people outside appeared dreary and downtrodden, those along the road were corpses, eyes blank, expressions dead.

What, in Ilumni's name, has become of my beloved city? Even as he asked the question, Stefan knew. The touch of shadelings was sucking the life from the living.

Soldiers patrolled by constantly, prodding one person or another with their tasseled spears, ordering them to move along before curfew set in. As one such guard put it, 'Either huddle a bundle, get off the road, or take a blade to the gut. Your choice.' The rule seemed to be no movement along the streets after a certain hour or face the dungeons or worse.

With the clop of their horses' hooves and snorts playing accompaniment, they ascended into the Upper City. Stefan fought hard to ignore the steady string of vibrations from his weapon. Several times, he resorted to yanking tight on his dartan's reins to dissuade it from attacking a person. The sights here were as depressing, with more than one notable villa now overrun with creepers and vines, their previously manicured gardens choked with weeds. Dust and debris blew along once pristine flagstones.

The few nobles out, who would be dressed in extravagant clothes, all wore darker colors. They pulled their cloaks tight around them, and kept their hoods up as they too hurried, averting their eyes from Cerny and the Kings' Guard. The way the nobles appeared to be in a rush and often made nervous peeks toward the guards, it was obvious the curfew applied here as well.

On more than once occasion, when his sword reacted, the person in question gave an almost reverent bow to Cerny and practically ignored Stefan. The dartan ensured they kept a safe distance. Stefan made note of every face he encountered during such occurrences.

Up ahead the Royal Palace loomed, dreary and foreboding. The effect wasn't simply from nightfall. The walls themselves appeared darker, not the near shining white Stefan remembered. Slowly spreading with night's advent, like some black creature encroaching on the lamps and torchlight, shadows clung to every crack, crevice, overhang, battlement, and murder hole.

To Stefan's surprise, a smaller than usual guard contingent kept watch along the colonnade leading to the stairs and wide entrance. Whereas the King once had several dozen servants greet visitors, only two did so, taking the reins of Stefan's and Cerny's mounts. The eyes of the one that took the dartan's chains flickered fearfully. With a few words, Stefan reassured the servant the mount would be fine, warning him not to tie it near the horses. The King's Guard dismounted and tethered their horses on nearby posts. Not saying a word, Cerny waited patiently.

Expressions somber, their boots echoing in the spacious courtyard, the King's Guard marched over to meet them. As they drew closer, Stefan's sword began a slight thrum. He rested his hand on the weapon, and the sensation subsided. They lined up five on each side, one row in front Cerny, and the other ahead of Stefan, and marched up the stairs.

The gigantic metal doors, at least twelve feet tall, inched open. Light pooled out from the interior to meet that of the torches hanging next to the entrance. Creaking on hinges as if they hadn't been oiled in ages, the doors swung inwards to reveal Kahar with his hood thrown back, silver and green eyes glinting.

"You men take to your patrols," Cerny ordered. "If I have need of you, I'll send for you."

The King's Guard bowed and turned stiffly to obey the command.

Behind Kahar stretched the main hall lined by pillars with lamps in sconces.

Cerny coughed into his gloved hand. "After you, the King—" He cut off when Kahar's eyes shifted in his direction.

The prospect of accompanying Kahar almost made

Stefan cringe, but he squared his shoulders and stepped inside. Cerny joined him and the doors groaned shut.

Stefan tried his best not to contemplate how they closed without Kahar touching them. Instead, he focused on a distant point down the hallway to give off the impression he was staring the bodyguard in the eye. Kahar turned and strode away; silky movements making it appear as if his feet never touched the carpeted floor.

A slow breath escaped Stefan's mouth, but his relief was short–lived as the pungent stench of rot and moldy fur made him cough. A sudden clamminess crept down his spine at the scent he recognized.

Wraithwolf.

His hand slid down to the comfort of his sword's hilt. Coupled with the carpet's stink, which reeked as if it had been wet but not cleaned in months, if not years, the long hall began to feel constrictive despite it being at least fifteen feet wide. With his other hand, Stefan loosened his collar trying to make it easier to breathe. Not once did Cerny react to the foul odor.

As they walked, Stefan kept his gaze shifting from the side to side into any shadowed alcove or corner. He started at what he thought was a flurry of movement only to realize it was a trick of the capering flames within the lamps when they played off the images of men, beasts, and battles on the many paintings and tapestries or off the statues along the hall. At any moment, he expected the shadelings the King employed to leap into the open and tear him limb from limb, but none did. In fact, not once did he notice so much as a guard by the time they traveled the length of the hall.

"You should not have returned," Kahar said as they entered an antechamber. Despite the palace's emptiness and silence, the man's voice lacked an echo.

"Why is that? I always return to the King, regardless of what happens." Stefan's voice reverberated.

"You were defeated. Again."

Stefan shrugged, trying to appear braver than he felt.

"Was this loss so different than the others? The Erastonians are stronger foes than Nerian anticipated."

Kahar said nothing.

They passed into a large room decorated with cushioned benches and chairs. The stark desolation of the castle only added to the chill that had crept into Stefan's bones upon reaching Benez. He wanted to hug himself. Instead, he drew the cloak tighter around him, making certain to keep the material clear of his sword.

"The Erastonians are not half as strong as they think," Kahar finally said when they entered another antechamber. "In another time and place, you would have defeated them."

Stefan bristled at the remark. "You mean if the King had bothered to give me the best of his Alzari or fought them in full force. Why would he let his armies face defeat after defeat?"

"Why indeed? Did the King not tell you about the hope, the belief he gained when he saved the Unvanquished?"

Stefan growled under his breath at the mention of the name. "He didn't save them. He killed them. Now look what's become of Benez. The people are without hope. They're fleeing. The soldiers themselves, all but the Alzari, appear as if they expect the end any day now."

"The end *is* soon, but not the one many expect."

"Nerian can't hope to win against the odds he faces. The Erastonians, the Felani, the Svenzar, the Tribunal's Ashishin with an allied Granadia at their back. He must—"

"You sound as if you side with them," Cerny interrupted.

In his mounting anger, Stefan had forgotten about the man. "No. I sound as if I have some sense."

"Whatever happened to the man who believed he could not lose?" Kahar asked. "The man who followed *the Disciplines*? The man who believed in perseverance?"

A twinge of sadness crept through Stefan. "He died," he whispered.

Cerny chuckled.

"We both know the dead can be reborn."

Stefan missed a step. *What did Kahar mean by that? Could he know …?*

They entered the last hallway and the long stretch before the throne room. Kahar stopped and faced Stefan. Heart thumping in his chest, Stefan met the man's silver–flecked gaze, not flinching once. *Demand bravery by overcoming your fear.*

"What happened with Garrick and his men was a warning to you that you could do no more here," Kahar said, face blank. "The Svenzar tried to warn you off, but you still would not listen. So no, I do not believe Stefan the Undefeated, Stefan the Steadfast is dead. He stands here before me, a living example of what a man who lives and breathes *the Disciplines* can become. You stand before me defiant, facing me down even though you know I am more than what I appear to be. You worked for years now to find a way to save your people, to defeat Nerian. Your presence here is proof of who you are."

"What—" Cerny blurted. He took several steps back.

Stefan reached for his sword.

Kahar's hand on his stopped him. He never saw the bodyguard move. "That will be of no help here. Do not attempt to draw on whatever meager power it gave you over the years. The *divya* was not meant for you but another. You are simply its carrier for now."

No matter how much he strained, Stefan could not break free of Kahar's hold. The man seemed not to exert any pressure, but his hand held fast all the same. Finally, Stefan gave in with a nod and relaxed.

Kahar leaned in closer. He had no scent. "Have faith in yourself. Ilumni will show you the way," he whispered.

Stefan frowned at the bodyguard's words. "Have you told any of this to the King?" he asked, matching Kahar's pitch.

"No, but King Nerian has a way of perceiving things. He always has. Not many can hide what they do from him."

"So what is it that you want?"

"For you to live … as you must. This is why I do not understand why you chose to return."

Stefan stared Kahar in the eye, his face becoming a mask of its own. "Because I have a people to defend. A wife, a son, and a daughter to save."

The corner of Kahar's lips twitched. He bowed. "Go. Save them then. They are in the throne room. But remember two things. Do not draw your sword against him, and no matter what he offers, no matter what you see or think you see, do not willingly give it to him. The weapon is your family's birthright." He turned and strode back the way they came, the door closing behind him of its own volition.